Praise for *Love Blind*

"Perfect pacing with spot-on character development that will leave readers empathizing with the characters from the very beginning."
—*School Library Journal*

"Readers will root for Kyle and Hailey to come together and admire their personal growth along the way."
—*Booklist*

"Like Desir's other books, [*Love Blind*] is forthright in its portrayal of older teens' emotional and sexual lives. Readers who enjoyed her earlier books will devour this latest offering, and those who love Ellen Hopkins will want to know Desir if they do not already."
—*VOYA*

Praise for *Other Broken Things*

"Fans of A. S. King, Laurie Halse Anderson, and John Green will appreciate this gritty, honest portrayal of the road to recovery."
—*VOYA*

"With edges sharper than a fragment of a vodka bottle, C. Desir reveals how far some of us go to run from the sorrows that have broken us, and how much it hurts to find a way to put the shards of ourselves back together again. Desir is hip to the truth that the broken edges let the light shine through. This book is a blinding beauty."
—Martha Brockenbrough, author of *The Game of Love and Death*

Praise for *Bleed Like Me*

"Edgy, dark, and turbulent with passion . . .
Be prepared to have your heart wrenched from your chest."
—*Booklist*

Also by

C. Desir

Fault Line

Bleed Like Me

Other Broken Things

Four-Letter Word (as Christa Desir)

LOVE

BLIND

C. Desir & Jolene Perry

SIMON PULSE

NEW YORK LONDON TORONTO SYDNEY NEW DELHI

SIMON PULSE
An imprint of Simon & Schuster Children's Publishing Division
1230 Avenue of the Americas, New York, New York 10020
First Simon Pulse paperback edition December 2017
Text copyright © 2016 by Christa Desir and Jolene Perry
Cover design and illustration by Karina Granda copyright © 2016 by Simon & Schuster, Inc.
Also available in a Simon Pulse hardcover edition.
All rights reserved, including the right of reproduction in whole or in part in any form.
SIMON PULSE and colophon are registered trademarks of Simon & Schuster, Inc.
For information about special discounts for bulk purchases, please contact Simon & Schuster
Special Sales at 1-866-506-1949 or business@simonandschuster.com.
The Simon & Schuster Speakers Bureau can bring authors to your live event.
For more information or to book an event contact the Simon & Schuster Speakers Bureau
at 1-866-248-3049 or visit our website at www.simonspeakers.com.
Interior designed by Tom Daly
The text of this book was set in Adobe Garamond Pro.
Manufactured in the United States of America
2 4 6 8 10 9 7 5 3 1
The Library of Congress has cataloged the hardcover edition as follows:
Names: Desir, Christa, author. | Perry, Jolene B. (Jolene Betty), 1976-, author.
Title: Love blind / C. Desir and Jolene Perry.
Description: First Simon Pulse hardcover edition. | New York : Simon Pulse, 2016.
Identifiers: LCCN 2015031920 | ISBN 9781481416931 (hc) |
ISBN 9781481416948 (pbk) | ISBN 9781481416955 (eBook)
Subjects: | CYAC: Self-confidence—Fiction. | Bashfulness—Fiction. | Friendship—Fiction. |
Fear—Fiction. | BISAC: JUVENILE FICTION / Social Issues / Adolescence. |
JUVENILE FICTION / Social Issues / Emotions & Feelings. | JUVENILE FICTION /
Social Issues / Special Needs.
Classification: LCC PZ7.D4506 Lo 2016 | DDC [Fic]—dc23
LC record available at http://lccn.loc.gov/2015031920

For those we've lost. And for those we've found.

Hailey's Fear List

~~Grocery shopping~~

Painting

Taking BLIND PEOPLE classes

Needing a service dog because
animals are kind of gross

Swimming

Spiders

~~Setting up/working in pottery shop~~

~~Walking down my street
with my eyes closed~~

~~Playing in a band~~

~~Playing guitar solo in front of a crowd~~

Cooking (for the moms)

~~Being on the radio~~

~~Being recorded in a studio~~

Tongue-kissing

Sex

Wardrobe switch

Bungee jumping or skydiving—
either is acceptable

Finding my way around an unknown place

Going blind

Chapter One: Kyle

Joining our high school radio station when I hated to talk was probably one of the worst decisions I'd ever made. Until I met Hailey Bosler.

Not that she was responsible for the state of my shitty life, but she certainly wasn't making it easier. Okay, that wasn't true. The bubblegum twin radio deejay talents of Lindsey and Lucy Latni weren't making it easier. It wasn't Hailey's fault said deejays were gushing about her band's arrival as if some pop star had autographed their not-insubstantial chests.

It also wasn't her fault the twins were ordering me around like a lackey, instead of respecting that I was the only one in the room actually certified to use the control board. And it wasn't her fault my head was pounding not only from girl squeals but also because I'd had a near panic attack earlier, forcing me to skip the minefield of lunch in our cafeteria.

Still, my afternoon was being sucked up by these girls, and I couldn't squelch my crap attitude toward Hailey and the rest of Blinders On.

Blinders On. Stupid name. Although I had to admit after hearing their GarageBand mix that as far as local bands went, they didn't suck like most of the usual talentless hacks the Latni twins frothed over.

"They're here," Lindsey squealed. Or maybe it was Lucy. "Girl band in the hoooussse."

A strange shimmy dance ensued wherein the twins proved yet again their astounding ability to derail the musical integrity of a band until it was the equivalent of a bowl of glitter-covered kibble.

I didn't say this, of course. Like I didn't say most things that popped in my head. Too many words. Out loud.

I looked down at the control board and bit the inside of my cheek, letting the high-decibel vapidity of the twins drown out my racing thoughts. I took a deep breath and pushed away the anxiety of meeting unknown people. Disappear. Fade into the background. Blend. Then I peeked at Hailey.

Holy shit.

Worn jeans, soft stretchy shirt, her blond hair pulled into a loose braid. Damn. She was exactly my type: hot in this really normal way, not done up, just casual, either too aware of her own beauty to care or not aware enough to realize the amount of space she filled in the room. Which was considerable.

My brain grabbed hold of an image of the two of us alone in the darkened radio studio, me actually being suave for once in my life and her drawn in by all my moves. Then, because it's my brain, it continued on to play the entire scenario out to its slightly inappropriate conclusion. God, what would that be like? I inched forward in my chair, more than a little aware of the semihard state of my junk. What was wrong with me? Three quick breaths, then I peeked at her again.

She eyed the girls dancing around her, brunette ponytails whipping in some sort of coordinated twin ritual, and crossed her arms as if she were observing animals at a zoo. Her nose scrunched and flared enough for me to read a hint of disgust.

I hid a smirk when I caught her slight head shake. She was hot and understood irony. I liked her already. Damn.

"Hey, guys," she said in a scratchy, low voice. I loved that kind of voice in girls. Equal parts Avril Lavigne, Elle King, and Melissa Etheridge. Classic. "Thanks for having us in."

"Of course," a twin chirped. "You all are so amazing." Then the Latnis clapped their hands and Hailey adjusted her braid as if she was well aware how damn awkward all this fangirling was, and was not in any way impressed.

I stared too long at her, barely even noticing the two girls behind her. Emo girls. All black clothes. Too much makeup. Too many piercings. Hailey was a wildflower in the midst of skunkweed. Sunny and warm and stupid sexy. Completely oblivious to my presence at the board. Which was probably best.

I likely would've stared even longer, enough to really embarrass myself, but my phone buzzed in my pocket. I jerked it out with so much impatience it half slipped from my grasp before my fingers closed around it. Only two people texted me, and one of them was at soccer practice.

Mom: Scrips are ready to pick up. Don't forget the rest of your to-do list.

As if I'd ever forget. My jaw tensed, and I typed a quick reply.

Kyle: Got it.

I shoved the phone back in my pocket and checked out the girls again.

Hailey's eyes moved back and forth, almost twitching as they searched the room. Beautiful eyes, blue green with big pupils, but something was wrong with them. They moved too much. Like she was on something, but that didn't match up with the rest of her.

She stepped deeper into the control room and scanned the space for a place to sit. Her eyes darted, darted. I sat up half an inch to help her, but then slumped down. What was I doing? The space wasn't that big. Not much to look at, and maybe a little dark, but she clearly had other people to help. Her eyes landed on me for less than a second. My hands shook a little as I watched her grope for the plastic seat. Not blindly grope, but sort of tipsy-drunk *I hope I'm not sitting in vomit* grope.

She planted herself slightly off center on the chair and laughed as she adjusted her position. "Sorry."

The vulnerability of it all damn near killed me. Those eyes. She was somehow broken. *Crap. Crap. Crap.* Beautiful, confident, and broken—the girl triple threat. She wasn't broken like me, but enough that I wanted to know her. I imagined a whole conversation between us.

"What's wrong with your eyes?"

"Why don't you speak?"

"I don't see so well."

"I don't talk so well."

And then I would ask her if she wanted to be the third person who texted me. One more name in my pathetic contact list. And she wouldn't even hesitate in saying yes.

For a second I allowed my thoughts to linger on the fantasy, our imagined conversation so real in my head I almost spoke. Almost introduced myself. But then, what the hell for? A third person who texted would be a third person I disappointed.

Instead, I turned back to the control board and cued up the next song. I let the voices of the twins swirl around me. They pointed Hailey's friends to the other chairs and started gossiping about the people from their last few interviews. I ignored it, pretended I didn't care. She was just another girl. High school was full of them, and they were all equally hard to deal with. Equally scary.

"Kyle," Lucy snapped. Or maybe it was Lindsey. "Are you ready?"

"Yeah," I mumbled.

"Well, what do we do?"

Speak into the microphone and try not to sound like an idiot.

I pointed to the two microphones set up in front of them, one for Hailey and her emo backup girls, one for Team Latni. "At the end of the song, start talking."

Lindsey clucked at me. Or maybe it was Lucy. Then she turned back to Hailey. Hailey's eyes narrowed, and she leaned forward slightly, peering at me. Peering like I wasn't another part of the equipment in the room. The feeling came back, the ache to connect with her, but just as quickly, panic took over my brain, spinning through the millions of reasons why connecting would be a terrible idea.

Nothing to see here. Move along. I didn't have it in me to get interested in a girl like Hailey, or any girl, really. I was too intrigued by her already and she'd barely said three words. I faded the song and engaged the microphones.

Chapter Two: Hailey

It was like he wanted to be invisible.

Wanted to be.

And he was doing a damn good job of it too, all hunched over the soundboard. Long arms and fast hands adjusting volume levels. Too fast for me to focus. His jet-black hair covered so much of his face I almost didn't notice him. Though it was hard to notice anything past the squeals of our school's most annoying deejays. At that moment, without my glasses, in weird lighting, with the Barbie twins gushing over our average music, I completely understood why he'd want to disappear, and I would have envied him, but I was about to play.

I had no idea how the hell to talk to two girls who were so obviously in love with music but still didn't get it. And even though I normally carried a spare pair of glasses with me everywhere, I was stuck without them after my graceful trip up the stairs. It made a place that already had crap for lighting even worse.

Nothing like being in a new situation, without being able to see, to put me in a foul mood. All I knew was that the room was dim, simple, and I hadn't tripped on anything getting to my plastic chair.

I pulled my guitar onto my lap and let everyone else fade away for a bit. The Les Paul '50s Tribute had been a present from my moms when I turned fourteen. I played for hours every day, and I loved the fifties vibe it held in the black lacquer. It felt like a true rock guitar.

Tucking a few loose strands of blond back into my braid, I started letting my fingers slide over the strings to tune up.

And when the guy whispered, "Anytime," I was already in the zone. I loved to sing, even though it always made me nervous, and neither of the other girls in the band were up to doing more than minimal backup vocals. Once we were a few bars in, it didn't matter. Didn't matter that I could barely see. Didn't matter that the three non–band members in here probably didn't get a tenth of the lyrics. It mattered that I hit every note. Every chord. And that I was brave enough to actually feel it. Even in this small room.

A hundred people were easier to block out than three. And I'd played for that many more than once. The radio station gig probably had more to do with being a "girl band" who played actual rock music than our talent, but playing for anyone was a rush. Besides, being on the radio was on my list, and I wanted to cross it off.

We finished to exaggerated praises and clapping from the twins. My girls, Mira and Tess, were already chatting them up—definitely better speakers for our band than me. I didn't have enough patience for squealing.

Besides, I wasn't sure how to react. I thought our song came off . . . okay. Not as good as we'd done it the night before, but still. Okay. And I should've sounded more grateful that the radio station at my high school wanted to have us on, but I swear, people get weird when they know you're in a band. Especially when they learn you play in places *off campus.*

Shit, playing a bat mitzvah might as well have been playing the Vic as far as most people at school were concerned.

"So, Hailey, is this what you see in your future?" one of the twins asked, tired of Mira and Tess dominating the mic, I guess. "Playing music?"

Yes. Maybe. God, that question was way too loaded for my current state of mind. And then, like he somehow saw me floundering, the silent guy at the board made a *wrap it up* signal with his hand, and the twins started in on promoting their next show.

"Sorry, that's all we have for today, everyone. We've had such a great time with Blinders On and hope great things happen for them! Be sure to tune in next week when we're doing a special show on local hip-hop artists." The twins even finished each other's sentences, which was obscenely clichéd and impossibly true.

So I guess we survived the interview unscathed, aside from my ears aching a bit at Muffy and Buffy's high-pitched voices. I needed to get to Individual Music Tutoring, which meant I was about to lock myself in a practice room in the music building for an hour and get a grade for it.

"Crap, Hailey. I totally forgot, I have a pair of your glasses." Tess, our drummer, and probably the only girl I'd call an actual friend, groped in her bag and slid glasses into my hands.

"Thanks." I owned a million pairs of glasses—all quirky enough to hopefully hide the way my eyes darted around trying to see, but I never knew where they all were.

I wasn't black-blind, just legally blind. Degenerative and "old-person" eyes as my ophthalmologist called it. "Legally blind" is a really professional way of saying one day I'll probably be black-blind. In-a-cave blind. Wave-my-hand-in-front-of-my-face-and-not-see-it blind.

Some days I shrugged that off. I could still see, and usually I could latch on to that. Besides, playing the campus radio station was supposed to be a good day.

Instead, as I slid on my glasses, I hated my eyes. The interview was officially over, but the twins, Mira, and Tess were still chatting. Screw patience—I'd pretty much run out of nice.

When I glanced around again, the fuzzy blur of the silent guy was gone.

The familiar weight of the Les Paul on my shoulder helped me relax as I stepped back into the hall. I waved and gave what I hoped was a smile to the two deejays, whose faces were still split from their embarrassing fangirling.

I cringed away from the light when I got outside, blinking over and over, willing my eyes to adjust. All I needed was to get to music class. From this side of our divided campus, it should have been easy.

Until my shoulder slammed into someone.

"Shit. Sorry." I scanned his face to see him better.

"Uh . . ." He held his hand between us, but no words came out.

"Hey. Disappearing guy." Good thing he was close or I'd have never recognized him in the bright light. Plain gray T-shirt. Jeans. Dirty white shoes. Like he was designed to blend. I breathed in, wondering why I was still standing there. Citrus tickled my nostrils. At least he was clean. For a guy, that really said something.

"Huh?"

"Nothing. So, thanks for putting up with the bullshit twins in there."

He looked down and his too-long hair hid his eyes. Nice eyes. Too bad.

"I'm Hailey." I thought about sticking out my hand, but

that sort of sucked, and anyway, he tucked his hands deeper into his pockets.

"'Kay."

We stood there for another beat. Me waiting for something from him and him apparently waiting for a large hole to swallow him. When nothing more happened, he shuffled his feet and darted off.

Guess he not only liked to disappear, but wasn't much for talking either. Kind of an odd guy. Something I could definitely appreciate.

I stepped into my mom's detached garage–turned–pottery shop. Rox had replaced all the garage door panels with windows, and added shelves across the new panes.

Every horizontal surface was lined with pottery. I squinted, but only fuzzy shadowed shapes appeared in front of the sunlight. She'd done some really great blue bowls the other day, but . . .

I squinted again at the pottery backdropped by the windows, and could still only see shapes. No colors. When had that happened? Had I lost colors when they were backlit?

"Hailey? Is that you?" Rox called from her workroom.

"Yup."

"How did it go?" she asked, still yelling from the back.

Rox sold tons of pottery out here, but she made it even faster. The extras ended up in our house—on every bookshelf, storage bin, and window ledge. There were days when the house looked more like a pottery shop than the pottery shop did.

I pulled my glasses off and set them on her sales counter, rubbing my nose and eyes. The yellow walls were supposed to be happy, but some days they were headache-inducing. "It's high school. Exactly how was it supposed to go?" I called.

"Oh, for goodness' sake." The irritation in her voice made me smile. "I was asking about the radio station."

"Fine." Such a great answer for so many situations.

Rox's wild black hair and tattooed arms appeared around the small door behind the sales counter. She scraped at her mud-covered hands in a gesture I'd seen a million times.

She pulled off her apron. I squinted at her jeans and black concert tee. No chance I could guess the band. My eyes were wrecked. My other mom, Lila, wore yoga gear. *A lot.* Ran a studio about a block away. The cliché of pottery-and-yoga lesbian moms did not go unnoticed, by basically everyone, but they always laughed about it and kept on being who they were, including being hoverers. Having one mom to smother me was a bit much, but two? Two who'd worked their asses off to adopt a little girl who'd come to them already damaged? Their smother-mothering could be a lot to take.

Rox frowned as she stepped toward me. "Your glasses are on the counter. Bad day?"

"No. Yes. I don't know." Why did she have to be so observant? It always brought out a weird, weighted feeling in my stomach, as if I was responsible for her.

"Let me get cleaned up and we can talk for a bit, okay?" Her smooth voice didn't match her rough exterior, but it was from Rox that I got my love of music.

I touched the guitar, still resting in its case on my back. "I'm gonna play for a bit. And besides, the doc says it's good for me to go without my glasses once in a while. Gives me practice." *For the day they won't do me any good.*

Rox let out a sigh she totally meant and wanted me to hear. Neither she nor Lila believed there would ever be a day when I couldn't see, but that's only because they didn't know what it was like to look through my eyes.

I opened my mouth to tell her I thought my eyes were worse again, but it would mean more ophthalmologist appointments, and maybe another small surgery. All the fighting against my terrible eyes was getting old.

"What's up?" she said more quietly.

I gestured toward all the rows of pottery on the shelves in front of the window. My lips pressed together.

"Hailey?"

"I can't . . ." I didn't want to do it. To say it out loud. "I can't really see what color they are anymore."

Rox walked around the counter and rested her hand on my shoulder. "Is it that way with everything, or . . . ?"

Her voice was the low cautious one the moms used when I had some new vision thing going on. It was the voice that was intended to calm me but really did the opposite.

"No." I shook my head, but my voice was sort of a whisper. "Just with the light behind them, I guess."

"Well." She gave my shoulder a squeeze before dropping her arm. "It's really bright out today."

"Yeah."

Her lips pursed for a moment, but after studying my face, she smiled—a sign that she was about to jump ship and change the subject.

Thank God.

"Lila will for sure be home for dinner. I'll let you know when she gets here." That was her nice way of telling me I would be joining them for dinner. Like every night. Family dinner. Mandatory. Grilling session of fifteen-year-old daughter. Not mandatory. Just a perk.

The gripping feeling in my chest over my vision started to dissipate, now replaced by what I'd tell the moms about my school day that didn't include anything about my eyes.

Maybe I could learn a lesson from the skinny guy in the sound booth and disappear.

Chapter Three: Kyle

I left money for dinner," Mom said as I dropped books into my bag. Calculus. History. *Beowulf.* My mom was a nurse. Mostly the night shift, although some days she covered for other nurses and was gone even longer. She was supposed to only work forty hours, but she had a second job as an in-home care nurse, so I was alone a lot. Which didn't always suck.

"'Kay. Thanks."

"Did you get my meds?"

"Yes."

I set her bag on the counter.

Mom hummed, sighed, and rifled through the bag to check. "And the other stuff I left for you to do?"

"Folded the laundry. The dishwasher isn't full enough to run."

"You should've run it anyway. The food will cake on otherwise." Her voice shook in that way that made me feel like shit. She looked at me, and her face changed, softened. *Damn.* The roller coaster of her emotions was not something I wanted to deal with today. "Thanks for picking up my things, Kyle. Sorry. I'm so sorry. It's *my* job to take care of *you*."

I grunted because what was I supposed to say? I'd like to interview other, more qualified candidates for the job.

She pressed out the creases of her uniform, her hands fluttering over her too-thin frame. Nothing fit her anymore. I couldn't remember the last time I'd seen her eat for real, not just standing in the kitchen scooping three spoonfuls of whatever into her mouth to get her through the next shift. She was definitely running toward another slip. Only thing worse than a pushy mom was one laid up, depressed and near catatonic, on the couch.

"Why don't you invite a friend over for dinner?" Flutter, smooth, flutter. "I hate that you're alone so much."

I hate that you are too. I didn't say it. Never would or could. But I felt it every minute we were together.

"I'll think about it."

"You haven't seen Pavel in a long time."

Pavel was pretty much my only friend, but I didn't see him with any sort of regularity. Homeschooled, Russian, a hell of a soccer player. And because he was a guy, he didn't ask me too many questions. Didn't talk about things in the past. Plus, he liked the right kind of music or at least pretended to.

"Yeah. Maybe I'll call him." I wouldn't. Pavel called me, mostly. Would send a random text with a half-naked girl or an obscure question about a song or an artist. And I usually texted back. But seeing him regularly was a different thing.

Mom pulled her salt-and-pepper hair into a ponytail at the back of her neck. She looked tired. Always. And sad. And sometimes angry. I wanted to make things better for her, but how the hell was I supposed to do that?

All the words we never said pounded in my head. Her sadness somehow seemed quieter, even though she cried in bed at night when she thought I was sleeping. Muffled sobs that split me apart until I had to put the Kinks too loud on my headphones and start reading Sartre's *Being and Nothingness* to make it go away.

"I saw the school is doing college testing prep classes." She'd gone from fluttering over her uniform to swiping at the kitchen counters in too-wide, too-hard strokes. "Did you want me to sign you up for them?"

More classes. More people. More questions to answer. Pass.

"I'm okay without them."

"Of course you are. But college is important, Kyle." The hardness was back in her clipped words. An almost unexplainable anger, except I could explain it.

God, I need to get out. I was such a dick for even thinking it, but there it was. The thought didn't matter. I wasn't leaving my mom. We both knew it. She talked about my future like she expected great things from me. Like I'd go off into the world and make her proud. But she withered every time she saw a catalogue come in the mail for an out-of-state college. So college was important, as long as it was close to home. Push-pull, push-pull.

"Hey. The guy with no name. Do you remember me?" Hailey asked as she stepped into the radio station control room.

Yes. "Uh."

She pushed some of her hair behind her ear and pressed her glasses back on her nose. Cute blue glasses with diamonds on the edges. Kind of fancy for the Converse she was wearing, but fuck if I get girls and their clothes.

I hadn't seen Hailey since the interview—a few days? A week? Our high school had two campuses, one for freshmen and sophomores, one for juniors and seniors. I was a junior and Hailey was a sophomore, so we never passed each other in the halls at school. And I *was* looking for her, even braved the main hallway after the final bell one day in hopes that she'd be practicing in one of the music rooms.

"Was that an answer?" she asked, head tilted to the side like she was trying to figure out what she was dealing with.

Crap. I hated that I couldn't say anything without wanting to curl inside and hide. I was like the sad turtle from that kids' book, the one not even the hippo wanted to hang around. Owen or Mzee. Whichever. I never understood that book.

"Can I help you?" Four words. Choked from the back of my throat, probably spoken too soft and too fast, but still. Four words.

She took a step closer. "Yeah. So what's your name?"

"Kyle," I mumbled because really, it was sort of the best I could do. The heat in the room was already getting uncomfortable.

I'd heard her voice in my head this week more than I wanted to admit—especially when I didn't want to think about other stuff. When my eyes twitched from reading. When I'd gone over my dumb life too many times. Her gravelly voice was like a whisper in my ear.

She licked her lips and my eyes dropped to the ground again. "So, Kyle. I'm wondering if I can get a copy of that interview."

I nodded and took a step back. Yeah. Interview. *Pull it together, K. Make a copy of the interview.* She followed me into the office with the main computer. Her eyes weren't darting around like they had the first time I saw her. The glasses must've helped. My fingers moved over the keyboard.

"It's kind of dark back here. How come you guys don't open any of the shades on the window?"

"The equipment gets too hot."

That was a reasonable answer, wasn't it? Five words. An entire sentence that was actually an answer to her question. Not much, but better than looking like a mute.

She tapped her fingers on her jeans and waited. *Tap. Tap. Tap.* A definite staccato. Did she always hear music in her head? I'd wondered that about musicians. Did she hear it like I heard words? I kept pressing buttons until I found the interview and copied it to a thumb drive.

"You're obviously not dumb. So are you shy or do you have a stutter or something?"

I shrugged.

"You don't need to be nervous around me. I'm half-blind with two moms. I'm probably the least judgmental person you'll ever meet."

Damn that low voice. Whiskey sexy, doing stuff to my junk that made me seriously glad I was sitting behind a computer.

I liked her. More. I liked her more. My eyes shut for a second and I shook my head. I couldn't like her. Girls didn't work for me. Or I didn't work for them. Plus, she was probably gay. That was stupid, right? Gay moms don't make you gay, but I wondered anyway. I wondered lots of things. Thoughts pressed into my brain all the time, pinged around and didn't go away until I wrote them down.

She blinked at me, waiting for something. I didn't really know what. Everything about being in the room with Hailey felt awkward. Like I had a giant sign over my head that said: NOT IN YOUR LEAGUE. Unless . . .

"Are you gay?" *Oh, Christ. I said it out loud.*

She laughed and tucked her hands into the back pockets of her jeans. It sort of made her boobs stick out, and I pretended I didn't notice, but I *am* a guy. And they *were* boobs. Kinda nice ones. Not ridiculously huge, but perfect in proportion to the rest of her.

"Am I gay? That's the first thing you're gonna ask me?" She let out a careless laugh. Loose. Like it cost her nothing. "Really?"

I refocused on the computer. "I didn't . . ."

She laughed again. "You're kinda weird. And I don't know if I'm gay. It's a little too soon to tell where I fall on the continuum. Are you interested in me?"

She said that. *Out loud.*

I shook my head and blinked at the computer screen.

"Okay. Good. That's cleared up. So are you asking because you wanna be friends?"

I glanced at her for a second, but then turned back to the computer. I quickly ejected the thumb drive and handed it to her.

"So maybe friends?" she asked as she tucked the drive into her bag.

My tongue was glued to the roof of my mouth.

She nodded. "Okay. Acquaintances for now, I guess." She patted her bag. "Thanks again. I had this list of stuff to do for the moms so I can go to this concert tonight. Portugal. The Man. You know them?"

I did, but I was surprised she did. I nodded.

"You going?"

Not likely. All those people.

"Okay, then." Hailey paused, maybe waiting to see if I'd say something. "I'll see you, Kyle."

"Yeah. Okay."

She spun on her heel and I'd be lying if I said I didn't watch her butt the entire time she walked out. I'd have to ask Pavel about the magnetism of girls' asses. He'd definitely have some hypotheses and supporting research on it.

Because Hailey was still on my mind when I left school, I didn't see them coming. Didn't see the subtle back-and-forth nods, winks, and chin tilts that packs do before they go on the attack. I knew better than to let my guard down, which was sort of the worst part. Because I had. Hung up on some girl's butt and glasses.

"Hey, douche, you've got something on your shirt."

I looked down. Stupid. It was a five-year-old trick and I fell for it every time. Tripped, sprawled on the floor, the sound of laughter and high fives echoing around me. Swiping at my brow, my finger spotted with blood. *Dammit.* I'd hit hard.

I knew enough not to take a hand when one guy offered to help me up. Just gathered my books and inched away, crawling out of reach before I finally stood, in case a fist or a boot wanted a piece of me too.

One more year in this place, and then I'd never look back.

Chapter Four: Hailey

Wow." Lila closed her eyes, and her soft blond hair fell back as she listened to me on the recording. She was in yoga wear. Of course. At dinner. But we were listening to my band in replacement of the usual fifteen-year-old-daughter grilling. Kyle had saved me from a round of questioning—something I might thank him for later. And something he might or might not respond to. I smirked as I thought about what his nonreaction/reaction would be.

"You're amazing." Rox touched my shoulder, bringing me back into the kitchen, where my voice and the band were just finishing the song.

On a recording, I didn't sound half-bad. Way older than fifteen, for sure. In my own ears, it was hard to tell how good I really was. I'd hated my lower voice until I'd realized that when I sang, it sorta worked. We weren't quite Halestorm or the Pretty Reckless, but there were only three of us.

I'd checked one more thing off my list. *The list.* The one my moms made me start at the beginning of freshman year—all the crap I was afraid of but still determined to do. Well, and some things I wanted to do before I went blind, but I'd never say that to the moms. "Overcoming fears" sounded way better, and they were into all that *be in touch with your feelings* stuff. I wanted to *feel* like I was kicking ass—that's why the list worked for me.

I'd done some really wimpy things so far—go to the grocery store by myself and sing in front of an audience. Okay. The second one wasn't exactly easy, and neither was the first, really, but still. Singing on the radio. Being recorded live. Huge mark off. It felt good. And I had the thumb drive proof I'd actually done it.

"You sound like Stevie Nicks." Rox smiled. "You know that?"

"Is that supposed to be a compliment?" I smirked. "'Cause she sounds like chick music for old people, not rock. I'm going for Taylor Momsen or the low version of Hayley Williams."

Rox slapped me on the shoulder, a pretend frown on her face. "Show some respect."

I laughed. "Okay. This was the last thing you all asked me to do. I can go out tonight, right? Portugal. The Man? They're from Portland or Alaska, or both. I forget. Incredible musicians.

I aced my math test. Sat through my eye appointment without cussing even once. And you've listened to the recording. So. *Please?*"

They exchanged tired looks over the worn dining room table. Lila looked like the softie, but she was always harder to convince.

"Please?" I'd been begging and doing extra chores ever since I heard they were coming to town.

"So. This is at an Irish bar? Which is dividing itself for underage?"

"Yes." I nodded, my heart thrumming with the anticipation that had been building for two weeks. Since Tess and Mira had shoved the flyer under my nose and told me what it was. "Totally divided." I stretched my arms out as wide as I could, when in reality, we all knew it would probably be a rope.

"And you expect us to believe you won't be drinking?" Lila raised a brow. "You look older than your age, so we worry."

"Come on! That was at Tess's house, and her birthday, and *one time*!" That they knew about. "Please? I spent almost a month's worth of allowance on this ticket!"

My legs jiggled under the table.

"Home by eleven." Lila's smooth voice made it sound like a privilege. Right. I knew better.

No way the band would be done by then. "But—"

"Eleven." Rox's dark eyes were hard on me. "That's final."

Lila cut in. "And you will answer each and every call—"

"No." I put my hand up between us. "I'll text. But no calls. I'd have to leave to hear you, and since I already have to come home before they finish, I don't want to miss any more than is absolutely necessary."

"And Tess and Mira will be there?" Rox said it more for me to confirm.

"Yes." Hope for my win spread fast.

"Okay. But—"

I didn't let Lila finish. "Thank you! I swear. I swear I'll be good, and thank you so much for not coming with me, and—"

"Well, that's not something I'd thought of." Rox raised a brow. "Coming with you."

My jaw dropped and my stomach sank before they both started laughing.

"You should have seen the look on your face." Rox cackled and held her sides. And even Lila snorted.

"Ha-ha." I let out a sigh. "Very funny." My gut slowly worked its way back to normal.

"Don't make us sorry, sweetie." Lila smiled her *I mean business but I love you* smile.

"Wouldn't dream of it." I bounded down the stairs to call Tess and Mira.

"I'm in," I said to Tess by way of hello.

"Thank God, because Mira's grounded. Again. Her parents are the worst. I thought I'd be stuck chatting up cute guys by myself."

I laughed. "I'm not going to chat up cute guys. I'm going for the band."

"These activities aren't mutually exclusive. I'd like to think a love of music and Portugal. The Man is a good way of vetting the caliber of possible suitors."

Tess said things like "vetting the caliber of possible suitors" a lot. It was as if she fell asleep reading either historical romance novels or enrich-your-vocabulary books.

"Pass. Anyway, what time are you picking me up?"

"I'll be there in a few to review wardrobe choices. I'm not giving up on finding someone cute for you. You keep telling me you have to be actively knocking stuff off that list of yours. I'm trying to be a supportive friend."

"Yeah, yeah. I'll see you soon."

When I hung up, I thought of maybe-cute Kyle and his halting speech. It was too bad he could barely string a sentence together. He might've been a good prospect otherwise. At the same time, there was something interesting about the idea of hanging out with someone who might be more messed up in the head than I was.

Chapter Five: Kyle

Being tossed around at school wasn't a new thing. Still, as I scrubbed blood off the neck of my T-shirt in the sink at home, I felt like I might start crying and never stop. I wanted to call Pavel. Have him tell me some stupid story about an article he'd read or about the power of positive thinking.

I scrubbed harder.

I wouldn't call him. Wouldn't because he'd had it so much worse than me and shrugged it off like nothing.

The front door opened and closed, so I flipped the lock on the bathroom to avoid another lecture from Mom.

I blinked in the mirror. A small cut on my brow. Swollen nose. Fat lip. A faint shadow under my eye that would be worse tomorrow. I'd hit the ground harder than I'd thought.

"Kyle?" Her thin voice carried from the living room.

"Bathroom," I called back.

"What are you doing in there?"

"Washing . . ." I didn't really want to admit I was hand-washing a T-shirt to make sure the blood didn't stain. "My face."

"Open up." She knocked. "I need you to run an errand for me."

I let my eyes fall closed and held in the groan that would bring on a lecture about respect and helpfulness and single parenthood. . . .

I rinsed a washcloth and carefully squeezed cool water over my face, flinching again as the water touched the cuts.

"Kyle."

I unlocked the door.

Mom pushed the door open, her frown echoed in the mirror. "What have I told you about fighting?"

Not to do it, obviously. I kept silent.

Her eyes narrowed. "You're not a fighter, Kyle. Don't be your father."

Yeah. *That* wasn't going to be a problem.

"I expect more from you. I'm killing myself at work. You can't be getting into this again."

For once, I agreed with her.

"You're not in trouble with the school, are you?"

"No."

A grocery/pharmacy list was flicked in my direction. The bags under her eyes, on top of how clipped and angry she was, said her shift hadn't gone well.

"Sorry, Mom. I'll take care of the list." At least no one had kicked my ribs this time. Carrying Mom's bags home with bruised ribs was the worst.

She sighed. "I'm doing the best I can here. I need you to work with me."

I stepped around her, wet T-shirt clutched in my hand. "Yes, ma'am."

"Sarcasm doesn't do anyone any good." Her words snapped. My head ducked.

Tonight wasn't a night to argue with her or say anything that didn't need to be said.

I dropped the wet T-shirt on top of the laundry pile in my room and stepped over a box of books to jerk open a dresser drawer. I put on a clean T-shirt. I needed five minutes to pull myself together. Five minutes. This wasn't her fault. It wasn't my fault either, but that was harder to believe.

Mom lay spread out on the couch when I finally emerged from my room, a remote in her right hand, her eyes glassed over and staring at the screen. "You can take my car." She gestured loosely toward the door.

Her eyes drooped farther. This was a drug-induced droop. Probably for the best.

She'd be asleep before I got home, which maybe meant I

had a few extra minutes tonight, or hours. With her car. A car she barely ever lent me.

After the day I'd had, and the headache that had only begun to fade, I figured I deserved something different. I could do different. Maybe. And maybe my bruised face would mean I'd be left alone for a while.

I slipped into Mom's car, her list in one pocket and her keys in the other. From this point, I could go anywhere. Just drive. Leave. I wouldn't, of course. Too afraid of too many things. But the *possibility* of a world being so open?

I might want something different.

Problem was there were no sure ways to get anything different without fucking it up along the way.

Chapter Six: Hailey

Even though the Irish bar where the concert was said the age limit was going to be enforced at the door, I figured eventually I'd be able to sneak under their stupid rope and past the few randomly placed bouncers.

Mira was home, unsuccessful in her efforts to get out of being grounded, which was fine with me. Tess tended to glom on to her when we were all together, both feeding off each other in their cute-guy quest, and I ended up playing the third wheel. Pissed me off.

Besides, hanging with one emo girl all in black was enough for me.

The room was dark enough that Tess would disappear if she moved more than a few feet away, but I could see the stage, I knew the direction of the door, and that was enough.

I'd gotten used to not having the specifics of my surroundings, but new places were still tricky. I could find a wall when I needed to get reoriented. All part of the "coping skills" that came from the few group sessions the moms had dragged me to for kids with "optical issues." The bullshit language really didn't do anything for me. I'd rather them say, *Let us tell you how to organize your life before you go blind and it gets a lot harder.*

The opening band was a group of locals I'd never heard before. Delayed. I didn't know if they realized their name immediately put them on the small bus, or if it was supposed to have some double meaning about getting laid that I didn't understand.

Regardless, they were good. Really good. Like killer-lead-guitarist good. I adjusted my glasses a million times but still couldn't make out much more than a few tattoos, crazy blond hair, and forms with guitars on the stage. That was the beautiful part about music, though—you didn't have to see to enjoy it. All you had to do was be smart enough to really let it in.

Bodies jostled. People cussed as they cheered. Tess got lost under the arm of some loser she was making googly eyes at, and I ran a hand through my hair, fluffing it up a bit to get some air. Maybe I should have let Rox braid it up—I mean, I'd been braiding my own hair forever, but she did designs with braids, and it gave her a bit of a mom thrill at the same time. A bead of sweat had already formed on my brow, but no one would even notice if I started to stink in here. Too many bodies. Too much buzzing energy. Too much drinking, sweating, and screaming.

Portugal. The Man took the stage, and nothing but stomping started their first song. I jumped up and down with half the crowd to stomp as loud as I could in Rox's old Frye boots, glad I'd thought to ask her for them. I might even start trading my Converse out for the knee-high kicks once in a while.

"You like?" A male voice made my heart jump a beat.

I turned to see one of the black-T-shirted bouncers. Talking. To me.

"Love." I laughed.

He wasn't one of the huge guys. If you weren't a huge guy and got hired as a bouncer, you could kick some serious ass. A lesson learned from Rox, who grew up in rock 'n' roll bars. The veins stood out on his arms, and I'd bet you couldn't find a pinch of fat on him—which I sorta wanted to try. His hair was almost military short, which added to his tough-guy image and made me want to run my palms over his head to feel the hairs pricking into my skin. So, yeah. Hot.

"Cool glasses. Green. Festive." His bright blue eyes shined in the dim light.

"To match my bra." I pulled the strap from under my tee, glad Tess had helped me dress.

"No. I already noticed that." He smiled a row of perfectly imperfect teeth. White but not totally even.

Flutters in my stomach. For the guy. The one who had to be at least five years older. Maybe more.

"So I'm supposed to be on that side of the room." The side that would show I was twenty-one. Older. Legal. Not in high school. I leaned close to see if he'd let me through.

His arm immediately went up with the rope so I could slide under, and maybe accidentally on purpose touch my back to his stomach. Which I did.

"Can I get you a drink?" he yelled in my ear. "We're allowed two drinks, as long as we drink them at the line."

I didn't even pause because while I wasn't looking for it, I also wasn't stupid. Hot older guy. That's major image cred in high school. Smoke and mirrors, just like being in a band, but whatever.

"Yeah. A beer?" I asked.

"Don't move. I'll be right back." He leaned in way closer than he needed to for his answer. He smelled musky. Like man. Not like boy. Man.

Score one for Hailey Bosler.

Portugal. The Man was three songs in by the time he made it back. Tess was now at the base of the stage with her new lackey, and I screamed when the band told me to scream, and stomped when they told me to stomp.

After three shots and two beers, I was also dancing with

Chaz. Yes. Chaz. My back to his chest, and his hand occasionally resting low on my stomach. Though he was supposed to be working, so I stepped away a few times to not make our closeness too obvious.

The night was turning out pretty damn perfect.

Except my phone buzzed in a text. And I had to pee. And I had no idea where the bathrooms were. And I definitely wasn't going to admit to this hot bouncer guy that I couldn't see far enough to catch a glimpse of the restroom sign.

I leaned back, pressing us together again. "I gotta take off pretty soon."

"Hey," Chaz yelled in my ear, pulling me even closer.

I turned, and he slid his arm low on my back until our stomachs touched. The room floated. I floated. His lips were so close.

What if he kissed me and I screwed it up?

No. No way. How hard could it be? Millions of dumbasses kissed every day.

"My boss is giving me the evil eye, and you're taking off, so how do I call you?"

I pulled out my phone, even though there was less space between us. "Give me your number."

He dialed in his number, and I hit send, then saved a blindly thumbed-in approximation of his name to my list.

"That's how you get me." I let my lips brush against his ear.

My boobs pressed into his chest, his hips pushed up against mine. Damn, I was brave.

"'Get you.' I like that."

I was close enough to see the corner of his mouth pull up in a smirk.

Without meaning to, I leaned in, and he closed the distance. His mouth crushed against mine, tasting like beer and a hint of barbecue, and feeling like something sexy, forbidden, and perfect with my night—really frickin' perfect. Wow. Kiss. Chaz. Tongues. Hands. Stomachs, chests, hips together. He pulled away too fast.

"See you soon, Hailey. Can't wait to see what glasses you wear next time." Only his eyes were on my chest. Not my face. I laughed, buzzing from the booze, the kiss, and another item to cross off my list.

Tongue-kissing.

As I pushed through the crowd, my stomach rolled, and I still had to pee, and I didn't see Tess, and my phone buzzed again.

Chaz was chatting with an enormous guy also in a black bouncer shirt, and I scanned the crowd for Tess, but there was no way I was going to find her and her stupid black hair in the dark. I needed air. *Out.* I could call her from the sidewalk. Or the bathroom.

I stumbled toward where I was pretty sure the door was, but it was even darker moving away from the stage than toward it. People were still yelling the songs with the band, and standing, jumping, shoving. I used my arms to guard my chest, but all the moving bodies made it even harder to get around. I hated my eyes. Hated that I was going blind. Hated that something as simple as finding a bathroom was a process. The whole night might make it onto my list.

I bumped into a familiar chest on the underage side of the room, standing against the wall. *Holy unexpected shit.*

"Acquaintance Kyle?" What the hell was he doing here?

"Uh . . ."

"Where's the bathroom? No. The door? No. The bathroom?" My body swam, only it was more wobbly swimming than the floaty, happy kind.

"Bathrooms are closer." His voice was barely loud enough for me to hear over the music.

"Which way?"

He pointed.

"Okay." I grabbed his arm. "Is the first door the ladies', or the second door?" In the dark, I'd probably have to stand there and squint for a moment. I wasn't into looking like an idiot in front of the bathrooms.

I expected a smart remark. Or a smile. Or a tease.

Nothing.

Relief.

"The first one."

"Thank you. So much." I put a hand on each of his narrow shoulders. "Can you stand here and wait for me for a sex? Sec?

Please?" When did words get so hard to form? When did my tongue get so sloppy? Tequila messed with my head a lot more than beer.

He nodded.

Perfect.

I stumbled toward the bathroom, glad he knew which was the ladies', and pulled out my phone as soon as I got inside. The lighting was no better in there. I couldn't see to get to the place in my phone that let me send texts.

Oh. I clutched my stomach as it rolled over.

Eleven twenty. Shit and back, I was in deep trouble.

No time for pee. No time for Tess. I needed home. Now.

I shoved the phone back into my pocket as I followed the wall back to Acquiesce Kyle. No. Action Kyle. No. Hilarious. I was laughing so hard when I reached him that I almost forgot what I needed. My stomach knotted up with each shake. And then my gut flipped over. *Oh, no.*

"Okay. I need out." I clutched Kyle's shoulder again as my stomach whirled.

He said nothing. Did nothing.

"Never mind." I didn't want to bother him, but the fear was that I needed someone just to find the door. Tears threatened my eyes, but no way was I going to cry on the awesomeness of this night. Just a door. Just a bar.

Kyle obviously didn't want to leave. Fine. Whatever.

I pushed past him, stumbled along the wall and then out

the door. Ah . . . night air. Cool air. The music still vibrated in my head. I ran my hands through my hair over and over, only it didn't feel right. Like my hands were tingly and my head was sort of floaty, and . . .

"Are you okay?" Kyle appeared next to me.

"Yeah. No worries. I'm totally fine," I said the second before I threw up all over his shoes.

Chapter Seven: Kyle

OhmyGod, I'm so sorry," she said for the thirty-fifth time. "I've never done that before. I'm so *sorry*."

"It's okay," I mumbled back for the thirty-fifth time. I was driving her home. Missing the rest of the set of the best band I'd heard in ages, in a place I'd never usually have had the courage to walk into, to drive a drunk girl home.

"I'll buy you new shoes. I swear. What size are you? I feel terrible. I'm such an asshole." She sucked in a short breath. "But I'm done puking. I mean, I feel way better now, so your car is totally safe."

Great.

My shoes were in the GO GREEN cloth bag I was supposed to use for groceries. Driving barefoot wasn't exactly the easiest, but it was better than dealing with the smell.

"Your eye?" She touched the small scrape left from the dickheads at our school.

I jerked away. "Slipped. No big."

"I'm such an asshole. What's your shoe size?" she asked again.

She'd been talking endlessly since the minute she'd puked. It was like all the vomit had uncorked some sort of plug and now she wouldn't shut up. Which, in truth, was sort of cute.

"How come you didn't have that guy take you home?" I asked between breaks in her monologue. It was easier to talk knowing she wouldn't remember any of it.

"Chaz?"

"Whatever. The bouncer."

For a second, a smile lit her face and a part of me felt incredibly jealous of a poseur named *Chaz*. I wanted to put a smile like that on her face. On anyone's face, really.

"Well, the obvious reason is he's still working, and of course, there're my moms," she said, her voice definitely more sober than when she'd first bumped into me. "But also, we kinda ended the night perfectly, you know? And I didn't want to screw it up."

"So he gets perfect and I get puke. Classic."

She laughed in her raspy way. "You're funny, Acquaintance Kyle. It's nice to hear you talk. You should do that more often."

No one had ever said that to me before. Even my own mom.

I grunted.

"Ack. Don't grunt. Don't be like all those guys. Either talk or don't, but for the love of cheese, don't grunt."

"Kinda hard to get a word in edgewise with you tonight."

She snorted. Slapped her hand against the dashboard of Mom's car. The car Mom told me to run her errands in.

"Your voice is nice," Hailey said. "Low but not weird low. Smooth. It's kind of hot. How come you don't deejay?"

Kind of hot. Oh, God. Too many synapses firing and misfiring. Too many fantasies clogging up the works. Which was fucking idiotic: she'd *just* been kissing another dude.

I shrugged. "Not my thing."

She slid her boots onto the dash and I gave her a sideways look. She didn't even notice, just shimmied and wiggled into a more comfortable position.

"Deejaying's not your thing or talking's not your thing?"

I eyed her again. The green bra was sort of ridiculous. Over-the-top and too expected for a lead singer of a girl band. But Jesus, I kept looking at it, like she'd worn it for me. Which was stupid. And not that my opinion mattered, but the day in the studio, when she wasn't all done up, she was hotter. Of course, she hadn't been tongue-fucking some random bouncer then.

"Both," I answered.

"You should have a list. And deejaying your own show should be the first thing on it. Well, that and maybe not freaking out every time someone says something to you. But that's sort of too general for the list. Deejaying is a very specific fear."

"What the hell are you talking about?"

She stomped her boot on the dash.

"Jesus, take it easy, will you?" Mom didn't have the money to fix the car if Drunk Hailey broke it. I didn't want to be a dick, but I was doing her a favor and the least she could do was not break the car.

"Sorry."

"S'okay. So you were saying?"

"Oh my God, haven't I told you about the list? Shit. Of course not. We don't talk. Well, we're talking now, but we're just acquaintances. Only my close friends and the moms know about it."

The list. Did I really want to know about the list?

"But maybe we'll be good friends now because I puked on your shoes and shit like that brings people closer."

I laughed, surprised. "Keep telling yourself that."

She grinned at me. "I knew I could get you to laugh. So anyway, the list. It's this thing I started last year. My moms wanted me to do it. Write down all the things I was afraid of and then start tackling them."

"Huh." Weird. Nothing my mom would ever suggest or, honestly, even care about. Her lists were very specific: *buy toilet paper, take out trash, pick up my Xanax* . . .

"Yeah, I know. It's kinda dumb, but it's sort of a rush when you actually do something on it."

"What have you done?" I blurted out.

"Well, nothing really great so far. But I sang on the radio. And tonight I had my first tongue kiss."

"Yeah. I caught that. Must have tasted outstanding."

She chuckled. "I thought you weren't interested in me."

Fuck. "I'm not."

"Then why do you give a shit what my first tongue kiss tasted like?"

I opened and closed my mouth. This was why I didn't get into friendly conversations. My brain screamed answers at me, but I couldn't articulate any of them without bumbling the whole thing. Or coming across as too interested. And I couldn't be into her. Could. Not. There were days when I thought my brain would explode just thinking about the shit Pavel had gone through. And Mom was a time bomb. Two people were enough. Mostly.

"It was just an observation," I settled on. "So singing on the radio and tongue-kissing. What else is on the list?"

She squinted at me. The greenness of her glasses made her eyes sort of sparkle bright green. Either that or the darkness of the night made the blue disappear. Stupid thing to notice, but her messed-up eyes intrigued me. Or maybe the fact that she was the only girl since second grade to be near me, curious about me—maybe that was the intriguing part.

"Nah," she said. "I don't think I'm gonna tell you. I think we should focus on your list."

"I don't have a list."

She shoved my shoulder. I gripped the steering wheel tighter.

"The point is that you *need* a list. You, of all people, need to start overcoming your fears or you're gonna have one hell of an effed-up life."

"You don't even know me," I snapped. Too harsh, but who the hell did this girl think she was to be making any sort of comment on my life? *I* couldn't objectively comment on my life, and I'd been stuck with myself for almost seventeen years.

"True. So tell me something that'd be on your list. If you had one. Something you're afraid of. Something that maybe no one knows about. Something different from deejaying."

"That's kind of an invasive question."

She nodded. "Hey. I puked on your shoes. I think we've moved past invasive."

I kept my gaze forward. Was I really gonna do this? I was so distracted I ended up blowing a stop sign.

But Hailey just laughed. Still drunk, then. Which was good. Fine. Safer to say whatever I wanted to. She'd forget.

"I'm afraid of going away to college."

She tilted her head. "Really? Yeah, I can see that. What else?"

"That's . . . it."

"Okay. Going to college: scary. All right. But, honestly, Kyle. Think about it. It might be good for you. Break you out of your shell or whatever. Okay, stop. Here's my house."

I pulled in front of a yellow house with a massive porch and a small detached garage. The glass front of the garage was a window into a pottery shop—Pottery Rox. I put the car in park but didn't turn off the ignition.

"This is it?"

She nodded and I noticed her hand shaking as she gripped the handle. Not so fearless when it came to her moms, then. Truthfully, I was curious about her moms. What kind of women raised a girl like Hailey? I hadn't met too many moms in my life. Mine, who was, well . . . yeah. And Pavel's mostly scolded, huffed, and cooked.

I considered leaving Hailey on the curb. Let her get out and then drive away. But I couldn't. I wasn't that guy. Never had been. Except maybe once.

"Dammit," she said. "I'm such an idiot. I'm so fucked."

"You want me to walk you inside?" I said. "Maybe it'll help distract them . . . ?"

She blinked at me and swallowed a few times, then whispered, "Thanks."

Her moms had the door open before we even got halfway from the car to the porch.

"You are so grounded," the blond mom said. Her face was open but held the small creases of mom worry. She had on flannel pj bottoms and a tank top. Thin and kind of muscly. "And who the hell is this? Where are Tess and Mira?"

"Um."

I looked at Hailey. Her fingers twisted in front of her. She'd suddenly lost her power of speech. The girl who'd spent twenty minutes talking nonstop in my car couldn't pull off anything other than "um." I wanted to laugh but didn't think it would help her case much.

"Hi," I said. "I'm Kyle," I added. The moms just stared, like that wasn't enough. "We know each other from school."

Hailey's dark-haired mom squinted at me, and I looked down. I didn't suck at talking to adults in the same way I did with people my own age, but it still wasn't easy.

The dark-haired mom sighed. I looked up and saw her touch the blonde's shoulder. Then she said, "Thanks for bringing her home, Kyle. We appreciate it."

I nodded and turned back to my car.

"Kyle," Hailey's low voice called out before I got into my car. I glanced back. "Sorry again about the shoes. Size eleven?"

I glanced at my bare feet. "Ten," I answered, and then slipped into the driver's seat. I couldn't look at her. Didn't want to know if she was looking at me. Didn't want to really hope for it.

All the way home, I ran through my night. I'd been puked on. Babbled at. Almost interrogated by two lesbians. And for a few minutes, it had felt like I had a real friend. I couldn't trust it. But I wanted to.

I walked into my lonely house and pulled out the journal I scribbled my overwhelming thoughts into. Lyrics from songs. Lines from poems. Quotes from philosophy I didn't understand but one day hoped to. Band names, podcast titles, ramblings from my own brain. Pages and pages of it. It was my third journal in eighteen months. I flipped to a new page and rubbed my fingers over the smooth paper. Then, before I could stop myself, I started my own list of fears.

Chapter Eight: Hailey

I found Kyle in the sound booth at the radio station. I was right to guess he probably hid there before school. It sucked because the place had crap for lighting, but he was the only one there. Big surprise.

"Hey, Friend Kyle." I smiled, wondering if he was still pissed about driving me home this past weekend. But maybe over the past few days, his annoyance had faded.

Kyle turned and stared. Solidly unreadable.

I was crap at apologizing, so I sat close enough to see his face better, which was pretty close—knees almost touching—and pulled out the box from my pack. Flipping off the lid with a flourish, I grinned.

"They're bright." He stared at the shoes I held between us, size ten, because I'm good like that and remembered.

We sat in silence for a moment.

But he still hadn't touched the shoes.

"I know. Green. Awesome, right? It's for you to remember the night we moved past acquaintances into friendship territory." I leaned forward on the small chair I'd scooted next to him. "This is good, sentimental stuff, Kyle. You should be more appreciative."

Mostly I wanted him in the damn shoes. They screamed Kyle. That color of green wasn't easy to find, and I'd had to beg the moms, telling them I was righting a wrong from my horrible night of mistakes and misfortunes, before they let me out of the house. Sadly, it hadn't been alone.

"Um . . ." His head still bent forward so far I couldn't see his eyes.

"I shopped with *two moms* for you. My very pissed two moms." Ungrateful. Seriously. His shoes could have been washed. They didn't need to be *replaced*. Why couldn't he see I was being nice?

"Oh."

"I get your whole blending thing, but maybe now you could sort of cheat and put 'Wearing bright shoes' on your fear list, and then you can get the high from crossing it off a minute later. Not every fear needs to be a huge one, you know?" I even waggled my brows for him, trying to get a reaction. And I knew I was probably sitting too close for whatever football-stadium-size comfort zone he had, but still. There was something fascinating about Kyle's disturbing silence, and I wanted him to talk. Give me clues as to what made him Kyle. "'Cause I know you wanna do it with me . . ."

"What?" He blushed. A bright-pink-cheeks-on-pale-skin kind of blush that made me realize I'd just innuendoed him.

I grinned. "The *list*, Kyle. Do the *list*."

I'd never convinced Tess or Mira, but at least they knew about my list. Kyle had to be desperate enough for friends that he'd join me. Or maybe he was a more hard-core loner than I'd given him credit for, which was fascinating in its own way.

"Kyle! I bought you new frickin' shoes. You drove me home, for shit's sake! I told you about my list! Like it or not, we're friends. Put on the damn shoes, and I'll see you later." I shoved them onto his lap and took off.

I sucked at finding non-annoying friends.

"Hailey! What the hell? I called you all weekend." Tess walked toward me, boots clomping, mouth in a scowl, and I knew I was screwed. Her short black hair stuck out on all sides today. Probably on purpose, but it was hard to tell with her. She had no problems rolling out of bed, putting on black, adding to the one- or three-day-old eyeliner, and coming to school.

In the whole Kyle/puke/shoe/car mess, I forgot to call. Or text. And the moms actually laughed when I asked if I could keep my phone.

"I got busted, and if you hadn't taken off under the arm of

that random guy, you would have known where I was." Arguing back was better than telling her I screwed up and should have called.

"I did know where you were. You were grinding with the bouncer guy, who was way hot. . . ." A small smile escaped before she found her pissed face again. Tess didn't just dress emo. She *was* emo. "And then you *bailed*!"

"You know I can't see well when it's dark like that. I had to be home at eleven, and when I found the bathroom, it was already after curfew. I didn't have time to find you. If you didn't need to wear black all the time, I might have been able to pick you out of the crowd." I knew that harassing her about her clothes was probably not the thing to do, but once I was on a roll, I kept on running. One of the perks/hazards of being me.

"You didn't have time to *not* find me. How the hell did you get home?" Tess's irritated voice always cracked me up, because she might dress like a bitch, but there was nothing she could do about her kitten voice. Mad Tess usually made me laugh, and that didn't always end well.

"I puked on Kyle's shoes, and he took me home." That was the easy version, anyway.

"Shit. I bet your moms were pissed." Tess sat back, hopefully a bit less angry.

"That doesn't even come close. Aside from school and a possible national emergency, I'm not allowed out of the house." The whole thing sucked, but as soon as I'd missed curfew, I'd known they'd freak. My being wasted and smelling like alcohol vomit also hadn't helped.

She leaned in. "So Kyle's the bouncer you hooked up with?"

"No. Kyle is the silent guy who does the engineering at the radio station here. He's cool." I adjusted the guitar on my back, knowing she probably wouldn't get my fascination with him. Hell, I was still figuring out why I hadn't left the guy alone already. Even if he did need to have those shoes.

Tess crossed her arms. "Really?"

"No. Not really." I laughed. "But he has potential."

And this is the great thing about Tess. She'd stomped up to me ready to be pissed, but once she'd found out I'd gotten home and that I was okay and in trouble, she wasn't pissed anymore.

This is an excellent trait to have in a friend.

"So what about bouncer guy?" She nudged my arm, and we started to walk toward class together.

"Chaz. Short for Charles." I knew I grinned like an idiot, but I was fifteen, and he was legal to get beer. *Con*quest.

Tess shook her head and laughed. "If you could see, you'd know how gorgeous you are, and you wouldn't be all that surprised."

What? That was maybe the only compliment I'd ever gotten from Tess outside of our band.

"I know what I look like." And I *was* surprised. And flattered. Hot bouncer and a sophomore in high school?

"So. We need to practice." She smacked her gum a few times. If she was in different clothes, with long brown hair, she'd have looked like one of the Barbie twins.

"Right. So I'm grounded hard-core for two weeks, 'at which point we'll reappraise'—so the moms say."

Tess released a way overdramatic sigh.

I opened my mouth to tell her to spare me another lecture, but she cut me off.

"Well, could you quit the attitude with the moms for those two weeks and let Rox do braids in your hair so we can play again?"

"Maybe." Perfect. Two moms and a sort-of best friend riding me. That's exactly what I needed. Though Rox sometimes let me off early if I was really, really cooperative. So the braids were probably a good idea.

The next two weeks would be filled with arranging pots on the shop's shelves, braided hair, and an occasional yoga class for quality time.

My girls better appreciate the sacrifices I made for the band.

Walking home was always thinking time. Running over songs in my head. Songs from my band, songs I loved. I needed my ears as much as my eyes for the mile walk—too many street crossings—so the iPod wasn't an option until I got close to home. By then, I rarely bothered.

A rhythm that Tess had been playing with flowed through

my head as I hit my street, and I tapped my thumbs on my
jeans while walking. Then I closed my eyes because I knew this
street well. Twenty steps to the Tanners' house, then a bump in
the sidewalk. The Masons had a big yard, so it was twenty-five
steps to pass their house, and their driveway had a bit of an odd
curve to it. All things that I'd thought were fun to practice in
middle school, but had started to become a reality when my
eyesight took another big leap down and my pressure-relieving
surgery hadn't helped as much as the doctors thought it would.

I hated it when my brain spanned away from something
I wanted to think about, so I focused on Tess's rhythm again.

When I heard bike tires behind me, I nearly jumped off
the sidewalk. I don't mess with bikes because they blend into
trees and basically anything upright, and bikers are generally
assholes.

Rox stood waiting on the porch for me, arms crossed, leaning against one of the posts. Exactly like she said she'd be doing
for at least the next two weeks. Special ~~torture~~ treatment after
my weekend.

Frickin' brilliant.

The bike slowed just past me, and I smelled citrus. Then a
flash of green caught my eye as he stopped in the driveway in
front of Rox's pottery shop.

"Kyle! The shoes!" He was actually wearing them. After
that morning, I'd sort of thought he might not, and honestly it
would have really pissed me off. It wasn't the easiest job to go

in search of the perfect Kyle shoes—especially because I didn't know him all that well with the whole barely talking thing he had going on. And they'd pretty much wiped this month's allowance.

"Yeah. Uh." He turned to face me.

"Now you need to scuff the shit out of them, okay? Otherwise you'll look like a total poseur." Even I could see how bright the rubber was. Not good.

His eyes almost, almost met mine, but he stared down again.

"So, you like 'em?"

He started to scuff, a black mark from our driveway marring the pristine rubber. "They're the color of your glasses from that night."

I grinned. *A whole sentence. Aces.* "Yeah. Funny. These seemed like good Kyle shoes. They're one of those limited-edition Converse colors."

"Huh." Silence. Painful, awkward silence.

"You've got some serious issues, Kyle. I'm cool with this. People with issues are good. I need to surround myself with people crazier than me. You're totally a safe bet." I reached out and punched his arm.

He didn't react.

Unfortunately, Tess and Mira only *dressed* like they had issues—most of their act was bullshit, but they could both play, so I let it slide. Kyle seemed to be pretty seriously messed up.

We definitely had to be friends. Even quiet, he wasn't boring.

"Wait." I looked up and down the street. "You don't normally go home this way, do you?"

His eyes widened a bit before he stared at the ground again, and his head shook once.

WORDS. I had to get the guy to use some *words*.

Rox cleared her throat. "No friends, Hailey." And she even used her *authority* voice.

Hell.

"This is Acquaintance Kyle, but I think maybe almost Friend Kyle. You don't need to worry about him. He's, like, one of the good guys. I mean . . ." I narrowed my eyes at him and leaned in 'cause I knew it made him uncomfortable. "There could be an ax murderer in there somewhere, but he did leave the awesomeness of Portugal. The Man early when I couldn't find Tess."

That comment, and the shoes, were about as much thank-you as he was going to get from me, so I figured a bit of flattery couldn't hurt. I also knew I made him uncomfortable. I wasn't blind enough not to see that. Probably I shouldn't have enjoyed making him squirm.

Rox sighed. "Thank you again, Kyle."

"No problem."

I let my gasp be heard. "Really? 'No problem' to her and a series of head shakes for me? Wait. You came home this way to show me you had the shoes on." It was good. Great. "That was very awesome of you, Kyle." I slugged him on the shoulder again. "You're, like, blossoming already."

"I gotta get home." He started to push off.

"Wait." I jogged a few steps so he couldn't get too far away. "The list?"

"Uh."

I touched his forearm and he shrank back. Serious issues. "The list. In or out?"

"I'm in," he mumbled before he started pedaling as if he'd robbed a bank.

Though a bike was a pretty dumbass way to rob a bank. Still, it was a cool picture. Kyle, in his bright green shoes, money bags on his back, cops chasing him. And he was in. I was going to get to learn a lot more about Possible-Ax-Murderer Kyle. Cool.

"Hailey!" Rox snapped. "You got two calls today from someone named Chaz?"

Don't smile. Don't react. Holy. Shit. Chaz called me. Me. Only a few days later. That had to be good in guy time, right?

"Tess's friend. Weird." I shrugged and slipped past her into the house, wondering if there was any way to sneak my phone to call him back.

Chapter Nine: Kyle

Fight! Fight! Fight!"

I hated those words more than almost any others in high school. I particularly hated them when they had to do with me. Which, unfortunately, they often did. And it wasn't always as easy as shuffling away from someone tripping me in the hall. Silence doesn't necessarily mean escape from the eyes of guys looking to whale on someone. Especially when everyone's all wired and stir-crazy right before spring break. My face bruises had *just* healed.

By the third punch in the gut, I was down, curled into a ball and protecting my head and face from kicks.

The salty flavor of blood filled my mouth. I kept as still as possible, waiting for a teacher to come along. Waiting for the bell to ring so everyone would scatter, and I could pull myself up and go clean off in the bathroom.

Another kick landed on my thigh. My hands clutched my junk from the next hit. It hurt to breathe deeply. I counted for distraction, but the numbers became a tally of blows or the seconds I'd have to stay down until the guys gave up.

So instead, I thought of Hailey and tried to remember the colors of the glasses I'd seen on her. Tried to decide which pair was my favorite. The blue ones, maybe. Or the green ones that matched her bra. God, I liked that green bra, even if it was sort of sleazy.

After many millions of years of pondering Hailey's bras and glasses and then even what she might look like naked, the bell rang and it was finally, finally over. For now. Before I could get up, Dave, I think his name was, coughed up a loogie and spat it in my hair. It was almost worse than the beating, but still I didn't say anything.

People left. Raced to classes. Moved on. Show's over.

I pulled myself into a crouched seated position and ran my hand over my face. Aside from the split lip, it wasn't too bad. Not nearly as bad as freshman year.

One day, I thought, I might fight back. Maybe. Maybe it would be something to put on the list. The list I'd written over a week ago and hadn't done one thing about. The list for Hailey, who I was maybe friends with. Particularly after that time on my bike. In the shoes she bought me that I didn't want to take off. That matched her green glasses.

Instead of suffering through teacher explanations or the whispers that would follow me, I eased my bag onto my shoulder and took off. Pavel would be outside playing soccer, like almost every afternoon. And as much as I never wanted to drag him into whatever shitty situation life handed me, his house was safe.

"Kyle, my friend. Finally you come to see me. And in the day. No school?"

Pavel wore a knockoff tracksuit, messing around with his soccer ball, flipping it off his foot and behind his back. Girl voices screamed from inside his one-story house, followed by his mom's sharp reprimand.

"No school. Not for me."

He nodded. "You bleed, eh? Fight?"

I shrugged. Pavel had seen me bloody before. Way more than this. When he still went to school with me. Before all the shit happened that made his parents pull him out.

He flipped the ball back up and headed it. "So we don't talk about the blood. Okay."

I looked down at my ripped shirt. I'd need to change before going home. Mom was probably having a sleeping day after pulling so many night shifts. Definitely not a good day to come home with a busted lip and a ripped shirt.

"But your mom will be upset. I'll lend you a soccer shirt. Tell her you saved a goal, but the guy on the opposite team ran into you. Good?" he offered.

Mom might buy that. Or maybe she'd be too tired to try to find the lie. "Thanks."

"Have you found a lady?"

Pavel always asked this, sometimes even before anything else. He was sort of obsessed with it in the way that only a guy trapped with his four younger sisters every day would be.

"No."

He dropped the ball and plopped down next to it, signaling for me to have a seat. I moved next to him, careful of the bruises and lumps already forming on my body. His eyes widened when I flinched, but he shook his head and released a great sigh.

"I found *Cosmopolitan* at the library. It has many tips for being a good lover."

I barked out a laugh. *Ouch.* Hurt to laugh. "Pavel. No one says 'lover.' And I've never met a teenage guy who reads women's magazines for advice."

Pavel shook his head. "Which is why they never have true love. They don't know how to talk to girls. *Cosmopolitan* has many good ideas."

"Dude. I'm not reading *Cosmo*. I'm not interested in girls. I mean, I am. But you know. I can't."

The weight of my words fell between us. Too many memories of Pavel held down in the freshman locker room and me fighting so hard to get to him. And the taunts about us not being able to get it up for girls. And all the blood. And his screaming. And me forced to watch. None of it mattered now. He'd still gotten pulled from school to study at home, less than a year after he'd gotten into the country. And here it was me being the one who couldn't say shit if I had a mouthful.

"You have nice shoes." Pavel pointed, always one to note some name-brand thing I was wearing, and I smiled at the memory of Hailey. I couldn't help it. The stupid awesome green shoes and Hailey's delighted face when she gave them to me. And my bike ride past her house. Something I should have put on my list but didn't think to.

"Yeah. They were a gift from a girl."

Pavel's eyebrows lifted almost to the top of his head.

"Don't get excited. She owed me because she sort of ruined my other ones."

"This was a good gift, though."

I nodded.

"She's a friend?"

I nodded again. "Maybe. I don't see her much. She's younger. South campus still."

Pavel flinched at "south campus" but shook it off a second later. "*Cosmopolitan* says that younger women like older men. You must learn the location of the G-spot. *Cosmopolitan* says it is essential for pleasing the ladies."

I burst out laughing, holding my aching side and trying not to move too much. I needed to see Pavel more. He was a good guy. I envied his ability to let go of all his crap and just be.

"I'm a ways off from finding the G-spot."

Pavel spun the ball on the tip of his finger.

"No. That's negative thinking. I told you, my mom is making us all listen to Zig Ziglar CDs from the library. We are only positive now. The power of positive thinking. It's very different for us. Different but good."

I was an asshole. I had nothing to cry about, considering what Pavel had been through. And I owed him more than a visit every few months. Part of why I didn't spend time with him was because I worried I reminded him of our freshman year too much. Just like I reminded Mom of my absent dad. And not to keep on with my own pity party, but it wasn't always easy being a magnet for shit.

"This is not a good face, Kyle." Pavel shook his head at me. "This doesn't seem like a positive-thinking face."

I shrugged. "Hard to put on a positive-thinking face when you've just had the crap beat out of you."

Pavel stood up. "So we will go inside and listen to your sad music and maybe one of my sisters will give you first aid."

I snorted. "Please, no."

Pavel laughed a little. His smiles were rare, only coming out when he found something funny. "If you marry one of my sisters, we will be brothers for real."

I wanted to say something good. Something about how Pavel would always be a brother to me no matter what. But the words wouldn't come out of my throat. Pavel didn't need a brother like me. He needed someone who could fight or at the very least speak. There was a fear in there somewhere that should probably go on my list, but there was no way I'd dig deep enough to find it.

Chapter Ten: Hailey

Two weeks of good behavior, on top of celebrating my "sweet sixteen" with the moms, got me band practice time and my cell phone. Having my phone meant phone calls with Chaz. And apparently phone calls with Chaz and texts with Chaz led to gigs. At bars. Like the one we had tonight. He'd listened to us practice over the phone and called a friend.

Tess slammed to a stop in front of a seedy, brick-front bar. No matter whose car we had, Tess always drove because Mira was always checking her phone. And I'd known since I was six that I'd never drive. The three of us stared at the façade for about ten seconds before grinning like fools. How many famous bands had started in shitty places like this?

The whole thing had fallen together perfectly. The moms thought me, Mira, and Tess were going to catch two movies at the theater. Actually, all our parents thought that. Sort of a perfect cover. No one's allowed to answer phones during movies, and we'd snagged some cash from the parents for snacks.

The second Tess pulled into a parking space, Chaz appeared outside of the van door, smiling wide. At me.

"Hey, gorgeous," he said as he slid open the door.

My body flushed with warmth. Excitement. "Hey."

Would whatever had attracted him to me before still work?

His hand slipped around my waist, his thumb tracing the skin at the top of my jeans. He pressed his lips to the corner of my mouth. "First time I've laid eyes on you in *weeks*. I'm not used to girls playing so hard to get."

I wasn't playing. The moms would have chained me up if I'd snuck out to see him. "I'm a busy girl."

"Still. I almost thought we were gonna be a no go."

I shook my head. He *had* been persistent on the phone, almost pushy and a little possessive. But here, now, the way he looked at me, my stomach swooped at being so wanted.

Tess and Mira opened the back of the van and let out a collective groan. "I love to play," Mira said, "but I wish it didn't involve so much shit."

"I got it," Chaz said.

And he did, along with a couple bouncer friends. We were ushered in backstage, shown the filthy excuse for a greenroom, and were set up to play in minutes.

The bar had us opening for another local band, people I'd

actually heard of. It felt like a giant step up from the small venues we'd played.

My girls and I stood backstage, shoulder to shoulder, like we always did. We weren't the praying kind of girls or the kind of girls to laugh and lock hands, but there was something about standing together before we went onstage that always helped us focus.

The bartender announced Blinders On, and when Mira and Tess jogged onstage, Chaz grabbed me from behind.

"It's going to be so hot watching you out there."

I tossed him a smile before stepping carefully onto the stage—at least the lighting was okay.

The crowd was decent, into the music, and the place was pretty packed. We'd been advertised as a girl band. It felt totally antifeminist or something using our ownership of boobs to get us an audience, but it worked. And my being grounded for two weeks with nothing to do but play my guitar had also paid off.

The lights fueled me. The crowd fueled me. The feeling of a song coming together the way I imagined when we wrote it fueled me. Knowing Chaz was watching backstage fueled me. God, all of it was heady and too amazing for words. Our set was over way too fast.

When we finished, the lights dropped. And my world turned black. "Shit."

Tess stepped to the front of the stage and took my hand.

Sucked, but on a dark stage, with cords, I needed the help. At least I didn't have to ask her.

"You were amazing." Chaz pulled me into him as soon as I was backstage, pinning me against the wall.

"Thanks," I said, my knees already jelly from how his fingers slid under my shirt to touch my sides, and then I melted further when he pushed his body against mine and kissed me.

Feeling his desperation was almost as big a rush as being onstage.

When we broke apart for breath, Tess had left to pack up. She'd always been totally anal about our equipment.

"You know, they're holding you back, baby." Chaz's stubble scratched my face, and then down my neck, but once his lips touched my collarbone, I couldn't breathe and my body started to take over, screaming at me for *more*.

"They're not holding me back. They're my girls." But I couldn't say much else because Chaz's lips and hands kept moving.

"Still, Hailey." His forehead touched mine, which was sweet even if I was sweaty, but he also had his hard-on pressed into my thigh, mostly to make the point that he was turned on and wouldn't mind finding somewhere to be. Did all twentysomething guys move this fast? It was definitely on my fear list, and another thing to cross off, just . . . not yet. This was only the second time I'd actually seen him, and phone flirtation didn't exactly translate to *feel free to punch my V-card.* "You're like a goddess up there, and those two are hiding in black."

"Maybe." I ran my hands down his chest, felt the hardness, and then the ridges of his abs, giving my amped-up body another inch to override any amount of fear of being closer to him that I had.

"I'm serious, baby. I could try to find someone else to hook you up with. People who might actually go somewhere. There's some good musicians around here who'd love to have a hot girl like you with a fuck-sexy voice in front."

"Maybe," I said again. The thought was exciting, but I wasn't about to ditch my two friends. Friends. *Damn.* I should have told Kyle to come. If I could get him to talk after, I bet he'd tell me the truth about our playing and not some line.

"Why don't you come back to my place tonight?" He took my hand and slid it to his crotch, as if I didn't already know he was hard. I felt the shape of him, the largeness of him, even through his jeans. I'd never touched a guy before, and looking up pictures of guys with Tess and Mira, and trying to figure out how *that* would fit in *us*, was one thing. Having my hand on that same something he wanted to shove inside me was another.

I blinked away my worry and pressed my hand against him harder. This rush was what the fear list was about. He grasped my wrist. "Careful, gorgeous. You're making a lot of promises here, and I'd rather get you back to my place to deliver."

"I'm sixteen," I blurted out. Chaz knew I wasn't twenty-one.

He'd known that the night we met, but sixteen was probably a lot younger than he was thinking. My heart still pounded, and I held my breath as I waited for his response.

"You're not going to tell anyone if I screw you, right?" He chuckled and pressed his dick against me again.

Umm . . . okay, then.

Chaz didn't care, which felt huge, though I wasn't completely sure which side of *really big deal* it fell on. "No. I wouldn't tell anyone." The blush crept up my face, and his hands slid under my bra. Any second someone could come back here. Panic and excitement swirled around my stomach, fighting for control.

"Fuck, Hailey. You're making me crazy." He kissed me hard and then ran another trail down my neck, and all I could think was, *Please don't give me a hickey*—no way I could explain that one away.

"Yeah." But I couldn't take a deep breath. Being around Chaz was addictive. His low voice, his firm hands. No bullshit about what he wanted to do with me. To me. I wasn't sure if it was him or the idea of blowing through so many of my fears at once, but God. *God.*

He hitched my legs around his waist, my back still against the wall, him still grinding into me, giving me rush after rush of heat so intense the room spun.

The other band had started to play. I hadn't even noticed them going onstage.

"Hailey!" Tess called out. "We gotta run. Mira's got curfew."

So did I, but I wasn't going to put any more age-restraint distance between me and Chaz. Way easier to blame it on her.

Chaz let my legs go, and the rush of heat began to slip away.

"Want a hand out to the car?" she yelled because the other band was crazy loud, and my eardrums already ached from the sound.

"Sure." I stepped around Chaz to take Tess's hand, and she moved close enough that our shoulders touched and she'd actually be able to help.

Chaz grabbed my arm and pulled me back toward him, making me stumble. "You're going to leave me here?"

"Yeah. I gotta go." I pulled my arm away. Now that I'd caught my breath and put some space between us, I started to feel a little gross about what we'd been doing, backstage, with the chance of at least a half a dozen people passing us. I wasn't ready for more with him, especially not here, and it was a lot easier to blame Mira than my inexperience. "I gotta get Mira home or we lose our other guitar player."

Even in the dim light backstage, I could see Chaz's face contort.

"Come on, Hailey." Tess gave my arm a tug.

"Shit, Hailey." He leaned against the wall, annoyance on every feature I could make out. "I wanted *time* with you. Alone time."

"Sorry. I gotta go." Worry settled into that awful place in my gut as Tess led me to the car. "But soon!" I added.

"If you can't spend time with me, then what the fuck are we doing? I got you this gig!" he yelled as he followed us to the back door.

I climbed into the car, all the tingling excitement now evaporated.

"Sorry," I mumbled as Tess threw him a look before sliding the van door closed between us.

I couldn't face him as we pulled away. Instead, I sank low into the backseat. He'd been fine, and then frustrated . . . and I got it. He'd thought he was gonna get to spend time with me, and all that had happened was I'd told him I was sixteen and run away.

Chaz called two minutes after we pulled out of the lot.

"Hello?" I answered slowly.

"Sorry," he said. "I was caught off guard. And now I'm wondering if I'm going to feel responsible for you or something because you're younger, but God, I wanna see you. I wanna be with you. Shit . . ."

He was thinking out loud, and I let him.

"I put my neck on the line to get you that gig. Off hearing your band *over the phone*. I mean, do you even get that?"

"I know. I do."

"Shit." He sighed.

I waited.

"Shit, Hailey. I like you, okay? That's why I'm so frustrated. I wanna see you. All of you. It's not gonna be weeks again, is it?"

"No." Because I didn't know what else to say. A crap ending to what should have been a kick-ass night.

"Okay, look." Another sigh. "I'll call you, okay? But my week's pretty busy."

"Whenever is fine," I said as my throat swelled up.

"Later." And the phone went dead.

So that kind of sucked, but after considering it for a few seconds, I didn't think my bouncer was a total lost cause—just horny and maybe a little frustrated and slightly drunk. He definitely was into me, so I figured I'd turn him back to my side. Besides, the more I sat in the back of Mira's mom's van, the more determined I was to keep him around. I could definitely add a few items to my fear list for him to help me tackle.

Chapter Eleven: Kyle

Friend Kyle." Hailey's unmistakable voice. "Start answering your emails."

I dropped the headphones I was holding and spun around.

"What . . . what are you doing here?" The booth off the main recording room was no bigger than a closet. A closet with only me and Hailey in it. Hailey in shorts with long-ass legs and one of those worn-to-the-point-of-see-through T-shirts. Sensory overload.

Her broken eyes took in the single mic and mini soundboard. "Are you recording yourself?"

"No. I'm editing prerecorded station IDs."

She leaned against the wall and I caught a whiff of her girl sweat. Sweet and a little rank. And there was definitely something wrong with me that it turned me on. I needed to hang out with more girls regularly or I was going to embarrass myself.

"You know, I'm sixteen now, so it's almost like I haven't seen you since last year."

"Uh, happy birthday?"

I ducked my head. Too much. Too too much. All in one little space.

"Hey, you looked at me for almost twenty seconds. We've made headway."

Maybe. "Why are you here?"

"I emailed you and you didn't respond."

"You emailed me?" I asked.

"After searching for your email for, like, an hour, yeah." She leaned in and squinted at me. "What happened to your face?"

Not answering that. "Did you need something?"

She raised her hand like she was going to touch my cheek, and I flinched. "Seriously. What happened?" she asked again.

"Nothing."

The silence stretched between us for so long that I started to sweat. I was pretty sure Hailey wouldn't like my smell as much as I liked hers.

"So . . . you wanna head to my house?"

That was unexpected. "Um . . ."

"Yes. You're coming. Finish up."

"What if I have plans?"

"Ha! He has a spine. Sorry. I was being pushy." She let out a small breath. "Kyle, will you please do me the honor of coming to my place?"

It shouldn't have taken me so long to work through this dilemma. It shouldn't have felt like a dilemma in the first place. Hot girl, house invite, seemed like a no-brainer. Only my pits were sweating balls just thinking about it, and my balls . . . well. "Um . . ."

She looked worried for a second, her forehead crinkling and eyebrows crunching together, which sealed it for me.

"Yeah. Okay. Let me shut down."

She nodded and tucked her thumbs into her shorts' pockets.

"Okay, um . . ." I glanced around behind me, even though I knew I was finished. Maybe there was something else to do.

"Kyle? Are you stalling?"

Obviously. "Nope. I'm good."

"Great." Hailey clapped her hands once.

The Latni twins froze and stared as I walked out of the booth with Hailey and her tiny shorts. I hoisted my pack higher on my back, shoved my hands in my pockets, and kept my eyes on the ground.

"You bike to school, yeah?" Hailey asked when we hit the main hall.

I nodded.

She bumped my shoulder, and damn if her touch didn't almost burn. I seriously needed to spend more time with girls who were not my mom. "Talk, Kyle."

"Yes. I have a bike."

She smirked. "Cool, so can I ride the handlebars or something? North campus is farther from my house."

"A block." One block farther. Not that I'd calculated the distance to her house from here.

"Exactly."

The only person who had ever tried to ride with me was Pavel, and it had not ended well. Third day of freshman year, both of us getting roughed up by a pack of seniors looking to steal my bike.

"You don't have your guitar?"

"Left it home today. Come on. Are you afraid?" she teased. "Because you could add that to your list, and then cross it off once we get to my house."

Her voice was so bright and hopeful, I couldn't say no. Wanted to. Wanted to avoid disaster, but Hailey didn't seem like the kind of person to attract disasters. So at least she was different. What the hell was I even doing with this girl?

"Do you have *any* friends?" she asked as we walked outside together. She blinked and blinked and swiped at her eyes for a moment.

"Yeah, uh, sort of." The ground was full of spidering cracks.

"Sort of? You strike me as the nerdy computer type. Are all your sort-of friends living in there?" she asked.

"No. Not computer friends. That's a lame excuse for people to be someone they're not. I don't have the patience for it."

"Holy shit, Kyle. That's a sentence I can't count in syllables." She swung her arm out and tagged my shoulder.

"Are you going to keep doing that? Bugging me about talking?" I asked, stopping next to my bike.

"Maybe. I like you more when you talk. So if I can get a rise out of you . . ." She lifted her shoulder, which made me look at her boobs. For a *second.*

I unlocked my bike, counting down the steps before she'd want to climb on my handlebars. Probably no way out of it at this point. "I hung out with Pavel the other day."

"Pavel, huh?" She leaned in, squinting at my bike. "He's a friend?"

"Yep." I slipped the lock in my pack and started pushing my bike around the rack onto the sidewalk.

"But no online friends."

"Too full of assholery."

"Damn, Kyle. That's a great word. You should talk more often. I've said this once or twice before, right?"

"Ha. You're hilarious."

"I am. And I like Sarcastic Kyle."

She liked me. I shifted behind my bike; no sense in making my semi completely obvious to the world.

"How bad are your eyes?" I asked.

Hailey barked out a half laugh. "Bad. Pretty soon I'm gonna have to feel people's faces so I can see them."

I'd seen that in movies, but people really did that? "For real?"

"Yeah. Glaucoma, macular degeneration, and generally really shitty vision, as well as a few other things thrown in for fun. My ophthalmologist says I have old-person eyes."

Huh.

"Stop for a sec," she said, and stood five feet in front of me. I was hopeful her eyes weren't that great, particularly if they were focused south.

She held still and stared at my face. Watching. Almost like she was memorizing the way I looked. My pits sweated even more. The traffic buzzed by. Again and again.

She slipped her glasses off, tucking them into a backpack pocket.

"What are you doing?"

"Come here." She waved me closer.

My heart slammed. "What?"

"Come. Here." I took a few steps forward.

Hailey's eyes looked different from other people's. Only not really. Maybe it was because I knew they were broken, so I could see something interesting in them. Maybe I wanted them, her, to be different from other people. "Your eyes look cool without your glasses."

"Really? 'Cause everyone says they move around weird, but I'm trying to keep them still. It's really frickin' disorienting." Her mouth twitched downward.

"Sorry."

"Don't be. Pity sucks. Let me feel your face."

"What?" I leaned back. We stood on a busy sidewalk next to our school with traffic running four lanes wide next to us.

"One day I won't be able to see, so let me feel your face, so I know how to see people when I'm blind. This is a perfectly reasonable request. Tess won't let me because she doesn't want me smearing her makeup, and I've done the moms a million times. They always wear those horrid pity smiles. Let me do you."

Let me do you. Jesus.

"But are you . . . are you really going blind?" I blinked. Blinked again. Breathed through my nose in case my breath smelled like fish tacos. We were so close.

"Yep. That's what macular degeneration is. Going blind, in the long run. My moms don't think it'll happen, but they're full of optimism in pretty much every way."

"Uh . . . sorry." Weak response, but Christ.

"I said I don't want your pity, and you should stop saying that."

"Saying what?"

"Uh . . ."

"*That* doesn't make me self-conscious."

"Sarcasm again." Hailey grinned. "I'm proud."

"Thanks." I grabbed the handles on my bike until my knuckles whitened.

"Okay. Now relax. We're doing this. I want to see how much of my bullshit you'll take."

"I—"

"I'm serious." She reached toward me.

"I don't . . ." But what was I going to do? Run away? Tell her no? Not likely.

"Look. I'm closing my eyes to make the experience more authentic." Eyes shut didn't make it much better, because the sun through her shirt outlined her shape and she was still way too close for me not to think about the skin that made those shadows.

She was going to touch me, and my whole body was a puddle of sweat. "Wait. How well can you see?"

"What do you mean?"

"Open your eyes. How much of me can you see? Up close like this."

Hailey's hands dropped and her eyes opened. "Without my glasses, you're a blurry mess of flesh-colored, egg-shaped blob with something dark on the top."

"That's it?" I couldn't even imagine. Squinted my eyes a little to see the world more blurry, but my head ached after only a couple seconds of trying to decipher the images.

"That's it."

"And with your glasses?"

"A little better. I mean, I know you have nice eyes." She smiled and then her hands were on my face.

Her calluses from playing guitar made her fingertips smooth but hard. Her fingers ran up the side of my face and touched my hairline, twisting some of the hairs.

Oh, God. My throat swelled. My balls twitched. My pits sweated. And everything got way hot.

She ran her thumbs over my eyebrows, around my eyes,

moving more slowly over my swollen cheek and then down my nose. "This is sort of fascinating, and I can't believe you're still standing here."

I wasn't planning on moving a muscle until Hailey gave me permission. Completely frozen was probably the only way to keep from melting into a pool of sweat or cum. Her fingers moved around my lips. I wanted her to touch me there. Wanted to be the kind of guy who could kiss her fingers, suck on the tips of them, and take in all her flavor. But that was a million kinds of douchey and only for pervy movie guys.

Her fingers paused on my chin. "I think you have a little zit right here. Want me to get it for you?"

I pushed her hands away.

"What?" Hailey laughed. "I'm trying to be helpful."

"No, you're not. You're teasing me. Do blind people even do that?" My hands tightened on my bike again, and I stepped back.

"Not really."

"Hailey." Why would she put me through that?

"Your sulking voice doesn't suit you, and I don't mean to tease."

"Of course you do."

"Sor-ry."

"Don't apologize when you don't mean it." I guess the touching thing didn't really mean anything to her. Maybe a thing on her list. *Stupid, stupid Kyle.*

"I was trying to lighten the mood." She slipped her glasses back on.

"Yeah, I got that." My shoulders tensed.

"You're pissed? Was I being a bitch?"

"You don't know me, Hailey, and . . ." I let out a breath. "You weren't being a bitch."

She laughed. "I know. You were being sensitive."

My phone vibrated in my pocket.

Not now, not now, not now . . .

Vibrated again.

I shifted away from Hailey, back to a more comfortable distance. "Just a sec."

Mom: Kyle. Please tell me you didn't forget to pick up my meds.

Mom: You know my dose was changed, right? New scrips, and I'm out of that hand cream that keeps my hands from getting chapped after washing them all day. You know the brand, right?

Oh. I knew.

"What's up?" Hailey asked.

"I have to go."

"Are you serious?" she asked.

I nodded once.

Hailey shrugged. "Well, okay, then. This was . . . interesting, Kyle. I'm not letting you off the hook, though. You promised to do the list. Pick something. Report. I'll report to you too, okay? Or maybe I'm covered since I told you about the tongue kiss? I don't know."

Yeah, 'cause I wanted to think about that again. "That's still on, then? With that guy?"

"Yep."

Great. "Look. I'm sorry I've got to go."

"You're also partially relieved. It's okay. You've put up with a lot from me today. We're good."

"I should walk you home or something?"

Hailey waved me off. "Nah. It's good. I could use the walk to work through a song I wanna make playable for our next gig."

"Okay." I stared at the phone, wishing I had the guts to throw it somewhere in the middle of the four lanes of traffic.

"This was weird. We for sure have to do it again." And with that, Hailey shifted her pack and started back in the opposite direction to campus. Back to where I couldn't follow her with my bike. And as abruptly as it had started, our afternoon was over.

Next time.

There would be a next time.

Next time I wasn't going to be so pathetic.

No. I probably would be. I had to go check my email.

I stepped onto my bike and pedaled so fast my calves cramped almost immediately.

I could still feel Hailey's hands on my face. And the fantasy of what could've happened slammed into my brain. Me moving toward her without any kind of hesitation. And kissing her like it was nothing, and then her hands all over me. Jesus Christ, I was not going to be able to make it home with this kind of wood. I needed to think of something else.

Her tongue kiss. With another dude. My junk started to go soft and I made it all the way to the pharmacy wondering what the hell she saw in a beefy bouncer. She didn't really seem like that kind of girl.

I stepped into the pharmacy. The whole place smelled like Icy Hot and ass, but the change of scene and the cool air completely squelched the memory of Hailey's fingers. Maybe Mom's increased Xanax dosage would mean a long nap for her on the couch so I could pick apart the details of this afternoon and jerk off in peace.

I shook my head. Not sure what about Hailey kept bringing out the sleaze factor in me. Maybe it was the idea of a real girl in my life. Maybe it was that her issues didn't seem to be my fault. Maybe I was fucking lonely.

She didn't want my pity, and I wasn't good about giving it to her in a way that could help. But the thought that she might not see one day left me feeling empty and out of sorts. Nothing I could do about it, but that was pretty much all of my life.

I waited in line for Mom's prescription, ignoring the judgy look from the pharmacist, grabbed the special Vaseline Intensive Care moisturizer, checked out, tucked everything in my backpack, and climbed back on my bike.

Hailey had a thing with the bouncer, so I was gonna need to try for friendship. Which shouldn't have scared the shit out of me but totally did. I had no idea why she wanted to hang out with me. But I wanted to be worthy of that. In a way that I hadn't been able to be for my mom or Pavel. My thoughts went back to Hailey's list. Maybe that was the key to feeling like I had something to offer.

The second I got home, I dropped Mom's things on the kitchen counter, ran to my room, and pulled out my most recent journal. I jotted a new item on my list. One that Hailey had first suggested. *DJ.* A weird rush hit me with those two letters. Because for the first time, I'd written something down that maybe I could do. Maybe.

A second later, I flipped my tablet open and refreshed email. Something I barely ever checked because Pavel's mom read all his correspondence now, so he stuck with texting. A bunch of spam about penile implants. And then there it was: an email from Hailey with a ten-digit number as the subject line.

To my friend with the green shoes,

I had to scour the Internet for an hour trying to find you, and that is seriously crap on my eyes. Even still, I ended up calling the IT guy at school to get your email address. Luckily, he owed me a favor.

I probably should have just showed up at the station, but I thought writing would be more effective. Didn't want to blindside you when you were working. ☺

You're kind of a reader, right? Tess said she's seen you at the library with some pretty big books. And journaling too. You write, Kyle? Lots of stuff to unpack with you, isn't there?

So you need to come to my house with your list. We gotta start tackling some of that shit if you're gonna make it to college.

I'll show you mine if you show me yours. Ha!

Don't talk yourself out of it. This is a good offer, and I might give up on your ass if you don't show up. Also, I'll be fifteen kinds of pissed if this bounces back as a bogus email. So call me. Write me. Tell me when works for you.

Affectionately,
The girl with the glasses

PS: I think I should have your phone number; if you can't find mine in this mess, then never mind about yours. ☺

She'd used her number for the subject line. Of course I had it. But what were the chances of me using it?

I read the letter probably thirty times. She'd had to show up at the station after all. Blindsiding me. Heh.

I used to check my email every day because Pavel sent me articles with love advice and they were the perfect mindless entertainment when my homework was done and I was tired of writing. Plus, sometimes he attached dirty pictures, and jerking off to those didn't feel as weird as trolling for porn on the Internet on my own. But then his mom read his "Hot Lady Soccer Players" email, and that was the end of that.

It was almost summer. School would be out soon, and I wouldn't see Hailey at all. We could email. Maybe. But then next year she'd be at north campus. And maybe everything would change. Or it wouldn't. She gave me her number, though.

"We got a letter from the village asking us to mow the lawn," Mom said from my doorway.

I flinched. Forgot to close the door. Jesus, where was my head?

I looked up from my tablet. "Why is it the village's business if we mow our lawn or not? What if we're doing one of those natural prairie lawns?" I hated our house. Our run-down shitty house, which hadn't been redecorated or really touched for ten years. It'd gotten too dated to even blend anymore.

Mom's lips dropped into a frown. "We're not growing a prairie lawn, Kyle. Mow the lawn, okay?"

No *thank you for picking up my things.* No *sorry if I interrupted something with your friends.*

"Why is this on me? You know how to use the mower." I shouldn't have said it. I never said shit like that to my mom. But having had to bail on Hailey bugged the crap out of me.

Mom blew a hair out of her face. "Because, Kyle, it's just

us. And I work all the time so we can live in this house. It's not easy being a single parent, you know?"

Yeah, so she'd reminded me. Constantly.

"So let's move to an apartment. We don't need all the space." The house wasn't huge, but big enough for emptiness to echo through the halls. Not exactly *home*.

Mom's jaw clenched. "I got this house in the divorce. We're not leaving."

She needed to find someone else. She needed to stop making everything about her and me. Or about my dad abandoning us. But I didn't know how to tell her. As it was, the reality of only one more year of high school hung like an albatross around both our necks.

I swallowed every thought down. Choked on it until it was a solid mass at the base of my throat. The real truth? It wasn't Mom's fault. Dad had left because of me. Not because he didn't want me or anything like that. Although he hadn't. He'd left because I'd told him to go. Told him he wasn't good for either of us. I'd thought it was true at the time. It probably was, but it hadn't made the past seven years any easier.

And I certainly hadn't realized that one conversation when I was ten would have the kind of impact on Mom that it did. A conversation that I could never talk about. That strangled me every time Mom and me spent more than ten minutes together. And now I knew I had another item to add to my list.

Talk to Mom about Dad.

Chapter Twelve: Hailey

My afternoon chat with Kyle felt unfinished. Instead of dwelling on something I couldn't change, I found some relief in knowing that he hadn't gotten my email instead of actively not answering.

To pass the time on my way home, I sent Chaz a text, but he was at the gym and couldn't talk. And that was fine. I mean, he was an adult. It wasn't like I wanted to wear someone's letter jacket or class ring or talk on the phone for hours only minutes after seeing each other at school.

"Hey there!" Rox called when I was a driveway away from home. "Wanna make something?"

I shrugged. I didn't have much homework, and I didn't care about what I did have. I wasn't going to need to know the details about the First World War to be a musician.

"I got fresh clay today." She grinned.

All the clay was sort of gross to me, and there was no way I'd ever be able to tell what clay was "fresh" and what wasn't.

But I followed her through the showroom and into her wheel room. The smell of earth and dirt clung to the air and walls. I dropped my pack to the floor and sat at the smaller wheel in the corner.

"Do you have any requests?" I asked.

Rox ripped off a chunk of clay and set it in front of me, placing a water bottle within reach—for me or the clay.

"You ready to try a plate?"

I made a face. "I think my brain is only up for something simple."

"Then do whatever you like." Rox sat at her own wheel.

I think sometimes she loved being out here alone, and other times Lila would come sit and read in the corner to fill space.

"Where's Lila?"

"Danielle called in sick."

Which meant Lila would be late.

"Pizza?" I asked. Lila never went for pizza, but Rox could sometimes be convinced. There were no vegan pizza delivery places, and in fantastic stereotype fashion my pottery and yoga moms were also weird about food.

Rox tilted her chin toward my wheel. "Let's see how you do first."

I grabbed the smock off a hook and slipped it on, pressing

my foot down to get the wheel moving. Maybe my hands would know what to do once I started. I pressed on the top of the clay and then the sides, letting the mud slip around my fingers. Even breathing was pretty important for this kind of thing because one small move could ruin the whole project.

I wish I were afraid of mud, because this would be such an easy thing to cross off my list. But that wasn't the point of my list, really. The point was empowerment. The idea that the things I was afraid of wouldn't control me.

Did I feel in control of my list?

I mean, spiders . . . How does one even conquer a fear like that? And seeing a spider in my room was nowhere near the feeling I got when I thought about living in a black world.

Did it even count?

Part of me wanted to add a few things about Chaz. He'd asked me for a picture of myself. One I hadn't taken or sent. I was afraid I couldn't see well enough to know if the picture was good or not. The moms might see it. Was it a real fear?

Dipping my fingers into the center of my mud cylinder, I started working on a mug. Or maybe just a cup. No handle.

"Close your eyes, Hailey. Might help," Rox said over the sound of our two spinning wheels.

My eyes fell closed, and instead of watching the clay move and shape, I felt it. Felt how it curved under my hands. Felt the cup begin to take shape. *One day this is how I'll see.*

I didn't want to live in the dark. My eyes flew open.

There was no air in the room. I needed air.

I took my foot off the pedal that spun the wheel, tugged off my smock, and walked out.

"Hailey?" Rox called.

I walked through the showroom, out the door, and sat on the driveway, resting my hands on either side of my face. Grasping the sides of my glasses, I wanted to rip them off and throw them at the house. Listen to them shatter. But these had been a gift from Lila's mother, my grandma who didn't want me to call her Grandma because it made her feel old. I couldn't do it. I forced my hands to relax.

"Hey, you." Rox sat next to me. "What's going on?"

I shook my head. The moms were great and all, but sometimes letting them inside my head meant a whole lot of talking and feeling and things I didn't want to deal with.

She nudged my shoulder with hers. "What do you want on your pizza, kiddo?"

"Olives. Lots and lots of olives."

My cheeks hurt from smiling as I squinted at my iPad. Messaging on phones really sucked. The text was always too small, and having a voice read it out loud could get embarrassing fast.

Chaz: I wanna see you. When can I see you?

Blinders On had no gigs coming up—who knew playing in a seedy bar wouldn't immediately put us on lists for more seedy bars?

Hailey: Not sure.

97

I hadn't come out and told him how particular the moms were. How there was no way in hell they'd ever approve of someone like him.

Chaz: your parents strict?

Hailey: "Strict" would be putting it mildly.

Chaz: that's ok. Makes things more fun ;-)

Hailey: Perv

Chaz: maybe you're the perv, preying on older men

I barked out a laugh. I considered myself pretty lucky.

Hailey: You wish.

Chaz: you tell me what time I can see you this week, and I'll be there.

Meanwhile, I still hadn't heard back from Kyle.

Hailey: Okay, let me figure it out

Chaz didn't know about my list—that was reserved for friends. Didn't know about my eyes, not really. And that was fine. That wasn't the part of my life Chaz belonged to. He belonged with the Hailey that played in a band and went to bars and wore boots instead of Converse. He fit there perfectly.

Chapter Thirteen: Kyle

Hailey probably didn't need to *see* my list.

I opened my notebook on the desk at the radio station. My hands shook a little as I leafed to the loose page I'd tucked in back. I'd have to leave soon to be on time. To be there when I said I'd make it in the very short email I finally sent back to her.

Wednesday after school?

She wrote back one word—probably making fun of me again, but the word was "yes," so it didn't matter.

"You're not engineering today, are you?" Mr. Schmidt, our faculty advisor, asked as he paused reading the paper spread before him. We'd transitioned to a twenty-four-hour radio station two years ago, though all the programming after ten was automated. By this point in the school year, our faculty advisor was more a babysitter than anything else.

I shook my head, snapped my notebook shut, and shoved it into my backpack. I could tell Hailey that she couldn't see my list. That I'd tackle the list with her, but we didn't need to review all the things. It didn't really change anything.

Backpack hoisted on my shoulder, I stepped into the school hallway and kept my eye out for anyone looking to break the monotony of their afternoon by scuffing me up. No one seemed interested.

My brain fogged in and out with each step I took toward the door. *List. Hailey. List. Hailey.*

I unlocked my bike, jumped on, and pedaled hard to stop myself from chickening out. I'd been to Hailey's house before. Today was no different. *Shouldn't* have been different. But her street felt like a full-on shift beneath my tires, pedaling through sludge until I finally got to her house.

Hailey was making out with the bouncer on her porch. His mouth looked like it was swallowing her entire face. *Jesus, dude, give the girl some air.* My bike brakes squeaked, and she pulled back, spit and lipstick smeared around her mouth. She was made up for him. Dark eyeliner and pink sparkly blush. I wanted to crawl into a hole and die. Stupid asshole. Him. And me.

"You came," she said. "We were . . ."

"Yeah. I see. Okay. I'll catch you later."

The bouncer. Jazz or Jizz or whatever the fuck his name was

stood up and shifted himself. Gearshifted his dick like I cared at all. Which I didn't. Not about him.

"I didn't realize you called in backup, babe," he said, and Hailey blushed.

She wasn't supposed to be the girl who fell for shit like that. And she'd made a goddamn plan—with me. I gripped my handlebars and situated my foot on the pedal.

"Kyle," she said. "Chaz has work. He was leaving anyway."

Was she playing us against each other? Christ, tell me she wasn't *that* girl. Every part of the afternoon was suddenly mired in shit.

Chaz leaned over and gave her a long openmouthed kiss. Then he nodded at me and took off without even saying good-bye to Hailey. Classy.

"I'd kiss you, I'm so proud of you for actually showing up, but I don't think I should with Chaz and all." She patted the spot next to her.

That was it? That was all she was gonna give me? Not *hey, sorry about the PDA* or *my bad for double-booking you when I had plans to hook up with my d-bag boyfriend*?

I should have left. Didn't need the aggravation. I stared at my feet. Green shoes, scuffed for real now because I'd worn them every day since Hailey had given them to me. My shoulders slumped. *Cultivating a friendship here. Need to try harder.*

I slid off my bike and parked it along her porch. I moved

to the spot next to her, not touching but close. What the hell was I doing?

"Don't make that face. You said you weren't interested. When you *are* interested, you need to say so." She grabbed my chin with her callused fingers. "You do it like this: *I'm interested in you, Hailey.*" She dropped her hand. "Speak up if you want me. But if not, don't give me any shit over Chaz because he gets me into clubs, he doesn't care that I'm sixteen, and he's hot."

"Yes. Those things will get him so far in life. There aren't enough dick-shifting bouncers with a thing for minors. Thank goodness he's filling that gap."

She nudged me with her shoulder. "Kyle made a funny. I like. Now, where's your list?"

I swallowed. "Where's yours?"

She lifted herself off the porch bench and pulled a wrinkled piece of paper from her back pocket. Tight cut-off skirt and a tank top. Almost-summer was the best time of the school year.

My hands shook again when I took the paper from her. Excitement maybe. What could a girl like Hailey have on her list of fears? I looked at the first two and handed the paper back.

"What?" she said, and I thought I saw hurt flash on her face.

"It's crap, Hailey. Those aren't fears. Grocery shopping? Painting? Really?"

She blinked and took her glasses off. She rubbed her eyes with both hands, smearing her eye makeup, and then put them back on.

"It's really fucking hard to read the signs. I'm already reading at three hundred percent on my iPad or getting my textbooks on audio. Grocery stores are a nightmare. That was a big damn thing to cross off my list."

"Oh."

"Yeah. Nice going, insensitive asshat." But she nudged me, so maybe it was okay.

I took the paper back and she smiled. A big smeary red-lipped grin to match her bright red glasses.

"So yeah, guess you've covered that tongue-kissing thing more than once." I tried to sound light, like I didn't give a shit that she had scrubby razor burn on her cheeks and chin from the d-bag's kiss.

"Have you?"

I looked down so she wouldn't see my cheeks. It was hard to say how much of my inner brain she could read with her eyes and all. Hopefully not that much.

"Um. No."

She giggled and leaned against me. "Guess you've got some catching up to do."

I shifted away and looked back at her list.

"Sex? You're afraid of sex? Haven't you? I mean, I figured with the bouncer guy or whatever. He doesn't seem the type to wait."

There was too much space between us. Too much quiet. I got up to leave because I was fucking up this friendship before it even really started. It was a stupid idea to come over. And what was I doing talking to her about sex? I was a babbling asshole. I knew better than this. I made a move to the steps, but she yanked me down and dropped her bare knee across my leg so I couldn't move.

"Chill, Kyle. Chill."

Yeah, that was gonna happen.

Chapter Fourteen: Hailey

I peered at Kyle, willing him to relax. He was so tense I wanted to toss him into Lila's yoga class until he turned into a jelly squid.

"So Chaz and I've only hooked up a few times, not for sex. And anyway, everyone should have sex on their list if they've never done it before."

"Why?"

"Because I don't know anyone who isn't afraid of fucking it up, you know?" I grinned and elbowed him a few times, but he shook his head, the same sort of petrified look on his face.

"Come on, Kyle. That's funny. Fuck up sex?" I laughed and knocked my knee on his thigh, refusing to let him ignore my hilarity.

The moms pulled into the driveway between the house

and the pottery shop in our boring, sensible gray Escort. Why couldn't grocery shopping take them as long as it took me?

"Wipe your mouth," Kyle said under his breath.

"What?"

"Lipstick."

"Oh. Shit." I rubbed it on the bottom of my tank, so when the moms came onto the porch, I was still wiping my lips, and Kyle was staring at my stomach.

"Kyle." Even from here I knew Lila's mouth was locked in her thin smile.

"Hi. Um . . ." He cleared his throat and rubbed his hands on his thighs a few times. "Hailey asked if I'd drop by."

It all was awkward, and needed to be over, but probably worked in my favor, because Kyle was a lot easier to bring home to the moms than Chaz. It wouldn't be horrible if they thought Kyle and I had been making out on the porch. I stood up and grabbed Kyle by the arm until he stood next to me. "Kyle's doing a fear list with me."

They were still half frowning. Not good.

Think. Think. Think.

"You know. Fear list. Like mine. *Therapeutic*," I choked out.

He was smart enough to hold up my list for them to see. The problem was they were nice enough to let me keep my list private, and then I realized that maybe it wasn't cool that he could see it, and they couldn't.

Rox readjusted her grip on the grocery bags before opening

the front door. "We're going to get started on dinner. You're welcome to stay, Kyle."

"They want to grill you," I warned.

"Oh." He stared down.

"We won't grill you, Kyle," Lila said.

"We're going to my room." I pulled him inside behind Rox. Kyle's face turned red.

Lila pointed to the downstairs. "Keep the door open."

Kyle looked again like he wanted the floor to swallow him.

"Lila. Seriously. My bed squeaks. I'm smart enough to make sure you're not home. Give me some credit." I smirked.

I'd be lying if I said I didn't love embarrassing Kyle.

"Jesus. Hailey. Don't." But that was all he could get out. It was like the blood rushing to his face drew the air from his lungs. Hilarious. Definitely worth doing again.

"Hailey. Mildred. Bosler." Lila's eyes widened.

"Ahhh!!" I screamed, holding my hand up between us, but kind of laughing too. "You win. I think I've been punished enough."

I ran down the stairs, dragging Kyle with me.

"Why did you do that?" Kyle asked as I pulled him into my room and shut the door behind us.

"Do what?" Even though I knew perfectly well what he meant, I wanted him to say it. Probably because I'm meaner than I should be, but also because it'd be good for him.

He stood for a minute, taking in my room. My plain white

walls. I'm sure he expected something different, but the plain-ness relaxed me. There would be nothing to miss when I couldn't see anymore. Hence *Painting* near the top of my fear list.

"Ever been in a girl's room before?" I teased as I elbowed his side.

He shook his head and took a step away from me. "Fear of paint?"

"Not a fear of paint. A fear of falling in love with whatever I do in my room and not being able to appreciate it when I can't see."

Kyle nodded, processing probably.

"It's a rush, though," I said. "Crossing something off your list. Especially when you're not sure what to tackle and how to do it. Like the paint? How do I take care of that?"

Kyle shrugged.

"Well, you think on it. But trust me, if you haven't crossed something off yet, look forward to it." It felt like control. Conquering. Strength.

He turned a half circle as if waiting for my room to turn into whatever picture he'd had in his head. That same after-noon, I hadn't even let Chaz in the house, but now . . . Kyle stood in my room, and it didn't feel weird or otherworldly like Chaz had. Chaz had expectations. Kyle was easier.

"So. You know I trust you, Kyle. We could do it. I mean, I'd have sex with you." I was half-joking, but it would be a simple, albeit awkward, cross off the list. Might be nice to get another one behind me. And Chaz might expect something different or fancy or experienced. Kyle would probably be on overload with being naked—assuming we stripped all the way down for it.

"Wha . . ." A million new shades of red hit his face. Or new to me. At any rate, I could tell he was seriously blushing. And his breath had gotten sort of raspy. "Jesus Christ. Are you serious? You said that out loud."

"Yeah, I know. But it's sort of an easy mark off the list. It's going to be awkward and weird no matter what, right? You and I could get it over with." I stepped forward and flattened my hand on his stomach. Then I realized it might be the furthest he'd ever gone with a girl and laughed.

"We're not going to . . . you know . . ."

Silence.

"Have sex?" I waited for him to blush more or walk away.

He shook his head like he didn't know what to do with me. Probably he didn't. The unbearable quiet made me push him further. How could he stand all the not-talking?

"What if we did?" I stood closer, facing him, putting my hands on his sides, more serious now. It didn't feel as weird as I thought it might to be so close. Probably having sex with Kyle wouldn't be half-bad. I bet he'd be really sweet about it, and it wasn't like Chaz and I were totally exclusive or anything. I didn't think.

"No." He squirmed under my hands. "Hailey."

"Think about it." I dropped my hands, and he immediately relaxed.

"Aren't you supposed to want it to be *special* or something? You barely know me."

"I'm a realist." I sat on the floor, giving him some space.

I wanted to hang out for a bit longer, and I knew he'd walk if I kept harassing him. Though maybe having to pass both moms upstairs would be enough to keep him in my room.

"Look, I'm not trying to be a dick, but it's a little insulting that you're suggesting we have sex when you just had your tongue down another guy's throat." He sat a few feet away, crossing his legs, and leaning forward enough to rest his elbows on his knees.

"Point taken. I wasn't trying to insult you. But this . . ." I leaned over to plant a kiss on his cheek. "This is why we're going to be friends."

Kyle didn't move.

"So. Anyway. I'm still adding to my list. I mean, 'Spiders' is pathetic, but I can't see them well, and they're fast. I have no idea how to cross it off, you know?"

He nodded.

"Doesn't have to be a huge fear to be on the list. Sometimes you need little things to cross off so you feel like you're doing something." I grabbed his arm. "Oh! Tess said she had an idea for that one. The spider thing. We could totally do it together."

"Um . . . that's not on my list. And I'm not sure how someone gets over a fear of spiders."

"You don't have to get over it, just conquer it." I shifted slightly closer to him. "What's on your list?" I asked as I took my folded-up list back from him. He could skim the rest later. Maybe.

"I . . . uh . . ."

He was totally bailing on me. Or backing out.

"No way, Kyle. I show you mine, you show me yours, remember?"

He scratched his head a few times, and I almost snatched his pack, but he opened it and slid out a notebook.

A big part of me didn't think he'd do it.

"I don't . . ." He held the notebook. Clutched it.

I snatched it and flipped through. Page after page of tiny writing. My jaw dropped. "Ho-ly . . . Did you do all of this?"

He grabbed it back before there was any chance of me focusing on his tiny script, and pulled a page from the back. But the single page seemed like nothing compared to the nearly filled notebook.

"What *is* all that?"

He scowled. "Do you want the list or not?"

"Wow, Kyle. You really don't want me seeing that. That's your writing, huh? I'm proud of you for sticking up for yourself like that."

"So . . . uh . . . the list."

I started to reach for the paper, but wondered how long it'd take me to read his writing. "Go ahead. You can read it."

He cleared his throat, and then we sat in silence.

Silence. Silence. Silence.

"I'm not asking you to *sing* it, Kyle. Read already." *Don't make me admit to you that I don't think I can.*

"Learntodriveastick. Askforaletter ofrecfrom ateacherat-school. Getthenumberof agirl in history. TalktoPavel about freshman . . ."

But he stopped.

We sat in silence for another moment, until I couldn't handle it anymore.

"You like a girl? No wonder you won't have sex with me." I grinned. "She'd better get how cool you are."

He stared down, and the paper shook a bit.

"I don't see why driving a stick would be scary; cars are almost never sticks anymore, so why would you even worry about learning? But whatever, that's cool. . . . At least you could cross it off, you know? Maybe it has more to do with you being afraid of *not* having that skill. Which, again, you don't need, but sure, fine. I can appreciate that. I mean, driving's sort of out altogether for me, so . . ." I wanted to give him hell over the list, but I couldn't. I hated it when I knew I'd be crossing a boundary and made myself stop. It went against everything Hailey.

"And you should put 'Making a friend' on there, and then cross it off." I kicked his foot with mine.

He nodded once. *Geez, Kyle. Always with the nodding.*

"So. What happened with Pavel?"

Chapter Fifteen: Kyle

I sort of expected it. I'd put it on the list and I'd brought the list over, even if I didn't think I was going to share it. And I said it out loud, even though I didn't say everything on the list. But there, in that minute, in her room, the words choked me worse than they ever had. Her big blinking eyes behind her glasses as thick as Coke bottles. It was sort of too much. Too much brokenness, and I wasn't ready to admit I sucked as Pavel's friend.

"It's not really my story to tell," I said.

"Screw that. You put it on your list, and you wanna talk to him about it. So start with me. It's easier. And I don't know Pavel, so it won't mean anything to me."

I stared at her long legs leading into her boots. Girl-band boots. Ass-kicking and sexy all at once. Boots with a cut-off skirt and tank top. Jesus, what was she trying to prove with this Chaz? My hands shoved themselves into my pockets and balled into fists. Awkward with how I was sitting, but I didn't want her to see them shaking so bad.

"I don't know where to start," I managed to choke out. Everything was too thick, heavy and warm and loaded. Her sad white walls almost burned my retinas, and I eyed the door for my escape. Flashes of Pavel pushed into my brain, and I blinked over and over. Maybe holding back tears.

Then I was talking. More than I'd talked to anyone. Blurting out the story of Pavel being on varsity soccer because he was so good as a freshman, had played in Russia since he was three, and the guys who came into the locker room with ski masks on and held him down and rammed a plunger up his ass and made me watch while I screamed. While Pavel screamed. While they laughed and I fought and got the shit kicked out of me. And Pavel shut down and stopped moving and I screamed louder and bled more.

Hailey pulled a thin, worn blanket around the two of us, wrapped her arms around me, and cried. Said it was the blanket that saved her as a kid. That still saved her when everything sucked. Told me I was a good fucking friend, even though I was actually worthless. She squeezed me so tight I thought I'd stop breathing and fall off the world and into her and it would finally, finally be okay, because sometimes people needed to be held so hard they hurt.

"Fuck, Kyle," she said eventually. "And you guys haven't talked about it?"

I shook my head because all the words were gone now. I had nothing else to give. Her arms loosened, but the blanket still rested over our shoulders.

"How is he now?" she said after I'd sopped her shirt with tears that I didn't really deserve to shed.

I choke-laughed. "He's Pavel. That's the thing. He's Pavel. He's fine, as if this was just another thing he had to deal with. It was totally messed up and he was in the hospital and his parents pulled him from school and he has to help teach his little sisters and everything. But he's fine. He reads *Cosmo* and wishes for girls and he's fine. I don't get it. I'm a wreck and Pavel is fine."

She put her hands on both my cheeks. I squeezed my eyes shut so that I wouldn't have to look at her beautiful broken eyes. But she tapped her finger along my jaw until I opened them and she released her warm breath along my face.

"This was good, Kyle. Hard. But good that you told me. And maybe Pavel is fine. Maybe he's not and he needs you to be a better friend. Show up more. Be present, you know? *Talk*." She smirked a little.

I nodded. He did deserve it. Deserved more than that.

She leaned forward and kissed my cheek. "But he wasn't the only victim in this shit. You were too."

I shook my head. "Nothing. Nothing happened to me."

She clucked her tongue and brushed a tear off my cheek. We were too close. I needed to extricate myself. From her warmth and her smell and her beautiful eyes. I shifted back, out from beneath the blanket, and she let me go.

"Something did happen to you. But now it's out. And I know. You've told a friend. And, holy hell, I can't believe you couldn't tell me your name when I first asked, and you trusted me with that." She paused, but only for a sec. "What happened to the guys? Do I want to know?"

"What you'd expect. Nothing. No one copped to it. School buried it. I didn't want to keep fighting. Pavel's parents didn't want to be a spectacle. They never talk about it, I don't think. My mom . . ." I shrugged. Didn't really know how to explain "got worse."

She pressed her glasses back up her face and nodded. "Yeah. So everyone at school turned a blind eye and that's why your face was messed up the other day?"

"Yep. Easy prey. Marked."

Before she could say anything more, her dark-haired mom popped her head into the doorway. No knock, just a *click*, and then she was there.

"Dinner in five. Kyle, you sure you don't want to stay?"

I swiped at my face and Hailey rolled the blanket into a ball. "Nah. I've got a lot of homework. I've been here too long anyway. Thanks, though."

She nodded and gave Hailey a pointed look. "Say your

good-byes, then. And next time, keep the door open when your boyfriend's over."

I laughed. "I'm hardly her boyfriend. She's got Chaz."

Hailey kicked me. Hard. *Crap.* They didn't know about Chaz. Of course. I should have considered it. Older guy. Bouncer. Even cool lesbian moms couldn't get behind something like that.

"I thought Chaz was Tess's guy?" her mom said.

"Well . . ." Hailey did the deer-in-headlights thing again, and if I was at all capable of it, I would've smiled at how funny she was with her moms. So different than she was with me or anyone else.

Her mom looked at me, but I dropped my gaze to my feet and kept my mouth shut. Easy for me—safe, familiar.

"Are you absolutely sure you can't stay for dinner?" her mom asked again, and I shook my head. I wanted to, but I didn't have the energy for a family dinner, particularly one that would clearly involve grilling. It'd been months since Mom and I had eaten together. I couldn't stand the thought of Hailey's sympathetic eyes blinking at me through an entire meal. Plus, after everything, the least I could do was call Pavel. Say something. Even if it didn't really mean anything to him now, too many years later.

"No. Thank you, though."

She nodded and pointed to Hailey before holding her five fingers out and signaling upstairs.

"Sorry," I mumbled as soon as she had left.

Hailey let out a loud sigh and flopped against the side of her bed. "I probably should have mentioned the moms don't know about Chaz. It's kind of code not to talk about personal stuff with other people's parents, but I guess you don't have much experience with that sort of thing, huh?"

"I've talked more in the last half hour than I have in the last month," I said.

"Yeah. I believe that. You should do more of it. Talking. You have a nice voice. It'd be a good deejay voice. How many times do I need to say this before you do something about it?" She leaned forward, staring.

When I didn't say anything, she shrugged and wrapped her hand into mine. "Okay, then, Friend Kyle. Lots of shit to process today. I'm glad you brought your list over. And I want to discuss this writing thing of yours someday soon. And keep at the list. Add more stuff."

"We haven't talked about all of yours. Maybe I could help with . . . I mean, not the sex thing." Though at the moment, I couldn't think of one damn thing I wanted more. "But other stuff."

"I'm gonna get back to you on the spider thing." She squeezed my hand again and still didn't drop it. "And, you know, even if I offended you, the sex thing remains on the table."

I swallowed. She had no idea what she was saying. My stomach tied itself into a huge knot. I was such an amateur with girls. Dick-shifting Chaz had way more experience than me. I'd end up disappointing Hailey. I wanted to have sex with her so much my junk nearly hopped when I thought about it. But the practical side of me understood my limitations better than anyone.

"Well, until I find the guts to go somewhere else, or it happens in the moment . . . ," she continued with a shrug. "I get that you're one of those guys who think girls want it to be special, but I'm pretty sure I don't care. Not for the first one. Maybe after I get good at it, I'll care. I don't know. Anyway. Point is, if you want, I'd have sex with you. You'd be a good candidate. Probably not an asshole about it. And you wouldn't care if I did it all wrong because you'd be in the same boat. I bet you'd even give me a card or something afterward."

A card? This girl. I shook my head. "I . . . I don't think so, Hailey. But thanks."

"Maybe you like History Girl too much to want to do it with me," she said when we reached the top of the steps. "Or maybe you're not sure after everything that happened with Pavel. I get that."

I released her hand and turned to her before we entered the kitchen. "Neither. History Girl . . . well, she's the only one who's ever said hi to me in class. It's stupid. But she noticed when I was out sick."

Hailey nodded. "Yeah. She's probably into you. Nice job."

I shook my head. "Doubt it. But still, it'd be a big deal to get her number. Maybe even meet her somewhere for coffee."

"It would," Hailey agreed, and started tapping her hands against her cut-off skirt. "Not quite sex, though."

It was the weirdest afternoon ever. All the stuff about Pavel and the tears and the list and the sex. God, the sex. I was so close to Hailey I could lean forward and touch my lips to hers. But I'd never even kissed a girl, and Hailey was dating a bouncer who could pummel me into a pea-size stain on the sidewalk. "Hailey. I'm not Chaz. And I couldn't ever be that for you."

She shrugged. "Huh. Well. Whatever. It's out there if you change your mind."

I slipped by her and waved at her moms as I left the kitchen. My feet couldn't get me out of the front door fast enough. Everything. Every single thing that normally ran through my lonely brain had spilled out of me onto Hailey's dull tan carpet. And it hadn't freaked her out. She even wanted to have sex with me. Kind of.

The thoughts jostled around my mind as I slipped onto my bike and headed home. I had a friend. A real one. And like a complete asshole, I was probably gonna fall in love with her.

Chapter Sixteen: Hailey

Y ou know the drill." Lila smiled over her plate of quinoa. "Give us the scoop on Kyle."

Both the moms' attention was focused entirely on me. Dinner inquisition.

I didn't even know how to explain Kyle. He'd sort of come out of nowhere, but he'd gotten the list. We were friends. I mean, he'd done some serious sharing that afternoon, so we had to be friends. And I'd meant it when I told him I'd have sex with him. It was a joke at first, but the longer he stayed, the more I didn't think it was that much of a joke. Was it crazy that I'd been making out with Chaz and then offered that up? Probably. But Kyle felt *different*, and he made me curious. Most people weren't interesting enough to make me curious.

"We're friends," I said.

"That's it?" Rox cocked a brow.

"Yeah."

"Because it looked like you two were . . . together on the porch before we came home. And you're wearing makeup." She pointed at me with her fork.

We all knew it was a big deal for me to wear makeup, because I couldn't do eyeliner or mascara by myself, at least not without making a mess of it. Tess had done it for me right after school because Chaz wanted to see me, and I'd promised to let him come over—especially since he wouldn't have to deal with meeting the moms if he didn't stay long.

"But Kyle said you were dating Chaz," Rox added.

Lila sighed. Apparently that part hadn't been discussed yet. *How to answer . . . how to answer . . .*

"Tess did my makeup after school for fun because I didn't feel like playing today. And Chaz is *her* boyfriend. Kyle must've misunderstood. It's not like he and I really hang out."

"You two were sitting under your blanket together." Rox leaned back and folded her arms. *Right.*

I figured I'd give being honest a shot. "We were talking about stuff on the list, and it got personal. That's all."

Rox nodded like she understood. Lila's small mouth pressed tight, and she stared a little too closely. "Something on the list put you two under your blanket?"

Crap. I'd finally actually come sort of clean, and she wasn't buying it.

"Some guys messed up his friend. And . . ." I released a long breath and stared at my plate. "I thought the list was supposed to be private."

"Lila," Rox whispered.

And then I knew all I had to do was not smile because Rox had taken my side, and I was off the hook.

After dinner I sat in my room and stared at my blank walls. I put my glasses on. I took them off. The white was still white. There was no difference aside from the edges of my door, or the tiny high-on-the-wall window, being a little blurrier. I was pissed at myself for putting *Painting* on the list. Who the hell cares what their room looks like? But I had a policy about not crossing items off the list unless I'd done them.

The whole painting thing started when I was twelve. I'd sat on my bed, and my *Buffy the Vampire Slayer* poster looked all messed up, but when I put my glasses on and stepped closer, it wasn't messed up at all. I was.

I spent all night cleaning my walls of the crap I'd put up since I was a little kid, and begged for white paint.

For the last four years, I hardly ever had to strain my eyes in my room. The walls were white, and I knew where I kept my stuff. But my room had gone from fun to sterile, and I'd been on the fence about changing it up again.

The moms had gotten this audio book about ways of coping with blindness, and it all had to do with being organized and knowing what's in your closet. Putting away clothes from light to dark, leaving clues like rolling up a sleeve of a shirt with print on it, or turning one shoe sideways in a pair that was the same but a different color.

I'd laughed at that last one, because I had about nine pairs of Converse in different colors, and there weren't enough combinations of shoes on their sides. I could still see the shoes, so it seemed like a wasted effort anyway.

It wasn't like I could pick my wardrobe out for the rest of my life before my eyes failed me. Or that I'd be able to feel Rox's pottery and know how she'd shaded the blues together. I'd only know how she'd attached the handles to mugs, and get a general idea of the shape she'd used.

One of the reasons the moms' optimism made no sense was that they still made me sign up for "Coping with Blindness" clinics once in a while. It felt backward. If they were honestly optimistic about my sight, I shouldn't need crap like that. But we all knew that there would almost definitely be a day when I'd see nothing but black.

I had to find more distraction because my big pity party was getting old, even for me.

"Okay." I stepped into the sound booth before school, guessing right that Kyle would be there. "I know last night was intense, so I had to come in here to make sure that you didn't get all weird and quiet on me again. As I've said a hundred times now,

I like your voice, and I think you're cool, and I also think the moms sort of dig you. Tess is totally for getting together after school so you can do the spider thing with me. Maybe next week?"

"We're cool. I'm still talking. And you were serious about the spider thing?"

"Yes."

"I guess next week's okay." He glanced up from the board of dials.

"Nice." I looked around the best I could in the dim light. "So do you just sit in here?"

"I . . . uh . . . set stuff up for the afternoon show, and organize all the digital files in case someone needs something recorded later . . . you know." He rubbed his hands up and down his thighs once or twice.

I nodded. "So will it bother you if I play? I should do my geometry, but playing sounds like more fun."

Kyle stared at me with wide eyes.

"You should show your eyes to History Girl. She'd totally go out with you. So can I play? I mean, it's cool. My band teacher always lets me use a practice room; it's that—"

"Don't you have to get to south campus?"

"Yeah. In a little bit. But my first class is health, which is a total joke and everyone rolls into class late. Even Mrs. Beck sometimes."

He gave me a nod. "You can play in here."

"'Kay. Thanks." I grabbed a stool, sat, and pulled out my guitar. The lighting sucked, but that didn't matter. I wasn't reading music today, just playing around to relax before school.

Kyle stared back at the computer, but his hands were kind of shaking. *Obviously* shaking, since I could see it. I thought of all that crap he'd let me in on the afternoon before and how he probably still felt exhausted from it. How maybe I should have left him alone today, but once I got to campus, I had to come up here.

"So Chaz signed me up for this big gig thing. He says I need to do a cover of an old love song and try to make it cool. I mean, he's into the music thing. It's a competition they do every year, so if you have any song suggestions over the next month or so, that would be great." The hard thing was I wanted to do something all me, so it was really a quest for kick-ass lyrics that came with really bad music. Or maybe uncheesing a song that had been sadly stuck in the cheese category, where it didn't belong.

Kyle froze his knob twisting. "Chaz wants you to sing him a love song?"

"Don't be an asshole." The Chaz thing was going to be a problem, because Kyle claimed not to be interested, but he got pissy when Chaz was brought into the convo. Was that a guy thing? Or a Kyle thing?

Kyle raised his eyebrows but didn't say anything. Of course.

"So will you think on it?" I asked. "You strike me as someone who's into music from whenever, so that would help. I mean, I play Bob Dylan because his lyrics are amazing, but aside from that, I know stuff from now."

Kyle nodded and turned, his fingers now ticking on the keys of the computer keyboard.

"Thanks." Maybe I'd play Dylan now instead of the Yellowcard song I was going to work on.

I relaxed onto the stool and played, and I meant to sing quietly, but there was no way to play Bob Dylan and not *really* sing his brilliant lyrics, so I decided I didn't care what Kyle thought. I was gonna sing for a bit. And having someone to sit and be silent while I played, someone who wasn't my moms, and didn't want anything from me, was a whole new level of awesome. But there was no way to explain this to Kyle, and he'd probably get red and maybe not understand anyway. Another time.

I let my eyes fall closed, my fingers move faster up the neck of the guitar. Definitely worth the walk to north campus.

Chapter Seventeen: Kyle

She sang Bob Dylan. Bob Dylan how it was meant to be sung. The poetry of his words coming out of her mouth with that amazing voice. The perfect low tremble, raspy and beautiful and sexy and unique . . . "It is not he or she or them or it that you belong to . . ." She sang Bob Dylan.

And all I could say when she finished was "Your voice is cool." As if I were one of the Barbie twins. As if I were Chaz, who wanted her to serenade him. Contest for a love song, my ass. He wanted her to go in front of people and sing to him. The dick-shifting a-hole.

The whole rest of the day, I walked through the halls with her voice in my head. And somehow, everything felt easier. I thought about the thing I'd added to my list last night, about being a good friend to Hailey. Every time I thought I'd made a step in the right direction, she turned me inside out and I was reminded yet again that I was the lucky one. I could walk away from Hailey and she'd shrug and go back to her life. But if Hailey walked away from me, I'd be gutted. I didn't want us to be like that. I'd resisted the inevitable unbalance between us, but every time I was with her, something changed.

And the offer to have sex still stood.

Even as I recognized being with Hailey was a terrible idea, one of the speeding thoughts in my head grabbed hold of *that* and ran. Me and Hailey in her room. On her tan carpet. Beneath her blanket. Her making me laugh at the awkwardness of it all and then kissing me and touching me. And me getting her to make sex noises with that low, low voice.

And maybe, if I could just get closer, if it didn't feel like such a huge leap from not even having a first kiss to actually having sex, I could do it. Maybe if I could keep from thinking of Chaz's hands all over her, I could wrap my mind around my hands getting to feel her skin, my mouth getting to lick her. Maybe if I could conquer my list . . . maybe then I'd deserve her.

Pavel hadn't returned my calls, so I went to the library after engineering the afternoon show. I'd written him a pathetically long email when I got home from Hailey's last night. Mostly, it was an apology for being unable to stop anything. For his having to leave school. For basically being a crap friend. I told him to call me. But he didn't. Hard to say what was going through his head. It was Pavel.

The town library was less than two blocks from school. I loved that because I never had to go out of my way to avoid home, but I didn't really have to deal with anyone from school either. Studying at the town library was arguably the best excuse for any kid to avoid interaction.

Mariah came out of the library when I was locking my bike out front. Mariah. History Girl. The list. It would be a perfect opportunity. After the Pavel dump, I felt like I could probably say anything to anyone. Hailey was right. The list made me feel like I had some control. Even for me.

"Hey, Kyle. I was wondering if you were going to be here."

"Hey."

She did the weird lip-nibble thing that girls do when they're nervous or maybe when they're teasing guys. Enough girls do it to make me think they can't all be nervous that often. But it wasn't like they got pointers in health class on how to make us think about their mouths. They just all somehow understood that lip biting made us go *there*. Maybe they got it from *Cosmo*. Maybe Pavel had the right idea.

"So have you decided what you're gonna do for the history final presentation?"

"No. Have you?"

I was having a conversation. With Mariah. The girl on my list. A girl who shouldn't even be here, but maybe was looking for me? I wished Hailey could've seen it. Which then made me feel like a huge dirtbag because I wanted Hailey to be there to watch me ask another girl out. Only I knew I couldn't ask Mariah out because I was still thinking about Hailey singing Bob Dylan and telling me the offer to have sex with her was still open. I wasn't stupid enough to get involved with someone else when I hadn't resolved anything on the Hailey front.

"No. Mr. Connor said we could do it with partners if we also did an oral presentation." She smiled and tucked the hair behind her ear. *What the hell was that?*

"So are you going to do it with someone?"

She blushed. Then I realized what I'd just said and I blushed. And it was horrible and awkward and I wanted her to go.

"The presentation? Well, I'm not sure. . . ."

This was the point where most guys would have realized a giant anvil of possibility was hitting them over the head and they'd have stepped in to partner with her. Even if a guy wasn't interested in a girl, he knew enough to accept an offer to partner with one because girls always did most of the work. And girls generally were way better at oral presentations than guys.

But the fact of the matter was, the entire thing pissed me off. It was like Mariah didn't know me at all. First, I would never do an oral presentation if I could avoid it, partner or no. Second, I spent most of my time reading, so doing any kind of report wasn't that hard for me. And it was frankly way easier than having to interact with someone for an indeterminate amount of time.

"Huh. Well, I'll see you."

Mariah sort of sputtered in this weird way. But if she'd known me better, she wouldn't have been surprised. Hailey wouldn't have been surprised. She probably just would have talked me into doing the oral presentation anyway by telling me to write it on my list.

I nodded good-bye, then took the elevator to the third floor and moved to where the public computers were located.

Be a good friend to Hailey.

I'd written it on my list. And I was committed to it, even if I wasn't sure how I could get there. The computer hummed to life when I started to punch in my library card number. I wanted to plan a playlist of songs for Hailey. Songs her voice would sound amazing on, songs that meant something to me because the words actually held some poetic weight instead of just bubblegum pop. A playlist starting with Bob Dylan.

Chapter Eighteen: Hailey

There was something about plugging my amp in on the front porch that made every afternoon better. The list Kyle had written up of song suggestions was pretty great, but I hadn't even *heard* of all the songs. I was right. Guy really knew his music. I'd played through about four so far. Played each of them enough that I didn't really need the chords or tabs anymore.

Clutching my iPad, I found the tabs for "In Your Eyes," a song that Kyle had marked for me to revive from cheeseland. I'd listened to the song a few times and figured that even with someone else's half-assed attempts at finding the chords, I could figure the rest out.

Making the tabs as big on my iPad as I could, I strummed down the chords. Fairly basic, but I had to add something. Probably the "something" would come as I played.

Starting at the beginning, my fingers slipped, and I dipped

my voice higher and lower, trying to find the right pitch. I slid my capo three frets up, started the song again, and a new riff fell perfectly into place. There wasn't a single song Kyle had picked that I hadn't loved.

"Whatcha playin'?" Tess asked.

My gaze snapped toward her, standing on the porch resting against one of the beams like she'd been watching awhile.

"Trying to come up with something for that competition."

"Without us, huh?" she asked. "Should I be worried? You quitting the band? Negating our awesome existence with your intrinsic drive to explore other options for personal growth?"

I snorted. "Nope. Didn't want to subject you and Mira to a night of love songs."

"And I thank you for it." Tess walked across the porch and flopped into one of the old wicker chairs. "And Mira would, if she were still going to be living here."

"What?"

Tess chomped her gum a few times and dragged an almost-black chunk of hair behind her ear. "Her parents caught her and her boyfriend in his car in their driveway—"

"Mira doesn't have a boyfriend."

"Okay. Some *guy* she met at that Movies in the Park thing," Tess clarified. It was just like Tess to go from "intrinsic drive" to "Movies in the Park thing." "Anyway, they freaked and are sending her to Dayton to live with her grandparents for a while. She's finishing her finals online."

I stood up. "Holy crap. We should go say good-bye."

Tess shook her head and waved me back down. "Nope. She's on lockdown from us. Her parents think we're 'bad influences' on her, wouldn't even let her call us. They're heading out this afternoon."

"How do you know?"

"She called her cousin and told him to call me."

"What a mess."

"Yeah. 'What a mess' is right."

There would be no more band. "What the hell are we gonna do now?"

My iPad pinged in a text.

"What the . . ." Tess sat up and squinted at my tablet. "Damn, is he hot, but how big an ego do you need to send someone a pic like this?"

I leaned forward to see a picture of Chaz at the gym. No shirt. Flexing in front of the mirror. That crazy-sexy grin of pure confidence on his face. "Kind of a weird move, huh?" I asked.

"If I looked like the female version of that, I'd go everywhere naked." Tess flopped backward again. "So maybe not all that weird. He wants you to want the goods."

My iPad pinged again.

Chaz: You next?

He'd continue to hint that the same kind of pictures from me might be fun. I'd continue to ignore the hints. Sending someone a half-naked picture could seriously backfire.

Tess laughed, able to read the text from ten feet away.

"I'm ignoring that," I said.

Chaz and my regular life didn't fit, and that was fine. He didn't have to fit into my everyday. There was really no way he would. Chaz was five years older than me. He'd finished high school three years ago. Keeping him separate was infinitely easier.

Tess and Mira fit into my everyday. So did Kyle, when I saw him. But Chaz held a wholly different purpose.

"Oh!" Tess's booted feet fell to the porch floor, rattling the table where my stuff sat.

"Oh?"

"I came to see if you and Kyle wanna do the spider thing today."

I had no desire to do the spider thing, but Tess swore it'd be an easy fear to cross off my list.

Setting my guitar down, I tugged my iPad onto my lap to text Kyle. "I'll ask."

"You know, I sort of hate your list, but today I might enjoy it."

"Is that why you're helping me?" I asked.

"No. I'm helping 'cause I'm your friend." She shrugged. "And because it's going to be a hell of a lot of fun to watch you squirm your way through this one. You should see how the spawn can go nuts over spiders. Like they're friends."

The spawn, or the reason for her job. As a nanny. She'd had

it since the beginning of the school year. Why someone was willing to trust Tess with their children was baffling.

My iPad pinged.

Kyle: I'm in. I can meet you?

Meet us? Why not ride with us?

Hailey: We can pick you up.

Kyle: That's okay. Where are we meeting?

"One of the spawn is with me," Tess warned.

"You left him in the car? This long?" I asked.

Tess waved. "He's got his tablet, and I cracked the window. I could leave him for two hours before he noticed."

"Where do I tell Kyle to meet us?" I asked.

Tess reached toward my iPad. "I wanna surprise you. Now pretend like you trust me and hand that thing over."

Oh, hell.

I smacked it into her hand and started wrapping up my amp cord to get my stuff in the house. Heaving my guitar over my shoulder and grabbing my amp, I stuck my head inside. "Tess is helping me with the fear list. I'll be back . . . later."

"Make sure you have your phone!" Lila called.

Of *course* I had my phone. But instead of being snarky, like I wanted, I brightened my voice as high as I could. "Got it!"

"Listen to you being all nice with the moms." Tess grinned, grabbed my arm, and ran me to the car. "Kyle wrote back. He's meeting us in twenty."

"Hi," I said to the kid in the backseat as I slid in.

No response. Head buried so deep in his tablet I could've been Santa Claus and he wouldn't have noticed.

I sat in the passenger's seat and tapped my foot. The thrill of crossing a new item off the list might not be worth whatever Tess had in mind. How do you tackle a spider fear?

We listened to music as we drove, and I tried to ignore the loud tablet beeping from the backseat. Tess pulled to a stop. I slowly leaned forward, squinting up at the sign. We were parked in front of a pet store.

"What . . . ?"

Tess ran around the car and jerked open my door. "They have great spiders here."

My gut dropped to the floor. "Really?"

"Come *on!*" She grabbed my hand and pulled me out of the car as my body screamed at me to turn and run. But I'd brought the list with me, and it felt wrong to walk away when I was so close.

She ducked her head into the backseat. "Riley? We're here. You don't want to miss this, do you?"

He slowly ambled out of the car, playing his tablet *as he walked.*

"Kyle!" Tess waved. "Awesome!"

I hated that she saw him before me.

"Hey," Kyle said as he got close. Shoved his hands in his pockets. Glanced down, letting his hair fall over his face.

"So Hailey's sucked you into her fear list, huh?"

Kyle shrugged. Typical. He pulled a hand out of his pocket and held open the door.

"Let me get Riley set up," Tess said. She marched him over to a bench by the fish and plopped him down. He didn't glance up once. *Kids.*

The smell of rodent poop and cedar bedding accosted my nose. "I don't like animals," I said to Kyle.

He stood in front of a glass case housing kittens. "My mom says she's allergic."

His words sounded tired, frustrated. There was some kind of history there. And he hadn't said she was allergic, he'd said that she'd *told* him she was allergic. That was a very bizarre distinction.

I stood next to Kyle, watching the small bundles of fur crawl over each other and mew with baby-cat voices. "I guess they're cute. But then they turn into cats that bring home dead mice and birds and stuff."

Kyle shifted his weight. "Not indoor cats."

"So there ya go. You should get a cat as a present to yourself when you leave home."

Kyle's body went so rigid next to me it almost felt like I was next to someone else.

"This way, you two!" Tess waved from next to a door with an unreadable sign above it.

"What are we in for?" Kyle asked.

My fingers got that numb, tingly thing that happened when a cross-off was close. "We're going to be able to check the spider thing off my list."

"I . . ." But he clamped his mouth shut.

A guy in a blue polo shirt with flame-red hair and blotchy skin followed us through a doorway into a very small room. I wasn't normally claustrophobic, but the heat combined with aquariums lining the walls made me wish for space. I hadn't looked in any of the small cages. I had exactly zero interest in seeing the blurred versions of what lived inside.

Kyle leaned forward, peering into one of the aquariums. "I'm not afraid of spiders."

I rubbed my temples, panic starting to set in. "What even is this room, Tess?"

Kyle continued. "I sweep spiders into dustpans and set them outside."

"So much talking, Kyle. I'd be impressed if I didn't want to throat punch Tess and run." I tried to laugh, but it turned into a cough. I blinked my eyes.

The redheaded guy had something large cradled in his hands. He licked his lips, and then again, and then again. "Okay. So. This is Chewbacca. I named him. 'Cause he has hair and likes—"

"Yeah." I nodded, tapping my hips. No beat. Just nerves tapping away. "I got the *Star Wars* reference." And wasn't at all surprised that this guy had named the thing.

"He's, um . . . really nice." He half turned toward the cage and then faced us again.

"He's a *spider*." I folded my arms, my stomach a mess of knots that I was determined not to show. Tess had definitely called ahead to set this up. In equal parts I wanted to hug and slap her.

Star Wars boy took another few deep breaths in. "He's a tarantula and a really nice one. I promise. *He's a funny little guy*." His voice turned all high-pitched and squealy.

"Is this for real?" Kyle asked.

"This is perfect, see?" Tess's voice had an excited edge that fed my nerves. "It's big enough for you to see, but still small enough to crush under your boot."

The kid gasped.

"Oh. Don't worry." Tess chuckled. "You break it, you buy it. We get it."

"I don't think . . ." His head shook so fast it turned into a blur in front of me.

Tess's hands went straight to her hips. "I'm about to buy that spider and take it to the spawn of the queen bitch I work for. Do you want me to tell your boss that you lost the sale of Chewbacca because you were worried about a blind girl touching a pet that isn't yours?"

He let out a sigh.

"I don't need to touch that thing. He's not on my list." Kyle backed up.

"Yeah . . . I don't think I care about this item on the list." I shook my head.

Tess's hand rested on my shoulder. "Don't be a wimp, Hailey. You can do this. Spiders are small. You're always going to be jumpy around them. This way, you'll have held the mother of all spiders, and—"

"Chewbacca is actually a male . . . ," red-haired guy piped in.

Kyle held his hands out. "Let's get it over with. I'll go. Then Hailey can go."

I tucked my hand under Kyle's arm. "I can experience by proxy."

"Nice try, Hailey." Tess snorted. "You're next."

And then this large, fuzzy thing sat on Kyle's outstretched hands.

"Woot, Kyle!" I squeezed his bicep. "You can cross this off!"

"I'd have to add it first." He shook his head. "I told you I'm not really afraid of spiders—well, maybe not until I saw this one."

I watched Kyle harder, wishing the edges of his face and hair were sharper, clearer. If Kyle actually worked his way down a fear list, he'd be something amazing. Someone people would have to take notice of. I guessed that mumbling, shy, quiet Kyle would start to disappear, and whatever would take his place would be pretty awesome.

The spider began to crawl up Kyle's arm. "I'm good! I'm good! Take it!" He laughed, though, instead of screeching.

"Your turn, girlie," Tess teased.

I closed my eyes and held out shaking hands, palm side up.

"You have this," Kyle whispered.

"He's real mellow." The kid's hands touched mine, and as they slid away, what felt like a ball of pipe cleaners rested on my palms.

"Chewbacca." The word squeaked out. "Holy shit, I'm holding a spider!"

And then he moved a leg. "He's moving!" I screeched.

"Calm, Hailey." Tess again. "Spiders move. Kyle survived."

I stretched my spider-holding hands away from my body. "You-can-take-him-back-now."

"I think he can handle you holding Chewy a few minutes longer." Tess mock punched the guy, but he didn't move, his eyes trained on me.

I kept my eyes on the spider, trying to sort out its legs and body, but Chewbacca was still a hideous furry blob. There was no way I was going to wimp out now. I had to cross off something else on my list.

Chapter Nineteen: Kyle

There was a very specific moment when Hailey's face moved from fear and disgust to determination. Not going to be brought down by a tarantula, this girl. The small window let in a bit of sun that shined off her dark blond hair. Her foot tapped the floor in a rhythm or maybe counting down. Hailey would probably never know how hot she was. Even if her eyesight were clear, she wouldn't be able to see herself the way I saw her.

One of Hailey's shoulders hitched. Like she was about to lose it.

"I think she's earned her cross-off now," I said.

Tess tapped her chin.

"Ted," I read off the pimply guy's name tag. "Take Chewbacca back before he gets tossed across the room, huh?"

He leapt forward and scooped up the spider. My fear of spiders was the same kind of fear most people had—I got grossed out when one crawled over my arm or something, but it wasn't like I was plagued by them. Still. To come here and watch this? Worth adding it to the list.

Hailey threw her arms in the air. "I did it! I held a motherfucking tarantula!"

"Ooh. That's a major swear, not even one of the minor ones." The kid Tess had brought with her stood at the door. "And my tablet's almost out of batteries. I need to recharge while we take Chewbacca home."

Hailey snorted, grabbed my hand, and dragged me from the small room. "I need a pen."

"What?"

She turned, her eyes wide, practically glowing with happiness. Over a spider. "A pen. To cross this off my list."

She was still holding my hand. And like a Pavlovian reaction, my palms started to sweat. I jerked my hand from hers and balled my fists in my pockets.

I borrowed a pen from the checkout girl and handed it to Hailey. "Here."

Hailey paused, her gaze ping-ponging from side to side. "Don't like holding hands, huh?"

"I sweat," I blurted out.

"We all do. It's a human thing. When I go blind, you're going to have to get over the sweating hang-up. I'll need hands."

It probably shouldn't have sounded as dirty to me as it did. But yeah . . . hands.

Her list was out of her pocket already. She uncapped the pen and sat down on the floor.

"See, Kyle? I'm in control. The things I'm afraid of, they're nothing. I can do this. Best feeling ever." She crossed it out a few times. "Aren't you gonna sit?"

I glanced around and thought about pointing out we were in a pet store, but of course she knew, and of course she didn't care.

As soon as my ass hit the ground next to her, Hailey held the pen toward me. "Your turn. Add it, Kyle. Cross it off. Feel the rush. Feel the control."

"You sound like a Sprite commercial." I pulled my list from my back pocket.

Her hands clapped together, and I smiled. A real, actual smile.

"You're so cute when you're smiling." She pinched my cheek.

My smile disappeared. "I'm not a toddler."

Her hand dropped and I felt like a dick, but this was not exactly the kind of territory I wanted to be in with Hailey. If I couldn't date her, at least I could be on the same level with her, not some project or little boy to be praised.

I flattened my list on the floor, feeling selfishly safe from Hailey being able to see it. Crossing off something on my list should feel . . . big. Instead it was a line on a piece of paper over an item I'd just written.

Being here with Hailey? Outside of school? With a friend of hers? That was bigger. Better. Should've probably written that.

The second I crossed out my newly added item, Hailey asked, "You mark it off?"

God, her eyes were shit. I nodded, and her arms wrapped around me. Not like I was a kid. Like I was more. My hands took too long to react, and she was gone and standing before I thought to tell my body to hug her back.

"I gotta get the spawn home," Tess said, waving the tablet around.

I stood, cock-blocked by my own stupid self and some kid who needed his tablet recharged.

"Stop calling me that," the kid said, clutching a box, which I could only assume held the beast we'd touched. "I wanna get Chewbacca home so I can play with him."

I waited for something in Hailey to shift when the kid said he *wanted* to touch the spider she'd been afraid of, but it never came. Maybe it was just me who thought my fears might be shit.

"Kyle. I can't believe you did this." Hailey bumped her shoulder against mine. "I love that you did this."

I loved that I'd done it too. With her. But I didn't have words. Words for her smile. Her broken eyes. Her excitement over a piece of paper. I wanted more of it. Of her. But it wasn't my place. Not yet. But maybe when I got farther down the list. Maybe when I started doing real stuff.

"Offer's still open," Hailey whispered, and raised her eyebrows. The sex thing again. "You know. Cross off something else? It's kind of a rush, yeah?"

And then what? She'd go and do it with her bouncer too? "I'm . . . I'm not the guy for that, Hailey."

I hated that I'd said the words. Hated even more that I'd only half meant them. Hated that I should have had better words to explain. Of course I did have better words, but getting them out was completely different.

"Fair enough." She shook her list a few times between us. "But another thing done! Nothing can bring me down today."

"Hailey! For real," Tess said. "You're worse than the spawn when he levels up on Candy Crush."

"Take it back, bitch!" Hailey yelled back.

"Um . . ." That Ted guy stopped next to Hailey. "Can you please not curse in the store?"

"Oh." Hailey slapped her hands over her mouth. But she was definitely smirking. "Fuck. I'm so sorry."

This time I made myself reach out and grab her arm. "Okay. Before Tess kicks both our asses or we're banned from this store for life."

Hailey laughed again as I pulled her toward the door.

148

"That's right, Kyle! It takes two of us to manage a Hailey," Tess said. And then she and the spawn were out the door with Hailey and me right behind her.

I dropped Hailey's arm as soon as we exited and she shook her head. "You're gonna need to figure out that touching thing, Kyle."

Then she gave me a wave and hopped into Tess's car, and kept waving as they backed out.

I had purposefully added and crossed out an item on my list of fears. Not a real fear, but something that got me closer to Hailey. Got me closer to actually being worth something to her. My shoulder, my hand, my cheek. Three points where Hailey touched me. And that damn hug. Probably I needed to go home and jerk off. Probably I needed to be less sleazy with Hailey and be a real friend. Probably neither of those things would happen and I'd be stuck with a lecture from Mom about not having texted her that I was going out.

I wanted . . . I wanted so much, but taking what I wanted, getting what I wanted, going after what I wanted, was going to be so much harder than adding something to a piece of paper only to cross it out seconds later.

A week after, school was finally out and I'd heard nothing from Hailey—though I guess I didn't reach out to her either. I was given a bunch of bullshit things to do every day for my mom. Couldn't she put all the groceries on one single list and send me in her car once a week, instead of this daily bike ride to the store to get a few things? I wanted to ask if she was trying to keep me busy. If my long summer with no job—I *was* applying to places every day because there was no way I could survive in my house alone for ten weeks—was going to be filled with stupid chores.

I didn't complain to her, though. Didn't say anything to anyone. For hours and hours at a time. I went into the radio station twice a week to engineer for our shortened summer hours. But I barely saw or spoke to anyone. Sometimes in the house alone, I'd read my journal out loud to hear my own voice. And every day I waited, checking email and hoping someone gave enough of a shit to see if I was alive.

Then, finally, a text from Pavel.

Pavel: Come over today, okay?

Kyle: On my way.

I'd been giving him space. I'd apologized and left the ball in his court. The wait had felt interminable, but maybe what I deserved.

When I got to his house, his mom hugged me hard, smashing me into her big arms and petting my hair like I was a puppy.

"He's in the back."

I passed through the kitchen with its delicious smells—Pavel's mom was always cooking Russian pastries—and his sisters hugged me too. I got more touch from Pavel's family than anywhere else. They used to seem stone-faced and unemotional, but once I was invited in, I was family.

When I stepped into the backyard, Pavel nodded at me. "Kyle. Perfect time. Play goalie."

I sighed. "I suck at goalie."

"Nonsense. Zig Ziglar says, 'You were born to win, but to be a winner, you must plan to win, prepare to win, and expect to win.'"

Since I wasn't quite sure how to respond, I moved to the front of the goal. "I sent you an email. A while ago."

Pavel lined up the ball and kicked it fast and hard. It whooshed past my ear before I could even move. "Yes. I received it. But not today, okay? Today, you maybe should tell me about your girl."

I sighed. Not forgiven, then.

"Don't look sad, friend. This is not for you to be sad over. Just not today, okay?"

I nodded. "'Kay."

"You still have the girlfriend?"

"Not a girlfriend. A friend who's a girl."

"Big boobs?"

I snorted. "Pavel."

"We're friends. Family. This isn't a question to ask?"

"It's maybe a question to ask. But maybe not the first question."

I tossed the ball back to him. He stopped it with his chest and let it roll down his body, smooth, like the ball was part of him. "Okay. Tell me something about her that's not boobs."

"Hailey. Her name is Hailey. She has a list of fears. She asked me to do a list too. That's why I sent you that letter."

"Because you're afraid?" He lined up the ball again and it whooshed past my other side, though this time at least I got a hand on it.

"Yeah. But not how you think."

"I should do a list maybe? Will this help me with the ladies? To show my soft side?"

I laughed hard. "Maybe. I don't know. I'm not the best person to ask about girls."

"But you see more of them than I do. I've been practicing, though. *Cosmopolitan* has great tips on oral pleasure. Also, they now say the G-spot is a myth. Do you believe it?"

"Uh, maybe. I don't have that much experience."

His eyes went wide, more excitement than Pavel's face usually expressed. "Do you have *any* experience?"

I almost told him about the sex offer. Almost. But Pavel would never let me live that down. He probably wouldn't speak to me for another month if I told him I'd passed on Hailey's suggestion. So instead, I tossed the ball back to him and said, "Nope."

I got home to a note from my mom: "You got the wrong kind of dishwashing soap. Cascade leaves streaks on the glasses. You'll need to get the streak-free kind today." *Great.*

I logged on to my computer—Jesus, why wouldn't Mom

let me have a smartphone?—and finally an email from Hailey. It was one line.

I've worked through every song you put on that playlist, and I love them all.

That was the moment I should have called her. Told her that Chaz was a stupid idea. Told her that I was in for crossing the sex thing off her list. That I needed time to prepare. Time to spend with her. That I wanted to hang out with her all the time. But I choked. I closed the email and did nothing. I couldn't.

I'd screwed up with Pavel. Screwed up with my mom. Of course I'd screw up with Hailey.

Chapter Twenty: Hailey

Chaz was still hot, and a perfect distraction from all the juvenile crap that went along with the rest of my life, even though I barely saw him. I finally texted him a picture of me in my bra, but not my face. Faceless boobs felt pretty safe.

He came over that night and I had to sneak out to meet him in his car. He had my shirt off within forty-five seconds.

"You have no idea how hot that picture made me. Your tits are perfect, baby."

Okay, gross. This shouldn't have been gross, but it totally was. "Baby" and "tits." I stopped him with a hand. "Do you want to . . . talk . . . for a little?"

He blinked. "Why? Do you? I never see you, and you sent me that picture. I thought you were into this. Into me."

"I am. . . . I don't know."

I shouldn't have been thinking of Kyle. Or the morning last week when he biked by and mumbled he'd seen Pavel but didn't have *the talk* because Pavel put him off. He asked if I was still trying to decide which song to use for the competition, so I guess he got my email, but he never said anything else about my multiple offers to cross sex off the list.

It shouldn't have affected me at all. Seriously, it was an offer of convenience, nothing else. But he barely acknowledged it. He didn't say, *Hey, Hailey, you're hot, but getting it over with that way just isn't my thing.* Only, he did look at me in this funny way, straddling his bike like it was the one thing keeping him from saying, *Hailey. I'm in.* I shook my head. No. That was wishful thinking. Because he didn't say it. I hated that it hurt. It shouldn't have. We were friends. But I wanted an explanation aside from "I'm not the guy for that."

"So do you not want this? Because, Hailey, a lot of girls . . . ," Chaz started, pulling back and adjusting his dick in case it wasn't totally clear what a lot of girls would be willing to do with him.

"No. I mean, I don't want to do it in your car in the middle of the night with my moms a hundred feet away."

Kyle would get this. Chaz looked baffled, like car sex with parental units close by was super normal. Kyle would be thoughtful about sex. God, why was I focusing on him? He'd said no. More than once.

The thing was, he could tell me about Pavel, and the most traumatic experience of his life, and cry all over my shirt, or stand next to me when I held a disgusting spider, but he couldn't man up and go for a sure thing. He knew it was still on the table. I'd told him it would be. I'd brought it up an embarrassing number of times. God, what was wrong with me?

"So we're not going to have sex?" Chaz asked.

I kissed him again, wet and way dirtier than I really wanted, but it was a holdover. A *not now but soon*. Because it would be soon.

It was ridiculous. I was almost two months into being sixteen. And maybe it was stupid to want to get sex over with. I mean, I knew I was going blind, and I wasn't eager for *that* to happen so I could mark it off my list. But I hated knowing that I would definitely someday have sex and not be able to see my partner. That's why I wanted it *off* the list. I'd crossed off nothing since the spider, and that was more than two weeks ago. I had a willing partner, and I also had an unwilling partner, which, I guess, didn't make him a partner at all.

"At the competition," I whispered in Chaz's ear. Then I shrugged my shirt on and snuck back into my house.

"I can't believe you're doing this, Hailey." But Tess grinned as wide as me.

"Me either." I stripped off my jeans in the passenger's seat of her car and slid on the denim miniskirt. I slipped Rox's boots back on, which looked killer with my short skirt.

"You remembered to wear black panties, right? Because if

you step too close to the edge of the stage, and guys try to look up your skirt, they might not be able to see the black."

I blushed, thinking about Chaz seeing them that night. The panties weren't black, they were green—Irish green. Matched my green bra. I'd planned this night since I'd promised Chaz two weeks ago.

"Promise you're not pissed?" I asked.

"That you're singing a love song for Chaz with another band?" We pulled into the parking lot near the bar. "No. Definitely not. Better them than me. Plus, it's not like we *have* a band. You need to be singing with someone."

I knotted up my T-shirt behind me, exposing my stomach and even more of my lower back. I'd rehearsed with these guys twice while "at Tess's house for dinner." Chaz insisted on me singing with them, and he was right, the band was probably really going somewhere, but they were picky as hell. I wouldn't be playing that night, just singing. Les Paul was at home.

"Okay. So, if the moms call, I'll just tell them that you're either in the shower or already asleep and then send you a text." Tess held her phone between us.

"Right."

"And"—she grabbed my leg as I opened the door—"if you need a ride after, call."

"I've got Chaz. I'm good." I pulled the braids out of my hair, letting it fall in loose waves, shoved the jeans into my bag, and ran to the back exit of the bar, where Chaz stood holding the door open and smiling.

"Have fun," Tess called as she gave me one last wave before pulling out.

I turned to wave back, but Chaz's hands were on my exposed stomach, sliding their way to my back. "Damn, Hailey. Every guy out there's going to want a piece of you tonight."

I shrugged because I didn't know what to say. Knotting my T-shirt up had been a great idea.

"We're on in thirty," one of the guys from the band snarled. "Where the hell have you been?"

"I told you she was working," Chaz barked.

So, yeah. They had no idea how young I was either. My age never seemed to matter when Chaz was around, 'cause he knew everyone.

"But I'm getting a piece of you, right? After you sing me my song?" He gave my neck a bite, but I was so nervous about performing with the guys that all the awesome anticipation of Chaz didn't hit me like it normally did.

"Maybe," I choked out.

"Not maybe. I am. Don't worry, Hailey." He brushed his hand across my cheek. "You're going to be amazing."

And the way he looked at me and touched me so carefully made me tingle all over, and I suddenly couldn't wait for my song to be over so we could cross something else off my list.

I sang hard. "In Your Eyes" was perfect for the crowd. They

even asked us to do two encores. Onstage Hailey was an animal, and I almost, *almost* wished that someone I knew had seen me. Anyone. Our mini-set flew by—there was something to be said for not having the stress of playing as well as singing.

The guys were bummed we only took second, but I thanked them for playing with me. They said they were maybe looking for a new lead singer but weren't ready to give anyone the spot yet. Probably best since the moms might not go for it, and then I'd have had to explain my age and curfew and all that.

Sometimes big chances were a one-time thing, and it felt okay. But I'd be lying if I said part of me didn't hope they'd get in touch with me again and ask me to sing lead.

The bar was closed, and Chaz and I were just about the last people left. The darkness of the small greenroom was both comforting and terrifying. Because Chaz and I were alone and my shirt was on the floor.

"Baby, that song. Every guy was wishing he was me tonight." He cupped my boobs and squeezed a little hard. "I can't wait."

I slipped my glasses back on my face and peered at Chaz. He was sweaty and flushed and breathing hard. Because of me. Because I turned him on.

I reached for my discarded shirt, but he stopped me.

"I'm not putting you off. It's that . . ." I looked down. "I wanna wait a little bit longer." I was being a baby. I'd just gotten completely high from singing, from a gig he'd gotten for me, and I was backing away from him? I had an *all-night* alibi. I felt totally pathetic.

"But you said . . ." He twirled my hair around his finger. "Why are you making this into a big deal? I promise to take care of you."

"Yeah, I know, you said."

He dropped his hand and slipped his fingers beneath the strap of my bra. I shivered because, honestly, he was hot. And I liked him.

He gripped my hips and pulled me closer to him, dropping kisses on my neck that made me shiver even more. "I want you to be able to see what I can do to you. *For* you."

Chaz did make me think I was sexy, and seriously, how many sixteen-year-old girls could say they were dating a hot bouncer? Who worked in bars that he got her into?

So taking all things into consideration—my need to get it over with, his horniness, and Kyle's lack thereof—the decision was pretty damn easy to make, and I finally took control, which was what I'd needed all along.

I shifted the skirt up my hips and stood, letting Chaz slip off my underwear.

"Leave the skirt and boots on." He kissed my stomach as I stepped out of my underwear. I was on top. I was doing this. I was in control.

He pulled a condom out of his pocket, unzipped his jeans, and gloved up. I'd seen a penis before—hello Internet porn and fifteen percent of Tumblr posts—but in that moment, I was sort of grateful for the dim lighting. Again. Thinking about that big thing being inside me was a lot to take.

His thumbs slid through my belt loops and he pulled me back down onto his lap. My legs shook. I tightened my jaw to keep my teeth from chattering in nerves.

"Take your shirt off," I said through tight teeth.

The same cocky smile that I'd fallen for on the first night lit his face. "You got it." He slipped off his shirt and guided me until I hovered over him.

I leaned forward and kissed him. I was on top. I was in control. I was shaking.

In a series of too quick motions, he grabbed my hips, tilted his hips upward, and pressed into me. I gasped at the sharpness of the pain.

"Hailey," he grunted. "You're so tight. Holy . . ."

Chaz rammed his hips into me over and over, telling me how amazing I felt. He jerked me toward him again and again as he mumbled incoherently, keeping his hands on my hips, forcing my movements. How long was this going to last?

I squeezed my eyes shut and clenched my jaw to keep from crying because it hurt like fire, and Chaz's hands gripped my hips tighter.

"Hai-ley, Hai-ley . . . ," he moaned, and I was about to tell him to stop already—because after all his sweet talk about taking care of me, there was only one person having fun here—

when his phone rang on the table next to the couch.

He paused, checked the phone, and then pushed his bristly mouth back into mine and started pumping away.

"Oh, come *on*." I shoved on his chest with both hands and scrambled to standing in the middle of the room, my body still burning.

"What the *hell*, Hailey?" His face turned down in an angry scowl. "You can't *stop* like that."

I opened my mouth to talk, but like when the moms had me cornered, nothing came out. When I stared at him, in that split second on the couch, I felt like an idiot for ever, *ever* taking the time to be with him. What kind of a pathetic loser of a twenty-one-year-old wants a sixteen-year-old virgin girlfriend? And how the hell didn't I see it sooner? The pictures. The being okay with not knowing the moms . . . I wasn't in control of this. Not at all. He wasn't my conquest. I was his.

I jerked my shirt back on, tucked my underwear in my pack, and took off. I didn't care what time it was. I needed home.

The problem with being me, and seeing for shit, is that it takes a long time to find a way home at three something in the morning, and even though Tess had offered, I could *not* call her after this.

The taxi dropped me off around five. I'd had to wait for ages at some random bus stop downtown. I dropped my bag under our coatrack and jogged down the stairs to my room, needing to be out of my clothes and into something clean. Probably I should have been quiet, but I wanted my bed and my blanket too much to care.

"Hailey?" Rox knocked on my bedroom door about two minutes later.

"Yeah."

"Why are you home so early?" she asked through the door.

"Just happened that way." I slid off my skirt—no panties. As I grabbed a pair from my dresser, I hissed because I was still sore. Another reminder of how stupid I was. My chest caved in deeper and I sucked in a few breaths to keep from crying. *Crying.* It was *my* idea.

I'm tougher than this. I am. I am. I am. I am. I had something else to check off the list. Checking things off my list was supposed to be amazing. Life-changing.

But Kyle was right.

It should have been special or something. Well, at least it *could* have been. I knew I locked feelings away I didn't want to think about. I also knew that once in a while all those feelings would crash around me, and they were *big*. Why hadn't I pushed Kyle? Why hadn't I waited for him? Was I so awful he wouldn't even consider me?

I pulled on my pajama bottoms and a clean tank, wondering if I had to get out of bed on Monday. My bed felt softer than it ever had, and I wrapped myself up in the familiar happy of my blanket. Five in the morning, and I was finally getting some rest.

"Hailey?" Rox knocked on my door again.

"What?" I didn't say *come in* because I knew she would eventually.

My door opened.

Double moms. Double concerned faces.

I was in deep shit. And I had no idea why.

"Your panties fell out of your pack when I brought it downstairs," Lila said quietly.

"Those aren't mine." I slid lower in my bed and pulled the blankets around my head like I'd done since I was five.

They glanced at each other, and then I realized how stupid I was because they'd bought that pair for me when they'd bought my green bra. How the hell did they fall out? Or maybe the moms went rummaging while I dug for underwear and pajama pants.

Shittty, shit, shit, shit. I couldn't think of a single way out.

"Why?" Rox asked. Her head tilted to the side, studying me.

I had to swallow. Not enough. Swallow again. Not enough.

I clasped my hands together. "Because I thought I was getting my period and it seemed like the easiest way to check?"

I really should've worked harder at not making that sound like a question.

Then they did the unthinkable. Rox sat next to me and put her arm around my shoulders, and Lila rested her hands on my feet.

My chest swelled. My stomach tightened. I couldn't breathe.

What was I supposed to do? How would I get rid of them? Why weren't they yelling at me?

No. I didn't want to feel the cracking and splintering. I wasn't sorry. I'd wanted it. I'd gone to Chaz and asked for it. It was no big deal. Thousands—no, probably millions—of people did it every day.

Instead I cried.

No one spoke. I knew the questions would start any minute. The first of which should've had something to do with how crazy I'd become.

"Did someone hurt you, Hailey?" Lila whispered.

My head shook, which made my body shake more, and made me feel worse instead of better. Whoever said a good cry makes you feel better is full of shit. Big piles of shit. "No one hurt me. It was my choice."

Rox wrapped me up in her arms, and I sobbed into her chest.

"I wish you guys didn't care about things so much." I punched my bed as tears streamed down my face.

"Why?" Lila massaged my feet.

"Because maybe then *I'd* care less."

"Why would you want to care less?" Rox gave me another squeeze.

"So I wouldn't hurt so much." I pulled my knees up, wishing to be alone.

The silence stretched for not nearly long enough.

"With who?" Lila asked.

"Chaz."

"The older guy? Fuck." Rox breathed out and her voice hardened. "That's statutory rape, or sexual assault of a minor, or something worth him being arrested. You know this, right?"

"Please don't." I shook my head.

"We'll talk about it." Lila gave me another squeeze. "You were careful?"

I nodded.

"Okay. Can we stay in here or do you want to be alone?"

"Alone."

They slowly left my room. Only I suddenly wasn't sure that I did want to be alone.

I reached around on my nightstand until I found my iPod, scrolled to Kyle's playlist, cranked it until my ears hurt, and wished to feel less.

I walked into the north campus building feeling like both everything and nothing had changed. My feet steered me past the empty practice rooms and the classes full of bored summer school kids. To Kyle. Alone in the studio. Where I knew he'd be engineering a music-only show with prerecorded station IDs. Not talking, still. I saw him and my stomach filled with guilt.

He was smart not to have sex with me. I wasn't even close to being worthy of a guy like Kyle. I was pushy and sometimes sort of awful. I didn't know how to be better. How to be different. How to be enough.

"You were right," I said the second he looked up from the computer. I stepped close to him. Enough to smell the citrus detergent and grab his hand if I wanted to.

I wanted to. But didn't.

A corner of his mouth pulled up. I loved that because it was so unusual for him. "About what?"

"When you have sex. Make it a big deal. It should be a big deal."

His face fell.

I felt dirty all over again.

Instead of trying to explain or trying to smooth things over or even figure out why I *should* smooth things over when he'd passed in the first place, I turned and walked away.

Chapter Twenty-One: Kyle

The look on her face crushed me. I'd let her down. She was more broken than I ever thought I'd see her. And angry. And hurt. I hated that she'd had sex with Chaz. Jesus, why didn't she know me well enough not to tell me about it? She should never have asked me to do it with her in the first place. She had to have known it would be nearly impossible for me. *Nearly*. I could have. I should have. God, I'd wanted to. That killed me the most. It wasn't impossible. I was just incapable of being what she needed.

Imagining Hailey with that douche was the worst kind of torture. But it was equally as bad imagining her with me. It almost hurt more. I wondered if she'd always feel outside of my grasp, or if that was a prison I'd built for myself.

I looked at the soundboard, switching it over to automated

so I could get out, out, out. I wasn't sure I was even breathing. When I hit the hallway, I sprinted out of the building. The second the sun hit my face, I stopped. I took a bunch of deep breaths. And could just barely see the top of her head as she walked around the corner in the direction of her house. Her shoulders slightly hunched.

I should have run to her. Pulled her into a hug. Told her I was sorry. Told her so many things. I had notebooks full of words at home. Stacks of them. But for a girl I cared about more than maybe anyone else, I didn't know what to say. Didn't know how to undo what had been done. What I'd done. What she'd done. What Chaz had done.

The farther away Hailey walked, the more I knew I couldn't follow. The more work I knew I had to make myself better. I had the beginnings of a list, but there was more. There should be more.

I let her go, and it was as if someone had stretched my body full of rubber bands, all of them too tightly pulled to really hold me together.

Hailey disappeared, and every band snapped. Instead of going back into the station, I walked for my bike, climbed on, and rode home. Mom got to have days in front of the TV. I could do the same. I knew it would do nothing to make me feel better, but I didn't give a shit. I'd lost something I could have had. For her and for me. Whatever misery Hailey felt, I deserved more.

◊ ◊ ◊

The front door slammed, and I jerked so hard my hand hit the floor, saving me from falling off the couch.

"Your teacher from the radio station called today," Mom snapped. "Care to guess why?"

"Shit," I muttered.

"Don't you dare use that language in my house. I'm trying to keep this family together by myself, Kyle. Do you understand?"

I understood all too well. I sat up and rubbed my eyes. Daytime TV was crap, even when all I wanted was the mindless chatter. "Yeah," I mumbled. I should have at least let Mr. Schmidt know I'd preset the show and bailed.

"Kyle." She actually stomped her foot. "Grow up and show me that you might be able to take care of yourself next year. You're not working. You're not doing anything except this small commitment to the radio station. Be your word."

Be my word. Ha.

I was less worried about me next year than how Mom would do, but that wasn't something I could say out loud. And I wasn't about to give Hailey up to the firing squad. Mom didn't deserve to know that part of me. I'd let her be angry. Furious. And hope it didn't spiral her down. Last time I thought she was teetering on the edge and was ready to spend a few days in bed, it had never happened.

"I needed to leave early today," I said. "I'm not feeling great."

Both true.

Mom frowned so deeply the lines of her face grew darker. "Honey, you need to take care of yourself. I don't want to worry about you."

There was no winning with Mom. Never would be. I rubbed my eyes. "What do you need from me, Mom?"

"I don't *need* anything, Kyle." Then she sighed.

"Sorry," I mumbled.

"It's okay. I'm tired. I didn't think everything would be this hard."

"Can I help?" The offer felt like a noose, but what was I going to do?

"Clean this up, okay?" She pointed to the water glass and cereal bowl on the coffee table.

"Okay."

Hailey had eviscerated me with her sad eyes and pathetic declaration. *Eviscerated me.* I woke up every morning thinking of her and realized I couldn't go back to her. Couldn't apologize for being angry at something that was my own fault. Couldn't explain that maybe I would have helped her cross that one item off her list if I'd been able to find the words and say them. Write them. Anything. She'd gotten hurt. And it was because of me. None of my words on the matter could alter that.

The whole event set me up for a shit summer. I'd let myself

hope for different. But I should have known not to build up expectations. It was the same as every summer since my dad left. Quiet. Lonely. Depressing.

I couldn't get a job because I sucked at interviews. So I volunteered at the library and read everything. I worked at the station twice a week. Listened to music. Saw Pavel, who still refused to discuss freshman year because it went against Zig Ziglar's positive-thinking philosophy. And every night, I thought about visiting Hailey. Stared at my bike and wondered if I could go see her and we could be how we were before. But every day that went by felt like another day too long. I should have followed her home. Should have shown up at her house and told her that the list meant something. That she meant something. That the world would right itself again, but I didn't have it in me. Didn't know if I could lie to her that way because I had no clue if the world would ever feel right in any way.

I relaxed against the wall of the library, *On the Road* resting on my lap. My mind faded from Kerouac's words to the monotony of the summer. The monotony was my fault, of course, I felt too paralyzed to change anything.

"Where is your girl, my friend?" Pavel asked as he stopped next to the bookshelf in front of me. He came often because he hated the heat, burned too easily, and got tired of taking his sisters to the pool every day.

"I don't have a girl. I've never had a girl."

Pavel narrowed his eyes in the same way his mom did when she disapproved of her daughters' language. "You've never had a *lover*. You've had a girl."

"I've had neither. Just me. And Mom. And the station. And the library."

He slid a book off the shelf. He placed it on top of his head and walked around like he was getting ready for a runway show, his long arms outstretched. "She has a new lover?"

I shrugged. Yes. No. I couldn't say. She'd *had* one.

Pavel placed the book back on the shelf. "You are always in the library or at the station for the summer. I think it is time for you to start reading *Cosmopolitan*. You know you can check them out from here?"

I shook my head. "I'm not reading *Cosmo*."

Pavel looked at the ceiling, then back at me. "You must stop pouting about losing the girl. You did not read *Cosmopolitan* as I told you, and now you're alone. You have done it to yourself."

And the messed-up thing was that Pavel was right. He didn't even know the whole story and still he was right. Except about the *Cosmo* part. I'd lost Hailey because of my own stupidity. Because I hadn't worked hard enough. Hadn't been what I wanted to be. Hadn't done the things on my fear list that would turn me into a guy who could speak. Say the right things at the right time.

"Have respect for the library, pick out a book, and read something," I said.

Pavel stared at me, his face expressionless. "I'll come back with a magazine. I know where to find you." And he stalked away like he had a mission.

Summer vacation was half over and I had nothing to show for it. I sat on the curb and stared at my list after working the station that day, half hating it. I'd started more than once to crumple up that piece of paper to throw it in the trash, but couldn't do it. Like I should have forgotten about Hailey and couldn't do that either. I held on to both, despite the sick feeling they sometimes left in my stomach.

I went over the list again. The one I had memorized. One item on my list wasn't doable right then, but I could do a trial run. Instead of driving across the country, I could drive across the state. My body twitched a few times, pushing me forward. Every time I crossed something off the list, I was better than before, right? Every item off the list was one step closer to deserving Hailey.

I couldn't get in the car and drive hundreds of miles without giving anyone warning. I couldn't. But when *I couldn't* ran through my head, so did Hailey. She'd laugh at *I can't* and ask me, *Why the hell not?* And then she'd probably scoot low in the seat to put her feet on the dash. In that brief second, I knew I was going to do it. I was going to take advantage of the car that Mom used for work most days, but hadn't today. I had hours. Almost a day and a half before she needed it again. I jumped up from my spot on the curb before I could chicken out. I climbed into Mom's car and turned the opposite way out of the parking lot than I normally did.

Two hundred miles outside of Chicago, the pressure finally began to fade. Who would even miss me if I didn't stop? Pavel? Maybe. All he'd need was a phone call, and even though I was his only friend the way he was mine, he'd say, *Good for you, Kyle, with the positive thinking and doing something drastic.* My Russian friend loved big, dramatic showmanship.

Mom. I was afraid to be too far away from her. But my guess was that it would take her two days to notice I was gone. She'd be more likely to call the cops about the missing car than her missing son. Though maybe that wasn't true. She'd be out of sorts without me around, but I knew after her schedule this week that tomorrow would be a sleep day.

It's not like I was actually considering continuing on, but with the road in front of me, I could understand why people did it. Climbed into their cars and never looked back. Understanding the need for escape was why I'd put a cross-country drive on the list in the first place.

I pulled into a random rest stop an hour or so after the sun had gone down, and finally understood the "rush" of checking something off the list. And I hadn't even checked this off, just gotten a taste of what it would be like when I did go all the way.

Hailey probably jumped into her items with both feet and eyes closed. Not me. Obviously. I climbed out of the driver's seat, stretching my stiff body. Mine was one of three cars in front of the bathrooms, whose stench filled the parking lot. But I was alone. The good kind of alone. I leaned against the hood and breathed in the hot and slightly rank summer air of a place I'd never been.

I'd been gone for hours. Just to drive. Told no one. And it felt good—no, *fucking fantastic*—to get in the car and run away.

For the first time all summer, I was glad I hadn't given up on the possibility of Hailey, even though it hurt to think about her. Listening to voices echo through the dark parking lot, I was even gladder I hadn't given up on the list.

Chapter Twenty-Two: Hailey

No band. No school. No Kyle. I would stare at the list every morning but hadn't even planned out what I'd do next.

Tess, despite her nannying job, and despite her attitude about my list, offered to help.

"I realize," she said as she pulled me from my house, "that you'd prefer to sit and mope in your morose state and continue to write songs."

I let my feet drag as the screen door slapped shut behind us. When had it gotten dark out? The days were beginning to blend.

"And don't get me wrong." She opened the passenger's side of her car. "The songs you're writing kick ass. But it's time for you to join the world again, Hailey."

I hadn't been nearly as bad as Tess was suggesting, but it

was pointless to argue with her when she got like this. She climbed into the car and pulled out of the driveway to my "surprise destination."

"Why do you hate my list again?" I asked as I slumped in the passenger's seat.

"It's like a bucket list, Hailey. And it makes you even more reckless than you already are. You don't need anything else to fuel your crazy." She poked my shoulder and chuckled. "Also, the list is little more than a bunch of dares. I get into enough trouble without daring myself to do crap I shouldn't be doing. At the same time, I miss that side of you."

"So that's why you're helping me?" I asked.

"Yes. Also, I'm your friend." She shrugged. "Once again, simplistic inspiration came from one of the spawn."

"Oh, brilliant. More tarantulas? The item only needs to be crossed off the list once, you know."

"Not spiders," Tess promised. "And it'll be a hell of a lot better than losing your virginity to Chaz in the greenroom."

She was correct on that count. It certainly couldn't be worse.

Tess stopped her car by the community center near her house.

"What are we doing here?"

"I've got swimsuits. We're getting in the water."

I shook my head. "No way. Not in the dark."

"No one else is here, Hailey." Tess even used her best

no-bullshit voice. "I pulled a lot of strings to get us an in."

"What kind of strings?"

She sighed. "Flipped up my shirt for the new lifeguard, okay?"

I scoffed and got out of the car. "Guys are so easy."

Unless they're really not interested . . .

I sat on the edge of the pool, resting my feet in the water. This was what I'd always done at the pool. Kicking in the water was fine. Being in deep enough that my body could pull me under and suffocate me? Not so cool.

Tess did another somersault in the chlorinated water. The empty bleachers stretched out on one side. The lights reflected off and in the water. The edges of everything blurred together, which was what had always made me paranoid. How would I know which way was up when I was underwater? How would I get air if I couldn't tell?

"Now slide down one step, okay?" Tess said.

The steps were small, made for children, and the full width of the pool. I slipped down one, letting my butt rest in the water, and then another, sinking in to my belly button, and then another, which reached the top of my chest.

I focused on breathing. On realizing that my shoulders weren't underwater. No one was around to push me. I was okay.

"How about we stop for the night?" Tess suggested. "Sit there for a few or something."

"And who will you flash to get us in here again?" I teased, still staring at the water, trying to make out the point where the air ended and the water began.

No luck.

"Nice one, Hailey." Tess snorted. "But I might kind of like the lifeguard, so we'll see. . . ."

"Oh, yeah?"

"Yeah. Maybe. Who knows."

I breathed through my nose. If I could sit underwater, I'd feel like I could cross this off, but I couldn't do it. How could I suddenly be so paranoid that I couldn't jump in and get this done?

Tess's blurry face bobbed up and down in deeper water.

I didn't want to feel like my fear was pathetic, but sitting on the edge of the kiddie steps, with my friend doing underwater somersaults, it was hard not to.

I hated admitting the Chaz thing had really knocked me down, though maybe not as much as the Kyle thing. I had to get out of my own head. Was this what it was like to be Kyle? Maybe I needed notebooks.

Since I was obviously not smart enough to make decisions regarding relationships, I decided to remain single until at least the end of junior year. I'd marked sex and tongue-kissing off the list, and really didn't want another Chaz mess, or pissed-off moms, or another doctor examining me in stirrups only to say that I was lucky enough to have joined the millions of people across the world with HPV. Apparently condoms aren't one hundred percent on that front. Damn lazy health teacher.

Yes. My summer was going *that* well. I'd made it to standing in the pool about shoulder deep, and every time I stood there, I thought that would be the day I'd let the water cover me, and every day, I ended up back on the steps.

I'd turned into a chicken, and I hated that more than anything else in my life. School was about to start, and I still didn't feel like I could cross this one thing off my list. Pathetic.

Chapter Twenty-Three: Kyle

Two weeks into my senior year, I saw her. Sort of inevitable now that we were on the same campus, but I was taking classes at Concordia University half my days, so I thought I could maybe avoid her. Too many days had passed. Weeks. Time.

In the hallway, she looked at me long and hard. Her messed-up eyes finally dropped to my feet.

"Acquaintance Kyle, who became Friend Kyle, who became Drop-the-Ball Kyle. You're still wearing the shoes?" A corner of her mouth twitched like she wanted to smile. God, I wanted her to smile.

Her hair was split into two braids behind her ears. Guitar strapped to her back and no makeup—simple Hailey. I wanted to say all the things to her. All the things my brain had been processing over the summer. But nothing came.

"Ah. So we're back to the not-talking?"

"H-How was your summer?" I stammered.

"Lonely. Mira stayed with her grandparents, and her parents sent her to Culver Academy this year so she could 'get serious' about music. Tess nannied the spawn for Queen B. And, well, I haven't talked to Chaz. So yeah, me and the moms and music on the porch. Pretty much."

I nodded. It was excruciating seeing her. Every minute I'd spent with her last year darted around my head, poking me with all the good things we could have been and reminding me that all I had left was shit.

"Okay, then. Nice not-talking to you." She moved past me, and I grabbed her wrist.

She blinked up at me. "Yes?"

"I'm sorry," I whispered.

"I can't hear you."

"I'm sorry, Hailey. I messed up. You came to me as a friend. I'm sorry. I screwed it up." What the hell was I doing? I should've let her walk away, but her face and the childish braids and her stupid purple glasses . . . I could *not* let go of her.

"You did," she said. Her bottom lip quivered, and I squished my eyes so I wouldn't have to see her cry and know why she was doing it.

"I'm a shitty friend. Ask Pavel."

She shook her head. "You weren't a shitty friend. Well, you kinda were the last time I saw you, but you weren't before that.

I was probably asking too much, huh? Or maybe telling you too much."

"Can we start over? Please." God, why did I even ask? She deserved better than me. But I couldn't watch her walk away again.

She scrubbed her eyes and nodded. "Okay," she finally said, and I released the breath I was holding. "Okay."

Then there was silence. The silence of expectation. Her waiting for me to tell her why I pulled away. Me unwilling to say the words that rammed against my lips. That clawed at my brain until I nearly shook from the pressure. *I'm interested in you, Hailey.*

People passed us in the hall. Nodded at Hailey, ignored me. I needed to go to class. So did Hailey. Instead we stood with the giant boulder of unspoken words between us until finally Hailey caved and let me off the hook.

"How'd you do with the list this summer?"

I swallowed. The list. Safe territory for us. Mostly. "Well, I've been trying to talk to Pavel. It hasn't really worked, but at least I've tried."

"He still reading *Cosmo* and asking you about 'the ladies'?"

I nodded.

She hooked her arm into mine and steered me down the hall. Like we were friends. Like nothing had happened. The rush of relief overwhelmed me, and I had to stop to catch my breath. Because it was so Hailey to stare down the pink elephant between us and move right past it like it meant nothing.

"*Cosmo*'s a good thing," she said as I dipped to take a drink of water from the fountain. "*Cosmo* means he's okay, I think."

I snorted. "That's weird, but you're probably right."

"Have you seen the girl? History Girl, who found you at the library?"

Jesus, when had I said all this to Hailey? And how did she remember it? "We have Calc together."

Hailey grinned. "Perfect. So this week, get her number."

"Uh."

She twirled me around and clutched my shoulders, inches from me, cinnamon breath in my face. I wanted to taste her, lick to see if the cinnamon flavored her lips. "Get her frickin' number, Kyle. I know you can do it. Even if you have to fake it and pretend it's so you can be study buddies or whatever. If she likes you, you should do something about it."

I nodded. Hailey was pushing me toward another girl. A girl more right for me. Probably. A girl who hadn't lost her virginity to a bouncer. I nodded again.

Friend Kyle,

I looked for you today after school but didn't find you at the radio station. I was told by the Man in Charge that you no longer worked afternoon shifts because of college. You are evidently going to college while still in high school? This is very cool and sort of weird, but maybe perfect. I almost think you can mark the college thing off your list. Because you're going. So there's that.

I am corresponding with your email because I have important things to say and don't think a dialogue would work after this morning's not-talking.

I have forgiven you for the summer bail. I imagine my news about Chaz was a bit disconcerting, even though you are NOT interested in me. I occasionally forget that you are a guy and likely don't want to hear about other dudes boning me. If it's any consolation, your general disapproval of the entire event pales in comparison to the judgment I've laid on myself about it. So it goes.

I have added to my list and am hoping you have too. I would like us to share where we are and make a REAL commitment to knocking these things off before you leave for actual college next year.

My moms would like to have you over for dinner. They evidently are of the opinion that I have done you wrong and think it perhaps is a good idea for amends to be made. Friday at 6. Vegan tacos. My moms are awesome cooks, but if you're a carnivore, you might want to eat something meaty first.

It was a very difficult summer. More than you know. I take partial responsibility for our estrangement. I could have gone to you. This not-talking thing won't happen to us again. Life can be shit, but I think we're good for each other. Please agree.

In earnestness,
Hailey

I rewrote my response to her ninety-seven times. Deleted. Rewrote. Deleted. Rewrote. Called Pavel. Laughed at his crappy advice. He'd bought that book *The Rules: Time-Tested Secrets for Capturing Mr. Right* and insisted that I wait to respond until next week since I wasn't given a three-day advance warning on the dinner invite. I snorted and hung up on him.

Girl-Band Hailey,

Friday is fine. I have a few new things on my list. And yes, we are good for each other.

K

Right after I hit send, my mom came home. I met her in the kitchen and she offered a tired smile. Good day, then.

I started to unload the dishwasher and she helped, still wearing her scrubs.

"I've got this," I mumbled.

"You've grown up so fast. I wish things had been easier for you. For us."

"It's been fine, Mom. We're fine."

She stacked a few plates and slid them into the cabinet. "No, it really hasn't, Kyle. It's been a lot of work and struggle."

Her words bore down on me. I wasn't even sure she realized the things she said and how they could be like tiny needles piercing my skin. I bit back my immediate retort.

"I'm having dinner with a friend on Friday."

"Pavel?"

"No."

Then I waited for her to ask. Waited for some little olive branch to spring up between us, but she went back to unloading glasses and I took the silverware and didn't say anything else.

Chapter Twenty-Four: Hailey

I stood by the pool with Tess while one of the two spawn ran to the changing room. Last of the outdoor swim practices for the season.

"So, you've seen Kyle and survived," she said.

I stared at the water. The kids were gone. Parents sat outside on the bleachers waiting. Every time the smallest breeze came by, the surface of the water became visible again in the ripples.

Who was I to ask Kyle about his list when I couldn't cross this one thing off mine?

"Hailey?" Tess asked.

"I can do this." Sliding my list from my pocket, I rested it in Tess's hands.

I sat down and grabbed the side of the pool.

Anyone else would have told me to stop or to change or something.

"You got this, Hailey," Tess whispered as she crouched next to me. "Do it before you think too much, or before you get caught."

Shoes and all, I held my breath, slipped into the pool, and let myself sink until my ass hit the bottom. The water burned my eyes, but I was underwater. Slipping my glasses from my face, I let out a few bubbles, which echoed in my ears. Moving my arms back and forth, I shifted my whole body. How had I been afraid of this? I felt weightless, strong. I pushed off the bottom and held the side of the pool again.

"Woot!" Tess yelled. "You made it!"

"You can't go in the pool like that!" someone shouted.

I held up my middle finger, having no idea which direction to point.

Like most things on my fear list, this would have been nothing for so many people. Even for the little kids who swam on the peewee team, but for me? I'd finally remembered what it was like to jump in and do something new.

And like that, my mojo was back. My fear list would be conquered.

"We still gotta pick up the other spawn." Tess laughed. "Hopefully I have dry clothes in the car."

I'd changed in Tess's car. Her sleep shirt with I WOKE UP LIKE THIS printed on the front and a pair of leggings she sometimes used under her skirts. My bra was still wet, and so were my shoes, but I wasn't about to go without either.

The soccer fields were a sea of green with colored, moving spots. I'd fail as a nanny on day one and probably go home with the wrong kid.

"I can't believe you're still a nanny." I laughed and poked her side.

"Whatever." Tess stepped up on a bench in her standard black and scanned the soccer field for spawn two.

Spawn one had his tablet poised in front of him and slowly sat as Tess tried to find his brother.

I stood next to her and pretended I could make sense of the small blobs on the enormous field. I could see well enough to know there were a lot of goal nets, which probably equaled a lot of people and places to look.

"Nannying pays for the gas, and I can eat all the snacks and soda I want after school. And Queen B doesn't care how I dress because she thinks it's a cultural thing, and that her kids should be exposed to all cultures." A snort followed that statement. Leave it to Tess to find something good in someone else's ignorance or overzealous parenting.

"Want help looking for the kid?" I teased.

"Funny." She sighed. "There are, like, six different fields out here. I don't know which one he's at today."

A guy near us was kicking and bouncing a soccer ball—off his head, on his knee, the other knee, foot. . . . I couldn't see the ball well, but it made these awesome blurs around his body without touching the ground.

He stopped and caught the ball. "You like?" Big eyes. Strong legs. Not bad. Pale skin. Accent, but I sucked with accents, so I couldn't even guess where he was from. Eastern Europe? Russia?

"It's cool. Are you showing off?" I asked.

"Yes. I'm Pavel."

"No way. *The* Pavel?" I jumped off the bench to get closer, to try and see him better. The moms were about to win the fight on when my next eye appointment would be. He nodded.

"*Kyle's* Pavel?" I squinted and leaned toward him a bit farther, but he smelled like a guy who'd been running in two-day-old soccer gear, so I backed off.

"I know Kyle," he said. He nodded, determined and sure, as if all was good with the world. Kyle was right. He seemed a lot less fucked up than Kyle did. Huh.

"I'm Hailey." I stuck out my hand.

"The gorgeous lady with glasses."

"Hey, Kyle said I was gorgeous? That was cool of him." All of my Hailey confidence had been found again after the leap into the pool. I got a stern lecture from the pool manager, but I didn't care anymore. That item was crossed off my list.

"Yes, and you are now friends again after his sad, negative-thinking summer?"

I nodded. "We're friends."

"But he has not found your G-spot? It's not a myth, you know. It's part of the clitoris."

Pavel was even better than Kyle said. "Dude. You can't say stuff like that to girls. Not right away, at least. And Kyle and I are nothing like that."

He frowned. "He has not listened to my advice."

I grinned. "Guess not. He's coming to hang with the moms tonight. And this is an awesome coincidence because I was going to tell Kyle that we had to meet. It's even better that we met without him. I'm sure it'll come up later at a really bad time."

I started planning the timing on my *I met Pavel and he asked about my G-spot* for full dramatic effect.

"Good." Pavel nodded, the soccer ball tucked under an arm. "Tell him to *think positive*." He even gave me a thumbs-up and a determined face to go with it.

I laughed because what the hell else do you do when someone busts out a slogan like that? "Keep up with *Cosmo*, Pavel. Maybe we'll run into you later on purpose."

"We'll see you, Hailey." He turned and jogged back out to the kids he was helping.

"Who the hell was that?" Tess frowned.

"Friend of Kyle's." I squinted to see if Pavel was hanging with anyone his own age, or if he was chasing the little kids around. He was far enough away that I couldn't tell.

"I still don't get your fascination with Kyle." She shook her head, but there wasn't enough irritation in her voice for me to take her seriously.

"He gets the list, he's more fucked up than me, and he's decided to come back for more. All good traits."

Tess pointed off in the distance. "I found the twerp."

"All right. I don't like kids, so I'm gonna head home now that we're closer to my house, and had our walk and girl bonding time, whatever that means. Have fun with your adopted children." I turned and started back toward the road.

"Not funny, Hailey," she called. "I get paid."

"Uh-huh. See you later." I waved without looking back.

"Later."

Huh. Big afternoon. And I met Pavel. Cool. I might save telling Kyle until a nice lull in dinnertime conversation.

Kyle showed up early for dinner.

With my moms. In the shoes.

"I think I told you . . . vegan," I said as soon as we sat. "Two moms—one's into pottery. One's a yoga teacher. The house is filled with drying herbs and homemade pots. It's almost disappointing the vegan thing is so expected. But no one rocks a stereotype like my moms."

Kyle smiled but didn't say anything.

The moms sat down on their side of the table. Like not only questioning us, but two-on-two interrogation.

I leaned toward Kyle and pretended to whisper. "The inquisition is next, and I'm hoping it'll be directed more at you than me. Partially because I like to watch you squirm, partially because I think it would be cool to learn more about you, but mostly because I'm tired of fielding their questions." I took my first bite of taco.

"Hailey." Lila's voice was full of the soft irritation she did so well. "Can you cut the poor guy some slack? I'm sure it's already awkward to come to dinner."

"I don't care that you're gay," Kyle blurted out.

"Way to open the convo, Kyle." I elbowed him, laughing.

"No . . . um, I mean, if that's why you thought I might be uncomfortable, or . . ."

Kyle already being uncomfortable needed a push off the edge. "I ran into Pavel today."

Kyle choked on his taco. I hit his back a few times.

"Cough it up. Pavel had a message for you."

Kyle's face turned red. Again. So predictable, but it still hadn't gotten old. "Um . . ."

"I didn't stalk him. I ran into him on the soccer field. He said to tell you to *think positive*, and that you think I'm gorgeous. It's sweet." I bit my tongue on the G-spot thing. No need to stir up the moms.

"Um . . ."

"Hailey." Rox gave me the mom wide eyes that said I should probably start behaving myself.

It felt so good to be myself again that I couldn't help it.

And then, when the questions started—in a way that the moms thought was normal conversation, but was too poorly disguised—Kyle handled the inquisition better than I ever expected him to. He told them about being half on the college campus for senior year, and about his mom working as a nurse, and that she was single, and I wondered if they heard any of the shaking behind his voice when he talked about her, like I did.

I guessed right then that his mom would end up on the list in some way. Or she needed to. But I was going to maybe be more like Sensitive Hailey this year. My single year. So I might not bring it up . . . tonight.

Hopefully Kyle and I would keep talking so I'd know how to talk about his mom. Probably at some point I'd ask, and it'd serve him right for letting silence hang between us for too long. I'd been right a long time ago: Kyle was already coming out of his shell. When he finished up that list, he'd be amazing. I wanted to help.

Once he and Rox started talking music, it was over. I gave up and ate four tacos. I loved music, but I didn't keep track of who drummed for who during what years. How exhausting. And boring.

Well. Unless you're suddenly Talkative Kyle and Rox, who chattered away like the Barbie twins from school.

◊ ◊ ◊

After dinner Lila stepped into Rox's arms, and they stood in the kitchen together in a nauseating display of affection. I'd pretty much given up trying to deter them by the time I was in fourth grade. The moment their lips touched, Kyle's eyes went to his lap.

"So does that turn you on, or is it weird? Because I think *no teenager should have to watch their parents make out*." No way they wouldn't get my hint.

"There are other rooms in this house." Rox laughed as she wrapped her arms more tightly around Lila's waist.

"I should go." Kyle stood.

"Nope. List." I took his hand and dragged him outside.

We lounged on the small bench on the porch, our feet on the pathetic excuse for a coffee table, with one another's lists in our hands. Kyle had folded his like mine, and I ran my fingers over the edges a few times, wondering how long it would take his to wear soft. I couldn't read it. He must have known but gave it to me anyway. My heart skipped when he did.

"Not to be mean, but this is a ridiculous fear, Hailey." He pointed to my list.

"Is not."

"Nobody is going to change out all your clothes." He shook his head, but the corner of his mouth was pulled up in a smile. One night and some direct questioning from the moms and I felt like I was finally really seeing him.

"They *might* change out all my clothes. Even I can see the disapproval on the moms' faces when I leave for school some mornings. And what if they made everything pink?"

"You're wearing pink right now." He tugged on the sleeve of my shirt. Kyle was totally sort of flirting with me. Definitely breaking out of his shell. He might be ready for Calc Girl soon—though she'd better realize what a good catch he was.

"Yes, but this is the *right* kind of pink. There's the right kind of pink and the wrong kind of pink. I need you to promise me that when I go blind—"

"If." His eyes met mine.

"Fine. *If* I go blind, you'll check my clothes once in a while, okay? Make sure no one has changed out my wardrobe. Because, yeah, fears don't always make sense, right? But this one has kept me up late more than once."

"Fine. I promise." Kyle thought I was ridiculous, and it was good to at least have his opinion, even if he thought I was crazy.

"Why did that have to be so hard?" I jutted out my chin and gave him a shove. "All I'm asking you to do is look in my closet every once in a while when I can't see."

He laughed a little. Awesome.

"So I thought of a way to help you with a different thing on your list. Or maybe something we could do together," he said. His eyes were fixed on the paper in front of him.

I leaned against his shoulder. "You have my curiosity piqued."

"I think I'm not going to tell you what it is yet, because it might not happen for a while."

"Huh. Kyle. I like it. But it is a *fear* list, you know. So as much as I want to jump in and cross something off, let's not do the bungee-jumping thing. I need some warning for that one. And you can spare me the lecture on it being generic. I don't care."

"Bungee jumping seems pretty normal as a fear. Kind of logical, actually. It's self-preservation, you know? It'd sort of suck if, in tackling this list, you got rid of your mechanism for self-preservation."

"Of course, it's on there because I think that jumping off a bridge while cabled to a rubber band is a fear that really digs deep, you know, into primal-fear territory, and I want to experience that."

"Well, that's not really normal, then. That's more insane."

"No. More kick-ass," I countered.

He flipped the paper over.

"What's this list? This isn't fear stuff."

"It's . . ." My chest tightened so much that I had to pull in a deep breath. "There are a few things I want to see before I can't see anymore."

"Paintings?" It was almost like he choked on the word.

"Impressionists—I mean, that's sorta how I see the world anyway. I want to see the real thing. The canvas they had their hands on. Before I can't. I've seen the ones at the Art Institute, but I want more."

His brow pulled down as he handed my list back to me. The mood had changed a bit—not bad, just a different kind of relaxation, one tinged with a little sadness.

I slumped even lower.

Kyle and I were hanging out. On the porch. No evil eye from my moms. No pressure to prepare for a new gig. He got me. And the shittiness of my summer was finally starting to dissipate.

"Kyle. I'm weirdly happy. You had dinner with the moms. Choked down not one, but two vegan tacos, and here you are talking with me like we didn't ignore each other for the past few months."

"You're happy?" he asked. And there was a lot more depth in his voice than I think he intended for there to be.

"I'm happy."

"Good." He even leaned into me a little.

And I mostly meant it. I still felt like a bit of a screwup, and it sucked that my girl band didn't exist anymore, but I was doing music, practicing every day. Still hung with Tess, was hanging with Kyle again. I knew something was missing, but maybe I'd always feel that way.

"Now, tell me more about the mini road trip you went on this summer."

Chapter Twenty-Five: Kyle

The first semester of senior year was exactly what I had wanted summer to be. I barely saw Hailey in school, but sometimes I'd catch flashes of her in the hallway. She invited me over to dinner again. And again. Three times altogether. The third time she invited me, I sprung my idea for helping with something on her list.

"I'm totally guessing on this soy milk." She leaned forward and squinted. "Is this a cup?"

Her skin was flushed, but in a good way. As if she was psyched that she was actually making dinner, and the endorphins poured off of her like palpable energy.

I sat on the counter, my legs dangling over the edge, and watched her pull ingredients from the fridge. "Looks like a cup to me."

"Maybe you should measure the stuff and I'll mix it all together."

I jumped down and touched her arm. It was us now. Sort of. Touching and not being weird or awkward. Too much. And my sleaze factor had dialed down considerably the more time I spent with her. I didn't think about all her pink parts whenever I laid a hand on her shoulder now. "The item on your list said 'Cooking (for the moms),' not 'Have Kyle make dinner for the moms.' You can do this. I'm here to make sure you don't burn the house down."

She laughed. Low and husky. So yeah, I wasn't completely oblivious to how she made me feel. But I was starting to actually be a good friend, and I wasn't letting go of that. There were more things to check off my list before I could try for Hailey anyway.

"I should have gone with spaghetti. Spaghetti pie is too complicated."

I wanted to rub the tension from her shoulders, but even I wasn't dumb enough to think that was innocent and friendly. So I hopped back on the counter. "Spaghetti pie is way better."

She blew a hair out of her face. "Do you think they'll like it?"

"I do."

"I want to make it good for them. Because, well, you know . . ."

It still made my throat close up to see her vulnerable about her eyes, about her moms. Such a strange disconnect in the

Hailey everyone saw, but I knew her so much better now that it made sense. All part of the package.

"It will be good. Don't worry. Go for it."

She pulled out the tomato sauce and reached past me for the can opener. "Thanks," she whispered. "This was a good one for you to help me with."

It got me closer to crossing *Be a good friend to Hailey* off the list, but I wasn't there. Not yet. There was too much to make up for.

I'd tackled a few of the things on my list. Asked for a letter of rec from my Calc teacher. Had Pavel teach me stick shift in his crappy family VW van. Which was hilarious and involved a lot of swear words. In the end, he pressed a Zig Ziglar cassette into the ancient player and took me to a cemetery to practice. Weird, but classic Pavel.

The problem was, I kept adding new stuff to do. Some I told Hailey about. Some I didn't. So when she asked, it always seemed like I hadn't accomplished anything.

"I've never had vegan noodles before," I said, watching her move across the kitchen. She didn't stumble for anything. This was comfortable. Home.

"Well, I hope you ate something before you got here. They feel a little like cardboard and taste a bit like paste."

"Nice. Meals at your house keep getting better and better."

She turned and smiled at me, though. Because we both knew it was the truth.

◊ ◊ ◊

We went to the movies one Friday night with Pavel and Tess. But it didn't really work because Pavel kept hitting on Tess with terrible pickup lines like, "It's a good thing I have a library card, because I'm checking you out." Only, he said "checking you in," and even I had to laugh. Afterward, Hailey convinced us to get ice cream and walk along the tracks.

"So, five things left on the list?" she asked as she stepped carefully from slat to slat. I knew she couldn't see what she was doing, but I didn't offer to help. Hailey was weird about that kind of stuff, and the line between pity and helpful assistance was pretty gray.

I sighed. "Maybe a few more than that."

Pavel had run to catch up with Tess, who'd bolted out of the van and onto the tracks as soon as I parked the crappy VW.

"But you've done some stuff, right?"

"Yep."

"Stop it with the one-word answers. Don't you ever volunteer stuff without me having to conduct an interview?"

I laughed. "You don't really give me a chance. You sort of start with the interview questions right off the bat."

She stopped and I bumped into her. My hands reached to steady her. And sort of landed on her ass instead. Which really was an accident.

Hailey barked out a laugh. "Did you just grab my ass?"

"No. Well, yes, but I didn't mean to."

"Hey, Pavel," Hailey called, "Kyle grabbed my ass."

Pavel raised a fist in the air. "Good going, brother. Now you find the G-spot."

Hailey laughed hard enough to snort. "Seriously," she finally said, "why would you even want other friends?"

I smiled. "Yeah. He's kinda great."

She nodded and I realized we'd sort of stopped when she'd stumbled. "So can I ask you something?"

"Aren't you already doing that?"

"You write all the time. In your notebooks. What're you writing?"

I released a deep breath. "Everything. Nothing. It's all sort of stupid. Sometimes song lyrics that remind me of things. Sometimes lines from books. Bands to check out. Podcasts I like. Sometimes the notebook is like a vacuum for my thoughts. You know, when they're circling around my head so much and won't really shut up? If I write them down, they aren't so loud."

"I kinda suspected as much. Journaling is sort of a weird hobby for guys."

She pulled off her glasses and scrubbed the lenses as if that would somehow help her peer at me better in the dark.

"I started after the locker-room thing with Pavel. Because I didn't really talk to anyone. And all the school guidance counselors told me I needed to move past it, but no one actually wanted to listen to get me past it. Not in the way that you did. My sort-of friends at the time turned into nonfriends. I was alone with my thoughts every day. And the locker room was the only thing I could think about. I'd relive it over and over. Know I wasn't doing enough to stop them, feeling hate and fear over and over. I could taste the blood. Hear Pavel's screams in my head. I started writing it all down, and it got a little better."

Her face softened and she reached out her hand to squeeze mine. I squished my eyes shut and wondered if it would always hurt to be with her and not with her at the same time. "I can't imagine you being in worse shape than what I found you in. I'm maybe glad I wasn't around that year."

"Yeah, you probably wouldn't have taken me under your wing in quite the same way."

She laughed. "Is that what I did?"

I released her hand and stuffed mine back in my pocket. "Something like that."

"So what else have you added to your list?"

I lifted my shoulder. Stupid. She couldn't see it. The worst kind of insensitive nonanswer.

"I don't think I'm ready to go there with you yet."

"Really? After the big journal reveal, you have even more secrets? Huh. I'm intrigued. Is it something dirty?"

I laughed. "Hardly."

She tapped her chin, then pressed the glasses back up on her nose. "Well, I guess I'll have to wait until we're best friends for full disclosure, huh?"

"Kyle," Pavel called from so far down the tracks that if it

were anyone else, I might not have heard. "Tess has agreed to introduce me to her lady friends. I'm looking after our interests, my friend."

Hailey laughed again. Addictive laugh. Addictive girl. "Looks like I won't be usurping Pavel's BFF title anytime soon."

"Unless he throws me over for one of the ladies."

"Well, as the only *ladies* Tess talks to are Mira and me, and Mira's not even around regularly, I don't see Pavel having a lot of luck in that area."

She started off down the tracks again and I watched her for a few seconds. She turned back and grinned at me. "Stop checking my ass out. You already copped a feel. That's all you're getting tonight."

I wasn't happy-happy, but I wasn't miserable. I had a friend who was a girl. And yes, maybe I wanted more, but it didn't matter because when I was with her, it was spectacular. And I had a friend who was a guy who snail-mailed me ridiculous photocopied articles and told me stupid theories about women. I wished his life were different, I wished our past together were different, but he didn't seem so bothered by all of it. So maybe I should've been able to let go some too.

And suddenly, life wasn't so incredibly lonely. Home became texts from Pavel and school became maybe seeing Hailey in the halls. And my thoughts quieted some. I still wrote. Especially in the house alone or on the train to Concordia. But it wasn't all depressing. I had people to talk about. Things in my life that sort of mattered that didn't have anything to do with the past or my mom.

Mom and I cooked a real Thanksgiving dinner, and even though it was out of cans, and done in silence, I felt like this new normal of my life was a totally livable one. Better than livable. Good.

So again, I let my guard down, walking between buildings at school, in the snow, and not paying attention.

"Nice backpack." My pack was ripped from my shoulders.

I swung around, just in time for a fist to connect with my jaw and knock me to the ground.

I was a senior. Was this still supposed to happen?

Someone kicked my thigh, and then my stomach. Instead of curling up and slamming my eyes closed until he or they finished, I opened my eyes to see legs within kicking distance.

I lashed out with both feet as hard and fast as I could, catching the faceless guy in the shins. The force knocked his feet out from underneath him. I scrambled to sitting just in time for a hand to clamp down on my shoulder.

"You three. Principal's office. Now."

The dull rumble of Mom's car wasn't enough to drum out my thoughts.

"I can't believe you would do this to me, Kyle. I need my

nursing job. Do you have *any* idea how embarrassing it is to be called out of work to pick up your delinquent son?" she snapped.

Of course I didn't, but it wasn't a question she meant for me to answer.

"Being a mother isn't easy. Being a single parent isn't easy!" She regripped the steering wheel. "I don't even know what to do with you!"

"Sorry," I mumbled.

I'd finally fought back, and earned myself a pissed-off mother and a three-day suspension.

"This will never happen again, Kyle. Do you understand me?"

"Yeah. Got it."

Then she glanced at me, anger draining away to defeat. "Please, Kyle. We *have* to work together. I need you to be better."

I nodded and felt my phone vibrate in my pocket. I'd sent Hailey a text about the fight and the suspension but hadn't heard back.

Hailey: Proud of you for standing up for yourself.

I smiled and shoved the phone back in my pocket, glancing at my mom's tight face. At least someone understood.

Chapter Twenty-Six: Hailey

The wind bit into my cheeks, and I shrugged deeper into my coat. Winter in Chicago could be a real bitch.

"Why do you keep making that weird face at me?" I asked Lila.

She laughed like I wasn't in on some joke. Kind of the best way to annoy someone, honestly.

"What?"

"We're out buying a present for Kyle," she said.

Oh, so that was what the look was about. She thought there might be something between us. "I think we're all painfully aware that I should not be dating."

The same smile pressed Lila's lips together and made her dimple grow deeper.

"Can I meet you back here in, like"—I glanced up the street—"an hour?"

She patted my shoulder like she used to do when I was ten. "Let me know if you need any help."

"No, thanks." When I found Kyle's gift, I'd know. But telling that to Lila would totally give her the wrong idea.

More knowing smiles from my mom wasn't going to help my irritation factor. And if I got tense, she'd try to drag me into another yoga class.

I paused at the streetlight, making sure I was okay to walk. Nothing would rile her up more than my confusing a DON'T WALK for a WALK.

This little crunchy part of town wasn't the best place to get something not patchouli-scented or without Bob Marley on the front, but still . . . I had options. Ideas.

I'd already done one thing for him, which was probably more self-serving than gifting. I wanted to gauge his reaction to my favor out of curiosity, I guess. But it was stupid to get someone a present that wasn't wrapped—at least it felt like it was. Which was why I'd ended up shopping in the cold to begin with.

I walked into a storefront that screamed *tourist trap*, but sometimes I got lucky.

Tapping my pockets, I wandered through the racks, squinting at the print on the bright-colored shirts. *Not right . . . not right . . . not right . . .*

"Can I help you with something?" A guy's voice, but slightly off. Sort of too smooth and higher-pitched.

"I'm good," I said without looking up.

Better that than squinting or stepping too close to make sure I was talking to the right person.

"I know the stock," he tried again. Closer.

I turned to face him.

Opposite of Chaz.

Blond hair. Bright blue eyes. A little scruffly on the chin, or maybe it was the way the light hit his tanned skin. He was pretty, with a pretty voice.

"I'd hope so." A corner of my mouth tilted up. I'm pretty sure I didn't give it permission to do that.

"So, you looking for someone in particular? Yourself?" He did the predictable glance at my chest. Guys could be so one-track.

"A friend." I rested my hand on the rack, unsure if I should keep thumbing through or talk to this guy.

He tilted his head, sort of looking at me sideways. "A . . . boyfriend?"

"No boyfriend," I blurted out.

Why was I half smiling and sort of chatting and not looking for shirts because I was staring at this blond guy? I'd sworn off guys.

"I'm Jaron."

"I . . ." I took a step back. "I'm late."

I'm late? Pathetic excuse.

"Uh . . ."

I turned back to the rack. "I'll let you know if I need help."

His shadow clouded a side of my vision for a moment before he took a few steps away and started rearranging merchandise.

I tugged out another T-shirt. And then another. And another.

Nope. Nope. Nope. Nope. Nope.

My shoulders sagged, and my scarf slipped off my neck. Maybe this was stupid. Maybe having a more solid plan for Kyle's present would have been a good idea.

"I want to innuendo a friend." I let out a breath of air. "So I guess I need a T-shirt that's wearable, but that's full of *suggestion.*"

"Ha!" Jaron again. "I can help with that."

Great.

"Size?" he asked.

"Ummm . . . medium?" Kyle seemed medium-ish, I thought.

I walked toward Jaron, who lined four T-shirts up on a round rack.

The second I saw the bright letters on green, I knew that was it. I was right to wait until I found "it."

"Perfect."

"This for a guy?" he asked.

"Hmm." Nonanswer. Kyle was right—talking was overrated. I clutched the shirt, picturing what Kyle's face would look like when he opened it. Perfect. So perfect.

"So . . . ," Jaron said. "You *do* have a guy."

I scoffed.

Right. Because the *only* reason I'd shoot this pretty guy down was if I had someone else. Guys and their egos. This. This was why I wasn't dating for the year.

I pulled out my wallet and handed him the shirt.

Chapter Twenty-Seven: Kyle

Wat are you doing here?" I said, standing stunned and immobile at my front door. Mom's bags were cutting into my wrists from my short walk home from the store. She'd called before leaving work and said she didn't have nearly enough energy to pick up groceries.

"Freezing my ass off and bringing you a Solstice present. Yes. Go ahead and laugh, the moms celebrate Solstice. It's gotten so ridiculous that I actually think they hunt for lesbian clichés to embrace."

Only I didn't laugh because I still couldn't get over Hailey at my house. My house. Panic cut through me worse than the bitter wind.

"I . . ."

She rubbed her mittened hands together and stomped her

snow-covered feet. Her long hair hung loose around her shoulders. "Come on, Kyle. Freezing here. Let me in."

"You've never been to my house before. How did you know where I live?"

She laughed. "There are these amazing things called computers. Some of us can actually find shit out from them. Now, are you letting me in or am I gonna head back home?"

"Uh." I pushed my key in, turned it, and then froze.

She grabbed the door and pushed past me. "You're not keeping a body in here, are you? I mean, seriously."

I stepped back, the bags clutched in my hands. "Gimme a sec."

Mom would be home any minute. *Any* minute. I couldn't imagine being in the same room with both of them. *Shit, shit, shit.*

"My mom'll be home soon," I said.

"She strict about girls or something?"

"Uh . . ." She was going to call me on that "uh" too. I was sure of it.

She groped around in her large purse and pulled out a lumpy package. "Here."

I set the bags on our kitchen counter and released a sigh. "Come on. We can talk in my room."

Hailey followed me to my room, pulling off her mittens and unwinding her scarf from her neck. "Your mom won't freak?"

"It's fine," I said. It was. I'd rather no one else meet my mom. Pavel was enough.

I waited for Hailey's next question, but she was too busy staring at my walls. She stepped closer and peered at all the things I had hanging there. She pressed her glasses up her nose and trailed a hand over one of my posters.

"You have the periodic table on your wall?"

"Yeah."

"And who's this?" She pointed.

"Cobain, back in the *Bleach* days." God, her eyes were getting worse. My insides turned over. The reality of her future blindness hit me in the gut and winded me.

"And this? What's it a map of?"

"The Pangaea. You know? When all of Earth was still one continent?"

She nodded. "Weird. Why do you have that?"

I dropped onto my unmade bed. "To remember how much things can change."

"Huh. Cool."

She sat next to me and I wished I hadn't been so lazy about cleaning my room. Too many books were stacked everywhere. Clothes on the floor. Clean unfolded laundry in a basket in the corner. Papers and notepads in piles on my desk. So different from the sparseness of her room.

"Your room's kind of a crap hole, Kyle."

I laughed. "Yeah. I guess."

"I'm surprised. Honestly. You normally smell kind of good, and I would have guessed fastidiousness for you."

I shrugged. "Sometimes it's hard to keep up with it all. No one sees my room, so I really don't care."

"Your mom sees it."

I shrugged again. Which I guess answered the question enough, because she didn't push it. My room was the one place in the house Mom never weighed in on. Too exhausted maybe. Or too overwhelmed by everything else.

Hailey took the lumpy present she'd been holding and placed it into my hand. "It's sort of a two-part gift, so don't open this one yet. Do you have your phone?"

I grabbed my phone from its spot on the side table.

"Okay. Open your contacts. Add these digits." She rattled off numbers fast with too much excitement in her voice. Hailey excitement brought out way too much worry on my part.

I eyed her. "And this number belongs to . . . ?"

"Mariah. That's her name, right? History-now-Calc Girl, whose number you've been too chickenshit to get."

My mouth dropped open and Hailey grinned at me.

"You're welcome."

"You know her? How did . . . ?"

"No. I don't actually know her. I saw her mooning over you in the hall one day. You're so oblivious. Her drool was blatant enough for even me to catch it. But you were so in your head you didn't even see her following you from class. Anyway, I asked her name and if she'd had history with you last year. . . . Wasn't too hard to put the pieces together and get her digits. I memorized them. Getting good at that, actually."

I stared at the phone number. So many conflicted emotions pounded me from all sides. It was wrong and right all at the same time.

"I can't believe you'd do this for me."

"Well, you held Chewbacca for me, so . . ." She slapped me on the back. "Now open the package."

My hands shook a little as I opened the odd-shaped present. "You wrapped this yourself, huh?"

"Shut up. It didn't come with a box, and I couldn't really see what I was doing."

I stopped and stared at her. "Hailey. Don't use your eyes as an excuse. Just say, 'I'm a crap wrapper.' It's unlike you to accept the shitty state of your sight and use it as a reason for mediocrity."

She flushed a deep red. "I'm a crap wrapper."

I leaned into her. I wanted to put my arm around her, but knew I couldn't. Not after she'd handed me Mariah's number.

I pulled a bright green shirt from the paper and unfolded it. GETTING LUCKY IN KENTUCKY. I made a weird *oh* sound in the back of my throat. Hailey busted out laughing and I joined her. She rested her hand on my thigh but quickly pulled it away. *Put it back. Please put it back.*

"I think this is a little bit of wishful thinking on the Mariah front," I said, and held the shirt up to my chest.

"You're almost eighteen, Kyle. And you aren't *so* shy anymore. I'm gonna give you the benefit of the doubt and think you might pull off tongue-kissing at the very least. You gotta nail some things on that list."

"Tongue-kissing isn't on my list," I said.

"Well, whatever. Do you know how much easier your list would be if you listened to me and did what I told you?" she teased.

She licked her lips. I leaned forward because my body wouldn't stop. Her eyes got big for a second and I thought maybe she understood everything. When she licked her lips again, I was certain of it. I'd never wanted to kiss anyone so much in my life.

The front door creaked open and slammed shut.

Hell. The groceries hadn't been put away. According to earlier texts, Mom was "exhausted" and needed my help tonight.

"Kyle?" Mom called.

"Just a sec," I called back, almost afraid to breathe.

"Why is nothing put away?" Mom's voice, louder.

Hailey's eyes shifted around the room.

"Just a sec!" I called again, getting up and moving toward my door.

Hailey folded her arms. Unfolded them. "I guess I should go."

Dammit, I didn't want her to go. Hailey was someone I actually wanted in my space.

"It's fine. She's just off shift, and—"

"Kyle?"

But this time Mom didn't wait before her footsteps came my way. I jerked open my door as she rounded the corner into the hallway and stopped at my room.

"Look, Mom . . . ," I started, but stopped at the sight of her holding up her hand cream with a frown.

"This isn't the right stuff, Kyle. I can't do the night cream. Only the day cream. You know this."

"They were out," I mumbled, hating that Hailey was here for this. But talking back to my mom wasn't something that would ever work—definitely not with Hailey ten feet away.

"But I can't handle the perfume in this one, and you know how raw my hands get."

"The label said unscent—"

"Kyle. Why do you insist on making more work for yourself? It's like you intentionally sabotage the things I ask of you," Mom said, crossing her arms and leaning against my doorjamb. She didn't even glance at Hailey. Didn't even acknowledge that someone was here. A girl. In my room. I might get that lecture later. "My life would be so much easier, and yours so much better, if you listened to me the first time."

Hailey flinched. I wanted to die.

"I'll go check somewhere else," I said, my voice too soft, too fucking pathetic.

And then Mom's stare flashed to Hailey.

"The suspension was enough," she said, obviously to me, but still staring at Hailey. When her eyes did turn to mine, I wasn't prepared for the hardness.

I flinched. *Coward.*

"You'd better not get anyone pregnant."

Even Hailey's cheeks flamed at that, but what could I say?

"I'll walk you out," I said to Hailey, hating that our night was ending this way.

Hailey waved her hand. "No. It's not necessary. I'm sorry I barged in on you over break. I'll catch you at school. It was nice meeting you, Ms. . . ."

Mom gave Hailey a curt nod. Nothing else. And then turned and walked back toward the living room. Either she'd overmedicate and crash in front of the TV or I'd get an earful as soon as Hailey was out the door.

Hailey stared at the floor.

"Hailey."

Her eyes began darting all over the place like they were avoiding mine. She focused on the periodic table.

"It's okay. She's tired. Anyway, I've got something for you too." I grabbed the small present from my dresser. "You can open it when you get home or whatever."

She nodded. "Yeah. Thanks."

I was sort of disappointed she was freaking out about my mom. She didn't think everyone had cool, conversational lesbian moms who actually gave a shit about something, did she?

I walked her to the door. Her boots stomping too loud over the silence between us.

Mom was shoving things into the refrigerator in jerking, slamming movements.

Hailey paused for a half second, but then kept walking. When I opened the front door, she reached out and pulled me into a big hug. So tight and fierce I almost lost my breath.

"I'm sorry I put pressure on you about the list. It was super shitty of me. I'm sorry," she said again.

"No, Hailey. It's—"

"Happy Solstice," she whispered in my ear. Then she was gone.

"Fine," I finished.

Chapter Twenty-Eight: Hailey

The wind and snow outside were nothing compared to the iciness in that house.

How had I not known about his mom? How had we been friends for so long without him ever saying anything about her? Was I any better than her? I mean, basically the same words came out of my mouth just minutes before they came out of his mom's.

The truth was that I'd been a shitty friend to Kyle when I was actually trying to be a good friend to him. Which was terrible, really.

It took me three days before I finally opened the note from Kyle that was attached to the present I didn't deserve. I told myself I was waiting for Christmas, but that was BS. Lying to myself was sort of pointless and stupid.

*I FEEL LIKE AN ASS WRITING HUGE, BUT . . .
WELL, SORRY.*

*SO YOU TAP YOUR JEANS WITH YOUR HANDS,
AND I'VE ALWAYS WANTED TO ASK YOU IF YOU
HEAR MUSIC ALL THE TIME, WHICH I THINK
YOU DO.*

*I SAW THESE GLASSES ON JOHN LENNON, AND
THEY STUCK WITH ME (I DON'T KNOW WHY)
AND I KNEW YOU HAD TO HAVE THEM. IT
TOOK ME A WHILE TO FIND A PLACE ONLINE
THAT SOLD THEM, AND I TALKED WITH YOUR
MOMS (HOPE THAT'S OKAY) ABOUT THEM
PUTTING YOUR SCRIP IN AND . . . THAT'S IT.*

KYLE

Wow. Kyle. I pulled out the glasses, and they were awe-some masculine sixties nerdy-cool and perfect. And he'd had to search for them. And he'd talked to the moms. It was . . . a lot.

Then I thought about his mom, and how crazy his whole situation was, and how I felt like an ass for barging in there like that. And I didn't know what to do with a guy who wasn't just self–fucked up, or situation-with-Pavel fucked up, but his whole life was fucked up. And he'd bought me glasses, and talked to the moms . . . and I knew my brain kept spinning back to the same things, but it all felt . . .

Intrusive. I'd thought he was close to saying, *Hailey, I might be interested in you*, when we sat on his bed together. I'd felt it, the hitched breath and the lean in, but maybe I'd imagined it all. Because he didn't say it.

And why would he when I obviously reminded him of his mom and how she spoke to him and pushed him, and holy shit, I was *such* an asshole.

It didn't matter anyway, because he had Mariah's number, and he'd smiled over it, which had answered any questions I'd had before giving it to him. And I was taking the year off of guys. Even if Kyle was a good enough guy to put up with me. I didn't want Kyle to *put up with me* if we were together.

I thought about him holding me the way Chaz had. Only it would be so different. So much better.

No.

I had to remind myself that Kyle had taken the number. Would probably use it. I'd been an asshole, and he deserved better. Probably should have some time without me dominating his life, pushing his decisions, and telling him what he should do next. My throat swelled.

No. No. I wasn't doing this achy feeling. Was not.

I went to see Kyle before school, knowing where I'd find him. Radio station.

"We should take a break," I said the second I made it through the door.

He stood up so fast his chair spun behind him.

My heart flipped. Damn, I wanted him. I couldn't, but I did. Screw our timing. Always off. Always not quite there. I had to make myself better. He had to gather the courage to call Mariah. We had things to do.

"What . . . what are you talking about?"

I shook my head. "You should work on your list on your own. It's not my place to interfere."

He swiped his hand over his forehead, slicking back his hair. "Uh . . . you're not interfering."

But he glanced at the floor.

"So you do your thing, and I'll do my thing, and I guess . . . I guess we'll report to each other when we do."

And then I ran away like a coward because I hated how I might have treated Kyle and I didn't know how to apologize to him. It would be good for him anyway, I thought. He was too invested in me. I was too invested in him. We weren't ready. I hadn't crossed anything off my list since dinner for my moms. I had to get back in control.

I found the chairs at my eye doctor to be suffocating—almost every time. My chin perched on the rest as Dr. Ricks flipped the little glass circles in front of me to try and force my eyes to see the letters projected onto the wall.

He should have known better.

"Can you read that one?" He tried to sound all official and

detached, but I'd seen him for too long and heard the strain in his voice. We'd been playing around with this for a while. Switch lenses, click, add another lens, click. Close to twenty minutes now.

"Uh . . . we're down to one letter, which means it's the *E*." I sighed and sat back.

Then it was his turn to sigh. His impatient look didn't match his overly neat exterior, tidy haircut, and abnormally large smile. "Sit back up. And I'll ask you about details, okay?"

Once again I rested my chin and stared at the single letter projected on the wall.

"Can you see the openings on the right side of the *E*? Or do those lines blur together?"

I blinked back my frustration, and knew I wasn't going to last much longer. As much as I tried to be relaxed, it wasn't going to work. My lungs were heavier with each breath, and I was using every trick I knew to hold back my tears. I paused, squinted, and tried to make that *E* look like an *E*. Everyone can read the biggest letter. *Everyone*. "Blurry enough that the ends sort of touch, but I still see the *E*." *Or my brain is filling in.*

"Okay." His forced smile looked painted on. "Thanks, Hailey. I'm done torturing you for today."

"No glaucoma test?" I asked. "No fun puffs of air?"

He shrugged. "Your eyes aren't bothering you, and you came in for one two months ago. Also, you give Kim a hard time for not controlling the tonometer when she has no control over it."

Then it was my turn to shrug. Getting your eyeball hit with air mostly unexpectedly had been known to unleash my varied vocabulary.

"I'm worried the most about the macular degeneration. You, my dear, have the eyes of a ninety-six-year-old." Same stuff he always said. Old-person eyes. Over and over. He leaned against the counter while on his tiny doctor stool—probably trying to look more relaxed than he was. I was a pro at that move.

"And still I have curfew." I threw a glare in the direction of the moms because it was easier to joke with them than to once again let the reality of my situation sink in.

A corner of his mouth pulled up in something that looked a little more genuine. "We're hoping we won't have to do anything to address your glaucoma for a while."

I nodded, relieved. Laser surgery to relieve pressure was about as fun as it sounded. I wasn't sure how long "a while" was, and in that moment, I didn't care. The appointment felt over, and I wanted home.

Lila handed me my glasses as we left the room together.

But even the moms were frowning as they talked with Dr. Ricks on our way to the front counter. Since I was ready to leave, and knew no one would be lasering my eyes anytime soon, I disengaged.

They were talking numbers, and changed prescriptions, and big glaucoma check, and how my eyes could possibly be so bad, so young, and that it was really difficult not having any genetic history because my birth mother had dropped me and run, and everyone was all politely discussing my future. All I could hear was *blind, blind, blind, blind, blind.*

And there were people walking around in the waiting room, trying on frames and smiling, and talking when I felt like I'd taken another huge dive toward being black-blind.

It all shook me too hard in places that were too deep for me to lock away. Not again. I could feel that aching start to take over, suck me in, pull me under, and all I knew was that I had to be home before it happened.

I grabbed one of the moms' hands and dragged her toward the door. Her arm came over my shoulder as we stepped into the light and air, only one of which would matter to me soon. Too soon.

"It's okay, Hailey," Lila said. "We're talking way in the future here. New developments are happening all the time, and people are working toward—"

"Don't," I snapped. "Just. Don't."

I climbed into the back of the Escort and wrapped my arms around my stomach. I hated that they volleyed from sending me to blind classes, to telling me it would never happen. And then here—how could anyone say I was lucky to see when it might not last all that long?

Home. All I could think was how I had to get home. Wanted to crawl into my bed and ignore the world. Had to.

◊ ◊ ◊

Kyle stepped into my room and froze. I'd barely seen him for a month. The moms must have called. Or maybe he'd just stopped by. I'd taken my glasses off, so I couldn't see his face, but he was very still, and probably staring.

"You're right. I hear music almost all the time." I sniffed, which I hated because, aside from the obvious fact that I'd mummified myself in my bed, it showed a weakness I didn't want to deal with. And Kyle was standing there like the best friend I'd ever had. I needed to give him something else. "I'll be better. Treat you better. Different from your mom. The glasses were perfect."

"Oh." He took another step toward me. Still stiff. Only half back out of Mumble Kyle.

"You remember this blanket fixes everything," I said as I pulled it more tightly around me.

"Really?"

"No. It doesn't fix jack, which really sucks." I pulled it even tighter, but a blanket wasn't going to solve anything. I knew this, and still the more I pulled without my chest loosening up, the harder I tugged on the thing. Desperate for two totally unconnected acts to make me better. Less pathetic.

"You look small."

"Your voice is small, and it shouldn't be." I didn't even know if it made sense, but Kyle should have a huge voice. Huge. And he didn't.

"You usually fill a room, but now it's like you've been swallowed." He shoved his hands into his pockets.

"There's a poet in there, Kyle," I said through my tears. "I hope this isn't your bullshit way of trying to make me feel better."

"No." But his voice was so quiet I barely heard.

Another sob hit me, which I hated, which I knew would lead to more, which I knew was going to make Kyle freak out.

Only he didn't freak out. He sat on my bed, and pulled me into him, crazy wrapped-up blanket and all. I breathed in his citrus and let my face rest on his chest as my body shook.

And then I started talking, and it all came out. All the ridiculous stuff, some of which he knew, but I said it again anyway, and all the real stuff, and all the stuff I tried not to think about when the rest of the world was too quiet to drown it out.

How I wouldn't be able to see the moms' faces anymore. How when I met people, I wouldn't know where to look. That I knew how to fold my money because one day I wouldn't know the difference between a one and a twenty if I didn't fold them the right way.

I hated dogs. I didn't want to walk around with a smelly dog to gain a little independence.

That maybe I'd marry some guy I'd never even seen. And if I ever decided I liked kids, I might not get to see my own.

Kyle didn't give me any of the bullshit that the moms did. He held me. Crushed me into his chest until my inability to breathe came from Kyle instead of my crazy. Because he knew me well enough to know that's what I needed.

I'd missed him.

I had to find a better word for him than "friend."

Lila let me stay home from school the next day.

"Sometimes when you drain that much energy," she'd said, "you need a break."

Which I did and I didn't. Because after Kyle, I kinda felt okay.

Also, Lila's ideas to "replenish my energy" always had to do with me following her to the yoga studio for her afternoon class.

The yoga studio was familiar and the lighting was good, the walls pale, and I for sure could have walked the place with a blindfold on. I waited outside Lila's office for her to make a few phone calls.

A girl in black yoga wear and lime-green hair walked around the corner and smiled. "You've got to be Hailey. Lila talks about you all the time."

Oh, great. "Sounds like her."

"I'm Annalise."

Her name had probably been mentioned over dinner or something, but it wasn't coming to me.

"Lila is so amazing. I've never met anyone with her strength and flexibility. I'm learning a lot."

Lila would never allow the kind of chemicals that could

create green hair in our house. I liked Annalise immediately.

"So you work here?" I asked.

"I'm about finished with my certificate to be an official teacher, and then I'm hoping for a job. Lila lets me teach once in a while, so sticking around here would be pretty ideal."

"How old are you, anyway?" I wanted to pick out more facial features, but all I knew was that she was small with big cheekbones.

"Twenty."

Twenty. Twenty sounded like a great age. No more high school, but you still got to hide under the mask of college or being young or whatever, so you could probably get away with doing a lot of stupid crap.

"No college?" I asked.

Annalise frowned. "When you have broke parents, and no money yourself, college loans are pretty intimidating. Anyway, who wouldn't want to do this all day?"

Me. But at least I could appreciate it.

"Must be awesome growing up with two moms." She leaned against the wall.

I laughed. Hard.

Lila's hand touched my shoulder. "This is my stretch-and-relax class. Come on." It wasn't a *you should come* kind of "come on," it was a *you're coming*.

I widened my eyes in exasperation at Annalise. "Yeah, see? It's awesome."

She smiled back as I was *gently led away* by my mom, who was determined to help me stretch away my fear of blindness.

I went to Starbucks on the way home because I needed some caffeine after all that relaxing. Reading the board was impossible, so I got the same thing. Every time. Coffee. Black. It was cheap and required no thought.

The song that Tess and I had played with the other day ran through my head, and I tapped my hips, waiting for some underpaid dealer of caffeine to get me my cup of plain black.

When I finally snagged my cup and headed for the door, a familiar shape came through.

"Friend Kyle." I smiled.

"Oh . . . ," he stammered. "Hey, Haileyum . . . thisis . . ."

He glanced to his right, where a girl stood. My chest tightened. I looked down just long enough to see they were holding hands. The girl. Calculus/History Girl, who I'd given him the number for. Mariah.

Right. Good. I mean, I was the one who'd given him the number, and then I'd sort of ditched him for a few weeks. And then he'd held me because he knew me well enough, and I'd started to understand how awesome it could be to date someone you know so well. But who knew he'd actually *use* the number? My stomach tightened up. And my chest felt heavy again. The thing Kyle couldn't do for me, he might do for her. The two hours of yoga were definitely wasted after Kyle, his Smartie Girl, and caffeine.

Was I so screwed up that I'd misread how Kyle had leaned in over Christmas break? I'd replayed it over and over, sure and unsure. And what he'd done for me yesterday—holding me until I was all cried out? Did he not see that I didn't let anyone in the way I did with him? Maybe I should have been the one to use the words, *Hey, I might be interested in you*, but the baggage I carried was too heavy. And the reminder of my words and his mom's words echoing over each other was too much. He didn't want me. And after everything, I didn't think I had it in me to be rejected by him again.

"Kyle. Nice to *see* you again." I smirked in a way I definitely wasn't feeling and bolted out of the coffee shop before I did something stupid. Like cry.

Chapter Twenty-Nine: Kyle

Mariah came home with me. I wasn't exactly sure how. It was stupid. The look on Hailey's face and the bitchy comment about *seeing* me and the anger that I couldn't quite figure out because she'd given me Mariah's number and she'd gone MIA after meeting my mom. But she'd also sobbed into my shirt and apologized and held me like I was the only thing that could save her. And I knew somehow I'd screwed up with her. It was a mess.

So I invited Mariah to my house. Because Mom was home and I wasn't going to go through keeping Mariah from my mom, only to have her freak out about her later. Cards on the table. And truthfully, part of me sort of wanted her to be appalled at my mom. So that Hailey's freak-out wasn't so hard to swallow. Mom was on a downswing now, so at least I didn't think there'd be any anger, though sometimes the quiet was worse.

"It's really nice to meet you, Ms. Jamieson," Mariah said. And it wasn't weird that my mom was on the couch. It was fine. "Kyle and I are in Calculus together."

My mom lifted her head. "Kyle's very good at math."

Mariah nodded. "Probably the best in the class."

Then Mom went back to the TV and the cocoon, and Mariah turned to me and asked if she could have a glass of water. It was all painfully fine and normal. Two mice surrounding me. Flapping and smoothing themselves out. Mariah brought my mom a glass of water too and then kissed me on the cheek and left.

She called later that night. We made a *plan*. I had no idea what I was doing or why, but Mariah seemed to. In her mousy way, she got my life and didn't want anything from me. She didn't push me to conquer my fears or bug me about talking more. She was there and happy with who I was.

And then after a shitty spring of semi-awkwardness with Hailey, and Mom in a terrible downswing more days than not, and Mariah just there and present and easy, I had to nut up and ask her to prom. Even though it wasn't on my list, Hailey convinced me that it was probably on Mariah's "mental list of awesome things" and since I'd gone through the effort of dating the girl and tongue-kissing her—badly—she deserved a dance.

Mariah actually giggled when I asked her. *Giggled*. I almost took it back, but she was so happy and I didn't think I'd ever made anyone that happy before. Except maybe Hailey when I'd biked past her house wearing the shoes. But that was different.

Hailey came over beforehand to take pictures of the two of us. Because Mom was working and Hailey thought she'd want a memento of her only son dressed in a tux. Hailey grinned so wide when she saw me that my junk kicked into overdrive. God, I'd thought I'd gotten past this with her.

"You clean up exceptionally," she said, and snapped a picture of me at the front door. "And you're wearing the shoes with a tux. I approve."

"Thanks. Did you want to come in?" I pulled the door open wide enough for Hailey to see it was okay. I'd cleaned the house. A little.

"That's okay. It's too nice out to go inside."

I stepped onto the cement steps beside Hailey. The night was perfect. The prom-night dream weather. Warm and pungent and spring-like. Hailey's presence beside me made me wish for too much, so I moved down the steps toward the sidewalk in the front of my house.

"When is the lovely Mariah arriving?" She walked up next to me and leaned in.

"The limo is picking her up and bringing her here at six. Then we have to go to her house for pictures."

Hailey whistled. "Limo. Very fancy. Perfect for the girls around here. But pricey, huh?"

I'd known Hailey long enough to understand the subtext of her question. "Pricey. But Mom's paying for it. She feels guilty about my deciding to go to Northwestern instead of Stanford." Though I suspected she'd known it would play out that way all along.

Hailey nodded. "You're still planning on living on campus though, right? Because I know you wanna be able to check in on your mom, but I think you'd really do well in the dorms."

"So you've said. About a billion times since I got my acceptance letter."

She squeezed my shoulder and I hated that I tingled still when she touched me. But at least I'd gotten used to it and usually I could keep the rest of me from reacting. I'd accepted being with Mariah and aching for Hailey and knowing I was with the "right girl" because I wasn't the "right guy" for Hailey. I'd convinced myself of the whole thing over and over. Journaled about it through most of the spring. Embraced my want in the same way I'd embraced my misery at school after Pavel had left.

"How many things do you have left on your list now?"

I shrugged. We hadn't talked much about our lists since she'd hugged me on Solstice. "Three or four." Lie. I'd stalled out on my list, but I didn't want to get into it with Hailey.

She waggled her eyebrows. "Prom night. Might knock out one of them in the limo." She paused for a second. "Actually. Don't. Don't be that guy. The one who takes a girl's virginity in a limo."

I laughed. "Yeah. Not likely."

She clicked another picture. "Nice smile. And yeah, I *know* you're not that guy. I wouldn't have stuck with you this long if you were *that* guy."

"Glad you did," I mumbled.

"You don't have to mumble that kind of stuff to me, Kyle. We're sort of past mumbling. And I know you're glad. I'm glad too."

It was painful being so close to her. The awkwardness between us so thick I could almost touch it. Especially in her silver glasses and sparkly, tight girl-band T-shirt, her hair down around her face. She was hotter to me than any girl could ever be. Even on prom night.

The moment between us was too long. Hailey stepped back and squinted up the street. "I think that's your girl."

Prom was on a boat. Stupid. But I think the plan was to deter people from getting drunk beforehand or hooking up in the too-small bathrooms. Which didn't work, at least in the bathroom I used. I hated dancing, and Mariah gave up on me after my third awkward attempt at swaying to a thumping hip-hop song. Elbows and bodies pressed against me, and I flushed with embarrassment at the number of couples making out on the dance floor. Mariah pouted and snipped at me that maybe I shouldn't have asked her in the first place. It was unusually honest for her.

And made me realize maybe I shouldn't have.

But that was asshole thinking, so I stuck to the slow dances and she danced with her friends during all the fast songs.

After the king and queen were crowned, our principal came up to the microphone and announced a special surprise from "one of our very own." My mouth dropped open when Hailey took the stage with her guitar. Her eyes were darting all over the place, but I was sure she couldn't see anything with the bright-colored lights.

She slung her guitar strap over her shoulder and leaned forward. I froze.

"So I got second place in this contest," she said, her voice raspy and sure and so Hailey. "With the help of a friend. Last year. It was for covering a love song. Whatever, doesn't matter. I probably would've gotten first if I'd done a different song. So yeah, here I am, trying again with a better song. I hope you like it."

"Breakeven." The song. One of the slightly newer ones I'd told her to sing for the contest forever ago, but she'd chosen "In Your Eyes" instead. When there was still Chaz. And not Mariah. The song that brought out all the best qualities in her voice and reminded me of every female singer whose singing had the power to crush me, from Janis Joplin to Nina Simone to Elle King. Hailey had *that* kind of a classic voice. Her face flashed uncertain for a second, and she peered out into the crowd. I inched forward. She blinked and adjusted the strap on her guitar.

Then there was nothing but her voice and her beautiful

eyes and her shiny-with-spit mouth, and prom became almost perfect. Almost.

When she was done, she ditched her guitar and came down to me. Cut through all the mob, whose faces I was sure she couldn't see, to get to me. Like she knew exactly where I'd be standing. She nodded at Mariah and made girl small talk that Hailey was really good at and Mariah wasn't. I told her I'd liked her song.

Then too much uncomfortability wrapped itself around us. Me and Hailey and the girl I'd come to prom with but couldn't for the life of me remember why.

I couldn't stop staring at Hailey.

"So, Friend Kyle, how about you dance with me?"

Before I could say anything, she grabbed my arm and pulled me onto the dance floor. I was so grateful I wanted to kiss her. Because everything was perfect with Hailey. She made *everything* perfect. Mariah probably noticed. Maybe. Definitely. I didn't care. I wrapped my arms around Hailey and pulled her into me.

She breathed in deeply when she slipped her arms around my neck.

"Are you sniffing me?"

She grinned. "Yeah. I like the citrus. I've told you that, right? I thought it was your detergent, but you're in a rented tux and still have the citrus. It's just you."

"My soap."

I wanted to pour myself into her. Give her all of me and pretend that Mariah wasn't standing on the edge of the dance floor waiting for me. That I wasn't leaving for college in a few months. That Hailey didn't have another year in high school. That things wouldn't be different next year. Again.

"Yeah," she said, and sighed. She pressed her face into my chest and I wondered if she heard my heart thumping. I heard it like a jackhammer, so she had to. But she tightened her arms and swayed closer to me.

For two minutes, it was her and me and warmth and bodies touching and everything I'd wanted since the moment she bumped into me outside of the radio station. I had so much to say. So much in me. All for her. God, we were so close.

"Prom's almost over," I finally choked out.

"Hmm . . ."

"Mariah's going to the beach with some of her friends after. But I told her I didn't want to go. Do you wanna get breakfast at Denny's?"

She pulled back slightly and I slid my hands lower on her back. Her breath stopped and then started again. I noticed. She licked her lips and I bit the inside of my cheek because I wanted, wanted, wanted so much to kiss her. But Mariah and everything I needed to say was still between us.

"Okay. Denny's. After prom. Go home and change and I'll meet you there."

She raised her hand and smoothed her thumb over my

cheek. Something a mom would do, but it didn't feel like that. It felt like an invitation. I leaned closer, breathed the scent of us in, stared at her mouth, her eyes behind the silver glasses. Eyes that weren't darting. Just studying my face.

Then the song was over, Hailey disappeared, and I was taking Mariah's hand and sending her off with her friends. And she hugged me tight before she slipped in the car with them and whispered it was okay and that we didn't have to be a thing because she was leaving and I was leaving. Mariah graciously gave me the out, which reminded me that she was the right and wrong girl for me all at once.

But I took it. And bolted home thinking about Hailey in her sparkly shirt and glasses and the possibility of a summer of me and Hailey. My body still tense and lit up from the dance in a ridiculous way. My heart pounded and the pool at the bottom of my gut worked itself around my system. A shot of adrenaline and lust and anticipation.

Then I walked into our house. Mom on the couch, sobbing. Letters in her hands. Letters from my dad that she'd kept for too long. Strewn everywhere I could see. I moved forward, forced Hailey out of my head, and wrapped Mom's thin frame in my arms.

"Why are you doing this? Why did you get these out?" I asked.

"I miss him so much, Kyle. You can't understand. It's like

a piece of me is gone and every morning I wake up and hope it'll be back in place. But it never is. It *never* is. And it takes everything I have to keep going."

"I know."

"I'm so tired. I hate that I feel so tired all the time."

"He was an asshole, Mom. He cheated on you. Disappeared over and over. Bailed on everything that was important to us all the time."

Sobs wracked her body. She sniffled into my tux shirt. "Why wasn't I enough for him? I didn't care about the cheating. He came back. He always came back."

Something inside of me snapped. Exhaustion and anger and all the emotions of the night rolled up into a ball of venom in my stomach.

"Yeah. Well, he didn't come back the last time."

"Why? I needed him. Need him still. Why would he leave us?"

I could *not* listen anymore. "Because I fucking told him not to come back."

Her mouth dropped open. "What?"

I raked my fingers through my hair. Pulled at it. "I told him to go. I told him never to come back."

"What are you talking about?"

"That last time, when he showed up after being AWOL for four fucking days, I stood at the front door and wouldn't let him in until he promised to pack up his shit and leave for good."

"No, you didn't."

"Yes, I did. I told him to go away forever."

"You were ten," she cried.

"And he was an asshole. He would have been an asshole when I was thirteen, fifteen, seventeen. It didn't matter. I told him he was ruining you and destroying our family."

"How could you?"

Accusation and fury lashed out at me. She pushed me away, curled deeper back into the couch. I leaned closer, but she shrank back. Like I was going to go after her. For a second, I realized her flinch was exactly how I must've looked every time some random asshole at school got the notion in his head to beat the crap out of me. It wasn't fair. It wasn't fair what she did to me when she yelled. What she did to me when she shut down. Tonight was going to be my night to talk to Hailey. Finally. I shouldn't have had to deal with this.

"Did you know I've never picked a fight with anyone, Mom? You'd know this if you asked about where my black eyes came from instead of making me feel like shit."

Mom blinked.

"I've come home after being jumped, having the shit kicked out of me, only to have you do it again!"

I'd snapped. And was being a fucking drama queen. But my night had been perfect and in less than five minutes it had gone to hell.

Talk to Mom about Dad was on my list, but not like this. And definitely not now with her past all over the room, scribbled on old letters.

"It's not fair for you to come down on me when I get straight fucking As on my report cards! When I'm such a good student they've sent me to the college for half days!"

Mom blinked again and again but said nothing.

"And I come home and let you berate me. Tell me I'm shit, and I'm terrified that if I ever talk back to you, ever try to explain, you'll hole up like you've been doing for a month! It's not fucking fair!"

It wasn't fair that I'd let Mariah go. It wasn't fair that Hailey had such a hold on my heart when I had so much to sort through first. I was worthless to both of them. To everyone, really.

Hailey had deserved better from the beginning, and when Mom broke out into keening sobs, I shut down.

I'd said the exact wrong thing at the exact wrong time. I'd held on to too many things for too long and they'd all come out in the worst possible way.

Mom jerked as she sobbed into her hands, and I watched. I couldn't even begin to know how to comfort her or even if I should.

I couldn't have Hailey. Couldn't have anything. I didn't deserve it. I'd destroyed my mom's life and ultimately my own. Tears wet my face, and I ran to my room and grabbed all the journals from my drawer. Years of "poor me" and pages of "I wish I could have Hailey." I shredded them. Pulling page after page out, ripping piece after piece until nothing was left of my sad, pathetic existence but the undeniable will to disappear altogether.

My arms ached. Mom's sobs had faded. I grabbed my phone from my tux pocket.

Kyle: Can't make it. Sorry.

Hailey might not forgive me for this one, and it was probably better that way. I'd screwed up everything.

Chapter Thirty: Hailey

I was pissed because Denny's wasn't a fun place to be at 2 a.m. Okay, so that was only half the reason I was pissed. My hands shook. *Shook.*

Did Kyle realize how hard it had been to pick him out of a sea of guys in black tuxes? I mean, there was no way for me not to walk directly toward him 'cause I'd have lost him in the crowd. And then we'd danced, and everything between us had finally fallen into place. His hands were nothing like a friend's hands on me.

I knew we weren't exactly there yet. I had more to work on. Things to make up to him, make me better, more deserving, but I did deserve better than this.

At least two times for sure since Solstice, Kyle had had the words right on the tip of his tongue. *I'm interested in you,*

Hailey. But he'd never let them out. Like there'd been two really good opportunities for him to kiss me, and he hadn't taken them. I understood the almost-kiss on the prom boat, because only a jackhole kisses a girl who isn't his date.

So I guess I had to give him props for that.

But he apparently didn't mind being a jackhole to me, leaving me alone at fucking Denny's.

The minutes slid by, each one scraping into me until too many hours of minutes had gone by for me to sit in the vinyl booth, which was making my ass itch from the heat. And then the text came.

Kyle: Can't make it. Sorry.

Kyle fucking bailed on me. Friend–turned–Maybe-More-Than-Friend Kyle left me at Denny's to deal with the after-bar-closing crowd, feeling like an idiot. I stomped too loud on my way to the door and started home by myself because apparently even nice guys are assholes.

I hated him even more for making me think that maybe, maybe a good guy would put up with my shit, and my eyes, and he . . . blew it.

The dark made it harder to see, and I knew I'd have to visit my eye doctor again. For him to tell me more about pressure and the finer points of my eyesight I'd tried to ignore since I was a kid. Fucking Kyle. It was fucking dark. And then I stopped at a stop sign because I had three more blocks to get home, and I knew the streetlight was out at one, and I did the unthinkable and called the moms to rescue me.

I was equal amounts pissed and heart-stomped-on. And I had no idea where Kyle and I stood. Again. So I went and found him at school the Monday after prom. Where I knew he'd be. In front of the radio station soundboard.

Leaning against the doorjamb to the studio, I folded my arms. "So."

His head snapped in my direction, his eyes sunken and shadowed with darkness. "I know I fucked up. I'm sorry."

What did I do with that?

He pressed a thumb drive together and inserted another one into the computer, furiously tapping the keys and sliding levers on the board.

Every part of the guy who'd held me at prom had morphed into . . . into whatever he was in this moment. A better friend would have sat next to him and begged for insight. Put their arms around him. But I'd been hurt by Kyle. Twice now. I'd pulled him under my wing and tried to help him be better.

God. Who the hell was I to make anyone better? I'd have made out with him on the dance floor, not even thinking about the girlfriend on the sidelines. I'd pushed and nagged at him like his mom had. It was stupid that I was even there.

"Okay, then." And I stepped back.

Kyle stood and started toward me, defeat lining his features. Whatever moment had tugged us together on that boat had passed. "Sorry," he whispered, but it was a thin "sorry."

The word that he knew he should say with none of the feeling to go with it.

He made me feel too much. Care too much. Want too much.

"You know where to find me," I said before I walked out.

After our nonconfrontation, I made sure I didn't see Kyle. It wasn't all that hard with only a few weeks left in school and him half on the college campus already. Mariah gave me a dirty look when I saw her in the hall, so I guessed they'd broken up, but I didn't know for sure, and wasn't going to check.

I didn't totally ignore the fact that Kyle graduated. I sent him an email, because as much as I wanted to walk away from him, I couldn't. And maybe I was going to sound pushy and forceful and exactly how I'd promised myself I wouldn't act around Kyle, but after he bailed on me, I didn't much care.

Kyle—it's bullshit that your voice isn't on the radio. Put it on the damn list and do it next year. No one there knows you. Don't be a mumbling asshole.

Hailey

Chapter Thirty-One: Kyle

I had a summer job. Unbelievably, I'd gotten a job at the library. Last year's volunteering paid off, and *they* called *me*. I didn't even have to apply anywhere else. And with my mom the worst I'd ever seen her, overmedicating and spending so much time on the couch when she wasn't at work, I needed to be out of the house in the worst way. The library was the one thing in the whole shit summer that wasn't terrible.

Okay, one of two things that weren't terrible.

"Kyle, my friend, we need to practice the stick shift," Pavel said as I was clocking out of the library one afternoon. "You only did it a few times."

"Thought you could only stand listening to me strip your clutch for so long." I followed him out to his family VW van in the parking lot.

"No. No. Zig Ziglar says, 'You can have anything you want in life if you will help enough other people get what they want.' I think I'm not having success finding a lover because I haven't helped you enough. So hop in."

I slid into the passenger's seat and fastened my seat belt. Probably I wasn't great at driving stick because Pavel drove as if no one else was on the road. He punched it out of the lot and I winced at the squeaking brakes behind us.

"Your hair's different," I said. Trendy. Cut short on the sides and left long on top. Both Pavel and not, at the same time.

He touched the sides quickly. "All for the ladies. I need to make a new profile picture. For that I needed the kind of hair to make the ladies swoon."

Of course this would be something he'd read somewhere.

"I don't think your success with the ladies should be contingent on me mastering stick-shift driving. Or your hair, for that matter."

He smacked me on the shoulder. "But it is. I have found an app. *Cosmopolitan* told me about it. It's called Tinder. All the ladies look for their lovers on this. But so far, they have not wanted to meet. I think maybe it's because I haven't proven myself a good friend to you. So this, and a new avatar, and I'll be in. I know it."

Jesus. Pavel *was* a good friend. He was a fucking great friend. I was the shitty one in this relationship. I opened my mouth, but he waved his hand. "No. No. No. None of that.

We're practicing driving, and you'll tell me what happened to Hailey. She's not around anymore. You two are possibly star-crossed lovers?"

"No. Not lovers at all. We could have been. But she met my mom, and that didn't go well."

Pavel frowned and shifted from second to fifth. The van lurched. "So she has broken your heart because of your mom?"

I rubbed the back of my neck. "No. Not exactly. We worked that out, but then there was prom with Mariah and her. And I was a dick to both of them, really."

Pavel's eyes widened. "Brother. You took two ladies to prom? That's a varsity move in *Cosmopolitan*. I'm proud of you, though maybe you leveled up a bit early?"

I laughed. Nothing seemed like a disaster around Pavel. The van could be on fire and he'd keep going and making the best of it. "Yeah. Probably. I mean, I might have pulled it off. Might have been able to come clean about everything with Hailey, but then I got in a fight with my mom. A really bad one. And I realized . . ."

Downshift back to second. Jesus, I wasn't the only one hard on his clutch. "You realized . . . ?"

"I'm not good enough for her yet. I have the list to finish. And I want to be worthy of her."

Pavel nodded. "Well, brother, that is admirable, but we are men. *Cosmopolitan* says that men are mostly dumb and it is the lady's job to help us. I don't think you need to be perfect for Hailey."

"You're wrong. I do. Because otherwise she won't keep me. She may start out with me and maybe even kiss me, but then when she realizes I'm such a fucking mess, she'll throw me out the door, and I don't think I could take it. Like then maybe the last piece of me will break off."

"So much poetry. You could be Russian. But this is crap. Because you're doing nothing now, and you have no one anyway. It would be better for you to say something. Apologize for trying to level up with two girls." He waved vaguely, and the van veered right.

"Maybe. I mean, I did apologize."

"Then what?" He turned too late into the cemetery parking lot, and the van choked and died. At least we weren't moving anymore.

"Then nothing. She told me I knew where to find her and walked out."

He shook his head. "You get in your own way, my friend. All the time. She wants you to find her. So we'll find her. Maybe double-date once I have my Tinder lover?"

I snorted. "Yeah. Maybe then."

"You need to make a grand gesture. Bring flowers and chocolates. Or Russian pastries. Surprise her. Perhaps her band will play? You should go see her." His eyes danced with excitement. Pavel was plenty expressive when he wanted to be. "I'll help you."

I thought about the email she'd sent. About being on the radio. How it would knock something off my list, get me closer to her, and be a grand gesture all at once. But the idea of it paralyzed me. Pavel was right. I always got in my own way.

"I could probably use your help," I admitted.

Pavel smacked the van ceiling three times. "Yes. Yes. Yes. I will be a good friend and you will get your lady back and I will get a Tinder lady because I am sensitive and good and have great hair."

"You probably don't need me for that. You're sensitive and good anyway."

He lifted a shoulder and for the first time in a long time, I saw a little of the Pavel from before. From after the locker room and before all the Zig Ziglar stuff. The broken Pavel. When he was doing everything he could to make it through the day. "I don't think I'll be going to college this fall. The money is too much. We need it for my sisters. And my parents don't think it is safe. So I'll still be here. You're leaving. It would be good if I had someone else."

"You deserve a better friend than me, Pavel. You always have."

"No. I deserve *more* friends, not a better friend. You are the very best. But I want to see other people than my sisters. And you may make new college friends."

I nodded. "Okay. Hand me your phone and explain how Tinder works."

His eyes lit up again. Hope was a good thing for him. "Yes. This is why you're the best friend. Good wingman."

Chapter Thirty-Two: Hailey

Mira came home from Culver for the summer totally different—no more black clothes or heavy makeup; she was more Gwen Stefani pinup girl now—but musically completely on her game. All she wanted to do was play with us again. We played for hours, almost every day. Tess was trying desperately to save enough money to get out of her house the moment she graduated next year, and I mostly tried not to think about Kyle or eyesight.

We landed a gig opening for a band from New York—Physicality. An *out-of-state band* that was like Milky Chance meets Audioslave. In other words—different and awesome. I was amped.

When Annalise heard that I was opening—through Lila, most likely—she begged to come and be our lackey if she could sit with us backstage. Cool girl that the moms already liked, with green hair? I was in.

"So, I swore off guys for all of last year," I told Annalise as I adjusted levels on my amp. Plucking strings, turning knobs. The worse my eyes got, the better my ears got, and it was taking me forever to get the tuning right. The room was practically black, only a few white lights were on to help us set up.

"Really?" Annalise sat cross-legged on the stage in front of me. In jeans and boots—normal clothes. I really wanted to make a note of that to Lila.

"Yeah. I've kind of decided guys are assholes, and I don't know if I want to deal with them anymore, but at the same time, I'm not sure I'm into girls either. Like maybe I'm just politically signing off of guys."

"Oh."

"I'm glad you came with me, but I didn't want to, like, lead you on or anything." I sang a few bars into the mic as my fingers plucked their way down the strings.

"Did Lila tell you I'm into girls?" Her head cocked to the side, and the green hair really glowed under the lights.

I laughed. "I have two moms. It's not hard to figure out."

"And so you also know that I think you're pretty?" Her eyes stayed focused on me.

"If you're interested in me, say so." I kept my eyes on the black nothing of the seating and plucked a few more strings.

"I'm interested in you." No hesitation. No pause.

I wanted to scream, *Fuck you, Kyle*, into the mic.

"Okay, but I'm not sure, is all. I mean, there's no point in leading you on, or starting something I'm not into." I played through the riff of our first song. Tuning felt perfect. Finally.

"I know." She shrugged. "Doesn't mean I don't like the view." Her smile was wide and open, and she leaned back on her hands to see me from her spot on the stage, and damn if the girl didn't seriously make me blush.

"Okay. Are we done with the lovefest over there? Because I'd like to be offstage when this place starts to fill up." Mira put her hands on her hips. Even with a black backdrop, I could see that.

"You want me to walk you to the mic when we come out?" Tess asked quietly as I set my guitar on its stand and made my way backstage.

I stepped carefully, knowing there were black wires on the black-painted stage.

"I'll do it." Annalise cut in as she held her arm out for me to take. "Since Hailey's still trying to figure out where she falls on the whole gay–straight spectrum."

"I'm only trying to avoid assholes for now." I laughed.

"I can help with that." Annalise bumped her hip against mine.

And it was odd walking next to her, knowing she was looking at me in a certain way, and still not being sure how I felt about it. But at least I knew what she wanted. After spending so much time around someone whose wants were always a mystery, she might actually be perfect.

The show was the biggest we'd ever played. Mira had all this pent-up pissed-off anger, maybe from ditching her black uniform and becoming a Culver girl. Tess had been sacked from her nannying job for swearing too much and getting caught calling the kids "spawn," and I was beyond pissed at MIA Kyle. At myself. At my eyes. It all added up to some really kick-ass girl-rock music.

The moms came, but they were good about staying off to the side. After their not listening to me play for the secret gigs that Chaz got me, I figured I owed them and wasn't even a pain in the ass about them coming.

Nothing beats standing in front of a pumped crowd. Nothing. We rocked. I felt every song. Every strum of my guitar, every solo. And we weren't perfect, but that crowd was there to have fun, and so were we.

The girls and I actually shared this sort of girly hug after our set, which we usually don't do on principle, but we were too high from our performance to give a shit.

The moms gave me the whole "not too late" thing, and "you were fabulous" thing, before heading for home. I wasn't going to miss a minute of Physicality. Especially since I got to watch from backstage. Hard-core rock I loved. Their set was over far too soon, and the crowd started to disperse.

Instead of riding with the band, Annalise offered to walk me home, which seemed like a sort of perfect way to end the night. Her arm wrapped around me, and she gave me a quick kiss on my cheek as we started toward my house.

"Can I for-real kiss you?" she asked, the engine noise from the cars leaving the parking lot echoing around us.

I stopped, turned my head, and brushed my lips against hers. I had seen Rox and Lila kiss about a thousand times but had never really thought about kissing a girl. It wasn't much different from kissing a guy aside from her being actually nice. Though maybe Chaz wasn't the best person to compare kisses with.

"Okay?" she asked.

I nodded.

She was cool warning me about steps and cracks in the sidewalk without being weird, and what normally would have been a crap walk home in the dark ended up being a sort of adventure.

"Thanks for letting me come." Annalise smiled her open smile again as we stood outside the door to my house. After she'd walked me home. And said she liked the view. And that she was interested in me. Because she was the kind of person who was open enough to talk, so I knew what she wanted, and could sort out what I wanted with all the right information.

It was all very actual-real-first-date-ish, and that made it sort of fun. But odd. And good. I thought. Nervous tingles floated through my stomach and chest.

"Thanks for the help." It was stupid, but I didn't know how to talk to a girl who was into me. Was it supposed to be the same as with a guy? Different? Should I want her hands all over me? Because I still wasn't sure.

"Don't stress so much, Hailey. It doesn't suit you."

"I know." I ran my hands through my hair, trying to relax, and then her lips were on mine again.

Soft, warm, slow. Her hand rested on the back of my neck, holding us together.

Our foreheads touched, and her breath brushed across my cheek when she spoke. "I want to kiss you more."

I took a hard swallow and we kissed again. Deeper, softer, longer.

Okay, so it was nice. She was so soft, and it wasn't like Chaz, who'd rammed his tongue into my mouth—it was like she wanted to actually taste me. And so we tasted each other. A lot. I'd missed being close to someone after my year of no guys.

Her eyes opened as she pulled away, keeping us close. "Any more ideas on where you fall yet?"

I shook my head, too confused to speak. It was good. Really good. If any girl would sway me, it would probably be her.

"Maybe we could go out again?" she asked. "While you sort it out?"

I nodded.

Hell. I'd turned into Kyle. That wasn't going to happen.

"If you can handle my bullshit and not being sure if I even like . . ." *Kissing girls*. But it was nice to kiss her. It wasn't fire-spreading-through-my-body-want-more, but maybe that was part of being with assholes, and I was trying to avoid them. Actually, I wasn't trying. I was determined.

I was also determined to spend more time at the Art Institute, and maybe travel a little to check some things off my "to see" list instead of the fear list. She didn't need to know I was working on the bucket part of my list. But looking at art and boating on the lake felt like fun things I'd do with friends *or* on a date.

"Yeah. Let's do it," I said. "Let's go out again."

Chapter Thirty-Three: Kyle

I hadn't seen Hailey since I'd watched her at the concert. And then found her outside, only to see her kissing a girl. My intestines tied into a thousand knots when I saw them, but I turned away, tossed Pavel's stupid flowers and Russian pastries in the trash, and walked home. That was my life. The girl I couldn't stop thinking about, couldn't have, didn't deserve, had gone from *maybe one day* to *never* in one girl kiss.

I went to Northwestern and my roommate never showed up. Our names were plastered on the dorm door and he never showed. For ten days. I asked my RA, but no one knew anything. So I was alone in my dorm room. Like I'd been alone at home. And after two weeks, I started to wonder how anything was different and if maybe I should move home and commute to campus.

But then Pavel moved in. It was all sort of unbelievable.

Out of a movie, but of course it would be—it was Pavel.

I screamed like a five-year-old girl when I found him in my room. And even he couldn't hide a real smile. Something cracked open inside me and I almost hugged him.

"What the hell are you doing here?"

"Kyle, my brother, we are roommates."

"What?"

He jumped off the bed and did a weird spin. "We are roommates. I am enrolled in Northwestern now."

So many thoughts spun out I couldn't hang on to any of them. "Your parents are letting you go to college?"

"Yes. Zig Ziglar convinced them with his talk of embracing the future and maximizing potential."

I dropped my bag onto my bed. "You're late. School started a few weeks ago."

He nodded. "Yes. It took some time working out the cost. But then I got a benefactor."

I laughed. "A what?"

He clapped his hands together once. "A benefactor. He will pay for Northwestern."

I blinked. "The whole thing?"

"Most of it. My parents will help a little too."

"A benefactor sounds a little dicey. What's the catch?"

He shook his head. "What is that?"

I snorted. Pavel could name every part of the female anatomy but somehow had missed out on the phrase "What's the catch?" "What do you have to do for your benefactor?"

"I have to tour high schools and talk about bullying and positive thinking. It is very good because I know about those things."

I gaped at Pavel. Of course. Of frickin' course. It's not like Pavel had a charmed life, but still, he was the kind of kid who turned a homeschool shit spiral into college tuition.

"And how the hell did you end up in my room?"

He jumped on his bed and bounced up and down like a kid. I'd never seen Pavel show this much enthusiasm for anything. Even the ladies. "This is God helping us with unexpected providence. Or perhaps we are getting our due. The man in charge of the resident halls said they were full up, but someone didn't arrive so I could have his spot. He gave me the keys. And then I saw your posters." He waved his arms at my wall. "And I thought, *This is my friend Kyle.*"

I reclined on my bed, my legs dangling off the side and Pavel still jumping next to me. For the first time in weeks, since I'd seen Hailey in a girl kiss, really, I felt like I could actually breathe.

"Wow, Pavel. That's fucking awesome. All of it. So tell me, what's been going on?"

"I have had Tinder success. I have been on thirteen dates and three times have given girls orgasm from oral pleasure."

I gaped. "No. Way."

"Yes. And one time a girl almost touched my penis. But then she stopped."

"Wait, so basically, you're making all these girls come and no one's even touched your junk yet?"

He jumped on the bed again. "They will want to touch my junk if I keep up with the oral pleasure. *Cosmopolitan* assures me of this. And I think I have a good Tinder reputation as a lover, because I am receiving referrals."

I laughed so hard tears came out of my eyes. Pavel was somehow getting a Tinder reputation because of his sex skills. *Jesus. This guy.* "Well, I think this is great news. But don't feel like you only have to be the one giving. Sex should go both ways."

He raised his eyebrows. "And you know this how? Do you read *Cosmopolitan*? Are you giving anyone oral pleasure?"

No. Of course not. Because the girl I wanted, the only girl I'd ever wanted, was apparently gay.

Even with Pavel as a roommate, I went home every weekend. Sometimes Mom was working. Sometimes she wasn't. She wasn't curled up on the couch as much, though, so I assumed something had been adjusted with her meds. Maybe her doctor wasn't prescribing emergency anxiety stuff anymore and had her on something more stabilizing.

One Saturday when I got off the train, she was waiting for me. A cup of coffee steaming in her bony fingers.

"You were ten when your dad left," she said before I could even open my mouth.

"I was."

"He didn't have to listen to a ten-year-old."

I nodded.

"Why didn't you ever tell me you had that conversation with him?" The whimper in her voice was almost lost in the wind.

"I thought you'd be happier. After the divorce. I thought it'd be better for us. But it wasn't. You didn't get better. You got worse. And it was my fault. At least partially."

"He would have left anyway." Her hands shook, and a drip of coffee splashed onto the ground.

"Yeah."

"I'm sorry, Kyle."

I swallowed past the lump in my throat. She couldn't possibly understand all that she'd cost me. But it wasn't her fault either. In the end, it was both of us.

"I'm sorry too, Mom."

Pavel talked all the fricking time. It was like his years with his sisters had taken the stoic Russian out of him and turned him into this tween girl who constantly had something to say. Late at night, I'd be exhausted from studying and he'd be back from another Tinder success with still-perfect hair and would start in with endless questions about the world. Then finally, finally, after midnight one night, he mentioned what had happened our freshman year.

"These are the things that carve us into the people we are,

Kyle," he said as we both sat reading on our beds. "To me, this horror has led to all the good things. It led me to Zig Ziglar. And Tinder. And school with you. I can't find regret in that."

It was too late. I was too tired. And lonely for my friend who was a girl. Would I go to her when I finished my list? I wasn't sure. Wasn't sure I had it in me to be turned away from her, even just as a friend.

"Well, then, you're lucky, Pavel. Because my life is plagued with regrets. Every single one of them punctuated by a list folded in the back of my desk. A list of things I haven't done. Things I'll never do."

"You are missing your great love."

I shook my head in denial, but the lie hurt too much.

"Yes. This is your problem. You have not seen her, then? Even when you've returned to visit your mom? And the grand gesture failed?"

"Yes. It failed. I dropped the ball with her. She's dating someone new. A girl, I think."

Pavel sat up quickly. "And you waited until now to tell me this? I told you about oral pleasure and you kept this information from me?"

I shrugged.

"You're angry at her?"

Yes. "No."

He nodded. "You are angry. You know what resentment is, Kyle?"

"I have no doubt you're about to tell me."

He moved to the edge of his bed and dropped his elbows to his knees. "Resentment is like swallowing poison and waiting for the other person to die."

I barked out a laugh. "Did you read that on a fortune cookie?"

He stared at me. "I can't remember. But it's good sense. You should go talk to Hailey. She's your great love. Even if you can never have her, she is a good friend for you. You can't only have me. Soon the ladies will grow interested in me for more than twenty minutes of oral pleasure and you'll be alone again."

The thing was, he was probably right. Pavel was sort of a dream guy. And as soon as girls got over his paradoxical optimism and stopped using him for his mad tongue game, one of them would snatch him up in a heartbeat. And I *would* be alone again.

Two weeks later, I pulled out my list of fears and drew a red line through number five. Then before I could think better of it, I emailed Hailey.

Wednesday, November 3. 6pm. 89.3 FM.

Chapter Thirty-Four: Hailey

W e didn't have a radio. Rox was too picky about music to trust any deejay to put on good selections, and honestly, who had a real radio anymore? I had two options: sit in the moms' car, or use my computer. I settled for the car, since even my laptop, with its ability to make everything huge, still hurt my eyes.

I knew he'd done it. Or at least I knew I was going to be pissed if he hadn't. If this was a lure for something stupid, like for someone making commentary on my "girl band," he was going to get a visit. If he *had* done it, if he had actually used his brains and his voice, he'd also probably get a visit, only I'd tackle him in a hug.

How close was Kyle to finishing his list? He had to be on the final few things.

I turned on the radio after dinner and reclined in the

driver's seat, resting my hands on the steering wheel. It was the first time I'd ever sat on this side of the car. I screamed when Kyle's voice came on.

"We're going to take a break from the indie scene to play some of the classics. We're kicking it off with the seventies and a little Janis Joplin, because she reminds me of a girl I know who I really hope is listening tonight."

I couldn't listen to the song. My hands covered my mouth and tears ran down my face.

Rox opened the passenger-side door. "What on earth are you doing out here?"

I pointed to the radio. "He did it. Kyle did it. Crossed something big off his list."

Rox sat next to me, her eyes not leaving mine. "You miss him, don't you?"

I nodded. God, I missed him. It pulled at my chest, and I was crying over hearing his voice on the radio. Pathetic.

"Why don't you go up this weekend and give him a visit?" Her hand rested on my shoulder.

"You'd let me?"

Rox shrugged. "Double-check which train you're on before it leaves. It's not too far."

"Yeah." I nodded. "Maybe I will."

Rox and I listened to all three hours of Kyle on the campus station. He'd done it. He'd actually done it. And maybe it was occasionally halting and a little uneven, but it didn't matter because it felt like everything. Or at the very least, it felt like the apology I deserved.

Kyle—

You were awesome. I would love to tell you I'm proud, but it would make me sound like the moms. But holy shit, you did it. I'm proud of you. I'm coming up this weekend to see you. If you'd like to tell me which dorm room you're in, it might save me a lot of trouble. Don't pick me up. I'll find you. That way I can cross something off my list, because big, new places really suck when you can't see. I figure worst-case scenario is that I'll have to call you from campus, but I won't know where I am and you'll have to come looking for me. That could be an interesting adventure on its own. Hope this is acceptable.

I'm coming. See you in a few days, Friend Kyle.

Hailey

◊ ◊ ◊

I walked to Lila's studio with the old playlist Kyle made me blasting in my ears. From Nirvana to 3 Doors Down to Milky Chance, and then a jump back in time to Dylan and

Marley. It made me think of when Kyle and I first met, and I was with Chaz, and the whole thing was such an unbelievable mess.

It also hit me how much I'd grown up since then. I was in my last year of high school and ready for something big. Something huge. Life-altering. More than crossing stuff off my list.

"There you are." Annalise smiled as I stepped inside, purple hair now.

Annalise and I weren't exactly going out, but we did spend time together, and we did a bit of kissing with that time. Most important, she wasn't an asshole, and gave me an excuse to say no to the occasional guy who asked me out in school.

We'd spent days at the Art Institute and the Field Museum and had even gone on a stupid tourist boat to see the city from the lake.

"Hey." I pulled out my earbuds and felt . . . different. Like I was almost where I was supposed to be, but hadn't quite gotten there yet.

It wasn't the studio. It wasn't my perfectly worn jeans and favorite boots. Rox had braided my hair up in some crazy design, but it wasn't that. Something was off.

Annalise's arms came around me, but I hadn't even realized she'd come so close. I hugged her tightly and breathed in, hoping to relax again.

Sweaty yoga wear hit my nose, and I pulled away. Weird. I never minded it when Kyle was off his bike and kind of ripe.

Kyle. His playlist echoed in my ears. This was . . . not right. Not for me.

She stepped back, her brows down. "What's going on?"

I couldn't look at her. Everything was off. Tilted. "I don't know."

There was suddenly no air.

I turned and sprinted for the door, then stood outside breathing in deeply.

Annalise stepped out behind me.

She kissed my shoulder through my sweater, and my body stiffened.

"Realization dawns." Annalise touched my cheek.

"What are you talking about?" I finally turned to face her.

"You. And me." She shook her head. "It's okay, Hailey. You told me you weren't sure, and I thought you were worth the risk."

I felt like complete shit. I'd hurt Annalise because I couldn't make up my mind. Because I'd wanted to try something different. I pulled a Kyle move and shoved my hands in my pockets. "I wasn't worth it. I'm sorry."

She laughed. "It was worth it, Hailey. It's always worth it when you give a shit about someone."

I swallowed, wondering if this was how painful having a normal conversation was for Kyle. Or if it was how it used to be for him and he'd grown out of it.

"Tell you what. I might use that guilt I see plastered all over your face if I need to make someone jealous sometime, okay?"

She sounded hurt but okay. And her smile. She was still smiling at me. I wondered if her eyes were watering up, but I couldn't see well enough to tell.

"For that, I'm your girl."

We stood in awkward silence for a few moments on the sidewalk in the biting fall wind.

"Well. I'll see you around." Annalise wrapped her arms around herself and stepped back inside.

And that was that. Not bad as far as breakups go. Beat the shit out of jumping off Chaz and standing in that dirty green-room with a million obvious realizations hitting me at once. Splitting from Annalise was also better than any of the times Kyle and I had drifted apart.

So I could check girls off as not a good option for me. Assholes were off, but they weren't always easy to recognize. I felt better, though, as I walked home. Not because Annalise and I were split, if we were ever really together, but because I felt like I was a step closer to filling that awkward nothing that clawed its way into my chest once in a while.

Happier. Lighter. Even those words made me sound way too much like the moms.

Kyle said in his email that they were on the fourth floor. That Pavel was his roommate—I knew there had to be a story behind that one—and I'd know their room by the sign on the door. Yes, he'd assured me, even I'd be able to see it.

A large white poster reading WELCOME, LADIES in huge block lettering was plastered on the third door on the right.

I laughed, because yeah. No way it wasn't the right room. I thought about barging in, and then thought about all the things single guys might be doing in their dorm room and knocked instead.

"Hailey!" Pavel's smile lit his face as he jerked open the door. "So good to see you!"

He kissed me on each cheek, then pulled me into a tight hug as Kyle smiled at me from his side of the room. Pavel's hands slid lower on my back, and then lower again until his fingertips brushed the skin between my T-shirt and my jeans.

"Pavel." I laughed as I pushed him away. "I don't think you should feel me up in front of Kyle."

He shrugged. "But it was nice? That soft spot of skin?"

"Yes." I nodded. "But only at the end of a date, okay? And only if she's hugging you back."

"That's an excellent tip. Tinder ladies are less discerning than you. I think I'm ready for real dating soon."

"Tinder ladies?"

"Yes, I have a good reputation for oral pleasure."

"Oh, yeah?" I teased. "How do you know?"

"I've heard from other Tinder ladies. And on Yik Yak. Almost all satisfied customers."

"This might be TMI, Pavel." And really, it was me avoiding talking to Kyle. Seeing Kyle. Even my small glimpse showed someone who looked more like a man than I expected.

"You will let me know if you hear anything not good about me? They shut my Yik Yak account down because they suspected me of being a troll."

"I'm not really on Yik Yak. It's for assholes." I'd evidently missed a lot on the Pavel front. "But good for you to be batting a thousand over there."

"Tell me if you're interested in me working the magic on you." Even I could see Pavel's eyebrows dancing—the guy had changed a lot.

"Get out." Kyle shoved him from behind.

Pavel left, laughing, and then the door closed.

And there I stood. In front of Kyle. In his dorm room.

"Holy shit, Kyle. It's been too long." I threw my arms around him, pressing my face into his chest, and he grabbed me back, almost knocking my glasses off.

"Hey."

"Hey? *Hey?* I took the train and wandered a new campus—I'm totally crossing that off my list, by the way—and I get a 'hey'?" I stood back to try and make out the changes in him.

He smiled that perfect Kyle smile, but only glanced at the ground for a quick second before putting his eyes back on me. Better. Kyle had grown up a lot and it suited him. Broader. His hair the perfect too-long black that I remembered.

"You were a brilliant deejay, by the way. The moms downloaded some new app so they can listen to your show. This is high praise from Rox, who doesn't let anyone pick her music."

"Crossed one off the list." He shrugged.

We stood in silence for a moment, and I almost started to panic that we weren't going to be the same. "The moms miss you too," I said to fill the silence.

His eyes darted around, almost confused. "I—"

I interrupted, needing us to be normal again. "So, which bed is yours?"

Kyle pointed and I jumped on. "Wow. Kyle. All grown up and gone to college. I'm proud."

"And you and . . . um . . . the girl, with the hair?" He gestured in circles, like his hands would somehow help him find the words. We were definitely still Hailey and Kyle, and I started to let myself really relax on Kyle's bed.

"Annalise? How do you even know about her?"

"I . . . saw you two, after your big show before Physicality."

"You came to my show and didn't say hi? What the *hell*? We're supposed to be friends." I hated it when Kyle backed away from me like that. Didn't say what he'd wanted to say or didn't do whatever it was he'd wanted to do when he came that night. He hadn't just ended up at my concert without a purpose.

He shrugged and blushed.

"Geez, Kyle. We're *way* past the not-talking bullshit."

"You were busy. With the girl." His hands stuffed in his pockets.

"Yeah." I sighed. "She was my first girl kiss. She was a great kisser. It's kind of too bad I'm not a lesbian."

He sat on the far corner of the bed. "But you . . ."

"All in my endeavor to stay away from assholes, Kyle. It's a good goal, and one I'm determined to stick to. But it's not going to happen with girls. At least now I know for sure." I was both sad and relieved about that. Mixed, I guessed, as most things had started to be.

"Oh."

I was dying to see his face better, to understand a little more the confusion in his voice, but on the opposite side of the bed, he was too far away.

"What else have you been up to?" he asked.

And that simple question was the jumping-off point for us. *Finally.*

"Well, Mira's back, not returning to Culver, but she's gone pinup girl and wants us to play rockabilly. Not the worst choice, but it's hardly what we're about." I elbowed him. "And you apparently saw me kissing Annalise, so that's kind of been who I've hung out with lately. I saw more paintings, went to the Field Museum, and holy shit, I can't believe that dinosaur. I'm doing this killer independent study on stringed instruments, so I'm stumbling through the mandolin right now. What about you?"

"Well, there's college. Which is okay. Pretty easy after high school. The station is good." Then there was this long pause, as if "the station is good" held enough layers to warrant the next part of our conversation. "And Pavel has a reputation on Tinder."

"Have you talked to him about the locker-room stuff?"

"Yeah. Sort of. He acts like it all happened for a reason. I'm not sure. . . ."

I nudged his knee. "Maybe that's why he's doing the Tinder stuff. Maybe he's finding something he lost."

He bit his bottom lip and nodded. "Makes sense."

"Are you going to tell me why it took this long to reach out to me? What happened after prom?"

He let out a long breath. "Well, so you know my mom. She's . . . complicated. She's not always pushy like she was when you met her on Solstice. My dad left a long time ago, and I think sometimes I'm a stand-in for him. And when I got home from prom to change, she'd pulled out all of his letters and she was kind of a wreck. And I wanted to meet you—Jesus, so much—but she and I fought. Because I admitted I'd told my dad to leave."

I blinked. "Wait, what?"

"My dad was a douche bag. Cheated on my mom. Treated her like shit. So the last time he left, I told him not to come back."

I put my head on his shoulder and felt a slight tremble. "And this all came out after prom?"

"Yeah. And Mom broke down. She does that a lot, but this was different. It felt almost dangerous. And she wasn't able to shake it completely until I went to school."

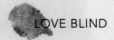

"And you couldn't tell me about your fight? Instead you leave it to me to come and find you?"

"I didn't know what to say. How to explain it all without it seeming like I was the same pathetic loser with a messed-up life that I was freshman year."

"This is a lot. And I don't want to push, but I think you need to talk to me more about it. Maybe not now, but sometime. Because I need to know how to act when this comes up with you and how to get you not to always panic around me. And how to help you stop worrying about being a pathetic loser."

"You kept asking me about my list. If I'd done anything. And I did stuff, but then I added more. And it was spinning my wheels, never moving forward or getting better or being worth anything."

"So instead of talking, explaining any of this to me, you went with a *can't make it* text and thought that was good?"

"No, I didn't think it was good. But anything else and you would have come over to my house."

I smiled. "Yeah, I would've."

"And I couldn't have you there. Not with everything between Mom and me. It's not your boat to be in, you know?"

"Yeah. Maybe. I guess. But still . . ." If we were friends, the way I thought we were, I should've been there. Maybe Kyle was right, and it had been his mess, not mine. The thing was, he should've told me, but I had known Kyle's limitations from the beginning and wanted him for a friend anyway. Not just *anyway*. If I was being honest, I liked him in part because of his limitations. The selfish part of me liked having the upper hand, but we weren't that way anymore. Kyle and I had definitely equaled out.

"I'm sorry, Hailey." Then he squeezed my shoulder and it was like the last of my anger melted into something else. Something good and warm and that I only felt with Kyle. It was like that day on the porch after his first dinner with the moms.

"Is your mom really better?"

He offered me a half smile. "Well, she's off Xanax and on Lexapro, which is way better long-term. So yeah. I guess she's better. She told me last weekend she might go see a therapist. She probably won't, but 'might' is a lot closer than where she was."

"We should sic Pavel on her."

Kyle laughed. He was still my Kyle, but better. More grown-up, less painfully awkward. I was staying away from jackholes, and he was living his own life in the dorm. I'd been right from the beginning. We were good for each other.

"I know you wanted to come up on your own, but it's dark. Can I walk you back to the train? Ride it home with you?" he asked.

"Don't ride it home with me. You'd have to pay for it, and then turn around and come back." That was ridiculous. It *was* dark, but the moms were ready to give me a ride if I needed one.

Kyle shrugged as he held the door open, notebook in hand.

I slid my arm through his as we stepped into the cold air.

"I know a place we can get pizza. We'll eat it on the way, and I'll have quiet thinking time on the way back. Maybe do some writing."

"But—"

"Nope. My mind's made up. We ride together."

I squeezed his arm tighter. "I like this side of you, Kyle. The guy who isn't afraid to say what he wants."

He shook his head and stared at the ground, a sure sign that he was still the Kyle I'd known, but with a little more confidence each time. In a few years, he might start to see how amazing he was, and then he'd be unstoppable.

Chapter Thirty-Five: Kyle

You like hanging out in my dorm room," I said to Hailey. I was on my bed studying while she sat cross-legged on the floor next to me.

"Yeah. It's sort of calming in this weird way. And gets me ready for next year."

"Have you decided where you're gonna go yet?" I'd had to hold my tongue so many times in the past few months. Keep myself from talking her into coming to Northwestern or at least staying close.

"No. I'm still waiting to hear from Berkeley."

Berkeley. In California. On the other side of the country. Forever away. Even with us emailing so much more, it wasn't the same. It wasn't Hailey's smile once a week, which wasn't enough for me but was better than nothing. It wasn't Hailey's different glasses and raspy voice and crazy fears.

I took a deep breath and tried to focus on my linear equations.

Hailey gnawed on her lip and tapped her hands on her thighs. "A few guys have asked me out."

I tensed, holding my breath, waiting for her to continue.

"I said no." Her eyes were on me. Way too still.

I nearly dropped my pen with relief.

"How come you never told me you were interested in me?" she blurted out.

The air whooshed out of the room. I placed my book to the side and looked at her.

"Can we have this conversation now?" she asked in a low voice, tentative and damn sexy. "Finally? Are we okay to talk about this?"

I nodded and slipped down to the floor so I could sit next to her, feel her warmth next to mine. I stretched my legs out in front of me, one green shoe crossed over the other.

"Which time are we talking about?"

She laughed. "That many?"

I nodded and she leaned her head against my shoulder. I inhaled. "I guess it always seemed like bad timing. That's dumb, isn't it? But there was Chaz. And then Mariah. And then Annalise. I sort of felt like we'd never happen. Plus . . ."

"Yes?"

"Our fear lists. They kind of seemed important, you know?

Like things we had to get through first, before we could deal with everything else."

"I was ready at prom."

I nodded. "I know. But I guess I wasn't ready. Everything got really complicated. Not just with Mariah. But with my mom. I didn't want to bring you into that. Felt like you deserved more."

She grabbed my hand and pressed it between her two. "I deserved the chance to say no."

"You did."

"And now, Kyle? What's stopping you now?"

I shut my eyes and released a deep breath. "Everything. Nothing. I don't know. It's like too much has happened. And I don't want to risk it. I don't want to risk you. Do you know that one of the things on my list is 'Be a good friend to Hailey'? Because I never felt like I was a good friend to anyone. And finally, now, I feel like I'm getting it right and I don't want to screw that up. I'm ready to cross it off my list. Going beyond friendship is a very big risk. And maybe you'll go away to school. Then I'll have lost everything."

"I think that's kind of bullshit."

I smiled. "Yeah. You would. But I sort of want you for life. And when you get into all this relationship stuff in high school, you don't keep people for life." There was so much I wasn't saying. So much I wanted to say, but my logic refused to be pushed aside. "I mean, how many people do you know who've stayed together when they started dating in high school? Too much changes. Look at you over the past two years. Look at me."

"I hate that you're being logical."

I released a bitter laugh. I hated it too. But I wanted so much more for us. I wanted everything, and I wasn't going to squander it on a quick hookup before she left. My imagination had shut down completely on that score.

"I'm interested in you, Hailey. But right now, I can't go there. Do you understand?"

She squeezed my hands and nodded. But I saw little tears on the edges of her lashes.

"Don't cry, Hailey. I won't be able to deal if you cry."

She sniffed. "I don't want to be the better man, Kyle. The responsible party. I'm the *instant access* generation. Everything I want, when I want it."

My heart beat too fast. "I know. But not this. Not now."

"But I'm determined now. I've learned so much. Like . . ." She took another sniff, trying to keep in her tears. For me. I knew she held them back to spare me and I loved her even more for it. "Like I'm not a lesbian for sure. I mean, I even tried it. She taught me some mad kissing skills. . . ."

My gaze locked on her lips. I wanted to kiss her. Was dying to kiss her. And not in the sleazy way anymore. I was so far beyond that. But I couldn't do it. Maybe still in my own way, or maybe for once, I was doing the right thing.

I took off her glasses with shaky fingers. Knowing that

she trusted me when she couldn't see, hoping that would be enough. Enough for what, I wasn't sure. Maybe to tide me over until I could have Hailey the way I wanted—even though I was still half-convinced it wouldn't happen until I'd finished the list.

"Why do you like my eyes so much?" She rubbed her eyes, then sandwiched my hand again.

"Because not everyone gets to see them the way I do." I'd gotten that much out at least.

She nodded, her eyes darting around my face, and I wondered if my face was a more distorted blob than it had been two years ago, when she'd rested her fingers there to *see* me.

"Kyle." She leaned in, touching her nose to my cheek, and I could feel my body starting to shake. Small tremors that hit me deep and then moved into the hand she held.

"Hmm." I couldn't look at her. Instead I focused on the way she held my hand between hers, on the part of Hailey I knew I could have without destroying us both. The only way I knew we could be together, and still like each other in five years. Ten years.

Her lips touched my jaw, and I nearly took her face in my hands and kissed her, hard, but I was smarter than that. Knew better.

"If you don't kiss me now, you're going to be another asshole I have to avoid." Typical Hailey.

"No. If I *do* kiss you, I will be another asshole. And I can't be that guy, Hailey. Not for you." The thought of us falling apart. Of not having her. I couldn't take it. Not ever again.

"Okay, Kyle, but I don't have a label for you anymore. You're More-Than-a-Friend Kyle, and Not-an-Asshole Kyle, and I . . ." She let out a breath, and I hated that I could hear the sadness in her voice, but she didn't know what she was asking.

"Maybe just Kyle."

She chuckled, but it was nervous, forced. "Spring break's in another week. Tess is coming with me to check a big one off the list."

I nodded. Because for some reason, the list still had a hold of her too. "Good. Let me know how it goes."

"Of course. You might not *want me*, want me. But you're stuck with me anyway. Because we've got these lists."

"The lists." Was that it? Was our connection to the lists what made her hang on? Seemed almost stupid now.

I hated myself for being scared, and I hated myself for wanting her the way I did. *I'm interested in you, Hailey.* I'd finally said the words, but couldn't do it. Not to her. Not to us.

Chapter Thirty-Six: Hailey

So the weirdest thing happened to me after my *big* convo with Kyle. I came home, pulled out Rox's old acoustic guitar, and played. Maybe it was because of my independent study, or maybe it was me evolving, but the longer my fingers went up and down the neck of the guitar, the more I realized that as much as I loved playing kick-ass rock music, when I finally let myself really play the acoustic guitar, I found home.

I sat on our front porch all day that Sunday with the old, beat-up thing, and I couldn't get enough. It hit my soul in a place I'd been forcing that electric guitar into for years. I'd been slamming the music into me, instead of letting it in to take over. Tess was going to be pissed. First rockabilly and now this.

That whole next week, my week before spring break, it's all I did. I wrote Kyle and told him. I expected him to sound surprised, but he didn't. He said he was proud of me. *Him*. Proud of *me*. And that it took guts to really let something in like that. When I finished reading his email, I cried a little, grateful he got me. That he knew it was a big deal.

That was the last straw—that letter from Kyle. I finally started caring a little less if I was playing something I'd have called "music for the moms" a couple of years ago. My voice slowed and flowed better. I wrote more than ten songs that week, and made another demo for Berkeley, even though it was probably too late for them to swap it out with my first one. I also, finally, looked into colleges close by. The moms were thrilled, and I didn't feel like I was doing it for Kyle. I felt like I was doing it for me. Before last weekend, if I would have stuck around here, it would have been out of fear of being away, but at that moment, I knew staying closer to home wouldn't be about being afraid, it would be about me both getting *and* doing what I wanted.

And as much as it scared the shit out of me to have a musical breakthrough in such a bizarre way, my world had shifted again and felt firmly underneath my feet for the first time ever.

I was Hailey. Hater of assholes. Player of chick music. Going blind, but slowly. A girl in love with her best friend. And I was okay with all of it. Mostly okay with it.

Tess laughed as she held the steering wheel with one hand and her Super Big Gulp with the other.

"What's so funny?"

"I was about to ask if you could drive for a bit because my ass hurts."

"Yeah. Not such a good idea. Plus, you hate when anyone else drives."

We drove in silence for a few, our last weekend of spring break and a list of adventures behind us and still in front of us.

"Does it suck? I mean, knowing that driving is something you'll never do?"

Tess and I didn't talk like that. Not really. We joked about me not seeing stop signs, or my missing the more subtle way a guy's nice ass moved by us because I couldn't fully appreciate the *deliciousness*, but not about real stuff.

"I'm scared of the little things. Living in black all the time. Like I've had all this practice using smells and sounds and touch, but not seeing feels like solitary confinement. All the blind people said you get used to it. I even talked to one guy who got his sight back for a while after a surgery, and said it felt so awkward."

"Oh."

"I think if you're with people you trust, it wouldn't be so bad."

"Can't live with the moms forever."

"And I don't want to." I laughed. Kyle's face flashed as I closed my eyes. "Damn him."

"Who?"

And then, even though I knew Tess didn't totally get my relationship with Kyle, I was *finally* starting to. "Kyle."

*first thing I need to say is that I'm sick of the coward
bullshit. If you're interested in me, then we're doing
something about it. I'm not taking no for an answer. I
have plans this summer, Kyle, and you're going to be a
part of them, because being in love with my best friend is
a combination of the scariest and most awesome things I
can imagine.*

*I'm crossing off a major thing over my last few days of
spring break, which I will share with you when I get
back. And we're going to have that conversation again.
The one where you say you're interested in me. And
this time we're getting past the coward BS. You've been
warned. Miss you.*

Hailey

*PS: Going blind wouldn't be as scary if I was doing it
with you.*

"Feel better?" Tess asked when I leaned back and sighed.
"Yeah. Much." I closed my eyes.
"Good. Because, you know . . ."
I opened my eyes and turned to Tess, but my eyes locked
in front of us. It was so fast. Everything was so fast. "Tess—"

Chapter Thirty-Seven: Kyle

Going blind wouldn't be as scary if I was doing it with you.
Her words shredded me. My body shook with need for her. I wanted to hop on my bike and find her. Go to her. Bring her everything: my list, my heart, everything.

But that wasn't my life. I didn't get to win. Ever. And even as my pulse skipped at the possibility of her note, I knew it would be taken away. I shoved things into my bag, felt the ticking of the clock in my gut, but the whole time it was like an anvil over my head. The phone buzzing in my hand confirmed it.

"She's in the hospital, Kyle," Rox said. "It was a bad accident, but she and Tess are going to be okay. They're both lucid. Broken bones and lots of bruising. Tess is in worse shape. . . ." Rox paused and I steeled myself. "She was driving. Swerved to avoid hitting a deer. She feels totally responsible."

"How's Hailey?"

"Kyle . . ."

Oh, God. "I need to see her. Please. I need to see Hailey."

Rox choked on a sob. "Not yet. It's her eyes. The trauma. She's in surgery. It doesn't look good."

I dropped to the ground then. I honestly didn't know how I'd managed to stay standing in the first place. "Rox," I whispered.

"I'll call you. When she's out. I'll call you."

She clicked off before I could say anything else.

I couldn't have made it through the summer without Pavel. Hailey went dark. Literally and figuratively. I called Rox and Lila constantly. They said she was rehabbing, doing better, but completely blind now. I begged to talk to her, but she wouldn't come to the phone. I showed up at the house, and Rox and Lila sent me away. She wasn't ready. She was still figuring things out.

Pavel kept me company. We started a lawn-mowing business together, him slathering himself with SPF 100 sunscreen as he talked on and on about all his different dates. Apparently Tinder was a bottomless source of women for Pavel. Two months in, though, and I was at my wits' end.

"Enough, for Christ's sake, Pavel. I don't fucking care what base you got to or how many dates you have this week."

Pavel stopped bagging grass and looked at me. "I was trying to distract you."

I pulled my shirt up and wiped the sweat from my forehead. "I know. I get it. But it's not working. Don't you see? She's all I think about. All I want. And it's like it's all been taken from me. She won't even talk to me."

"Always with the sprint, never with the marathon." He sat cross-legged and stared up at me. "Don't you think it's maybe meant to be this way? Like this is your test. The journey to get the prize. And it will be all that much sweeter now."

"No. I don't think that. I'm done with that. I've had enough of a journey. I want Hailey. I'm tired of all these character-building life lessons."

Pavel shrugged. "Then talk her into you. Surely my friend Kyle can talk one girl into him."

I shook my head and stared at the sweat stains on my shirt. "I don't know how. It's like she's seen everything. I don't know what else I have to offer."

Pavel rolled his eyes like a tween and popped up. "You have patience. That is all. And if you exercise it, give it as much of a workout as you've given your heart, it will be enough."

"Jesus," I mumbled, "I can't believe you're still on the Zig Ziglar." But even as I said it, the kernel took hold. For the first time in weeks, I grabbed on to a spark of hope.

Chapter Thirty-Eight: Hailey

Timing was always off with us. Maybe it always would be. I wasn't ready. Wasn't ready to sit in the same room as him and not be able to see his shape. His smile. The way his hair always swooped over his eyes.

I couldn't do that. Couldn't be so close to something I was desperate to see and not see it.

Kyle didn't stop calling all summer. I thought he would, but he kept at it. He didn't come over, except the one time I wouldn't talk to him, but it didn't matter. I heard Lila and Rox on the phone with him daily, giving an update. I didn't know how I felt about it, but that was becoming a theme in my new life.

I thought I'd be prepared for the darkness. But working with available light was so much different from total black. Every day was a test of feeling my way into blindness. At night,

I played my guitar because I could do it by touch. But everything else I had to learn all over. iPads were practically impossible for me to figure out. Even with the audio prompt, I kept screwing up my messages. I started figuring out braille, but it was all painfully slow. More often than not, I felt like an infant, unable to do the most basic things by myself.

But still Kyle called and asked. Rox didn't bullshit him. Told him it was going slow. I wasn't adjusting as well as they hoped. Who could? I was strapped without sight. It wasn't going to be resolved at the end of the half hour. The only luck I had was that school didn't make me finish up any classes after spring break. My grades stood, and I graduated but didn't go to the ceremony.

I deferred Berkeley, of course. They said they had a lot of services for the disabled. Which I was now labeled. They said it wouldn't be a problem to accommodate me. Audio textbooks and all the rest of it. I told them maybe next year. But I couldn't imagine going.

By September, Rox was officially done with me. She forced me to get out of the house almost every day, even if I only made it to the porch. Lila was softer about it, encouraging me in her warm voice with a bunch of bullshit platitudes. Neither tactic worked. I played music in my room, went to occupational therapy, and otherwise never left. I allowed myself one indulgence. Kyle on the radio every week. Me in the dark, listening to him as if he was sitting next to me.

One night in October, I finally snapped. He'd signed off his show and my body flushed with fury. I wanted more of him. I didn't want his show to be over. I missed him like I missed my sight. And as tears dripped down my cheeks, I realized he was something I could have, but I was going to have to do something big.

The next day, I had Rox drop me off at the college. I had a dog to take me everywhere now. I named him Basic. He'd only been with me a week and a half, but I'd grown attached. I didn't go upstairs without him. I didn't go to the bathroom without making sure he was outside my door. His fur was soft and his smile slobbery enough that I could form what he looked like in my head. I made him blue because my eyes couldn't tell me otherwise.

Someone from Student Services led the two of us to Kyle's dorm and let us in. I had her leave me at the stairs. Three flights up, two doors down on the left. Basic and I could handle it. But my mouth dried out a little, and I searched my memory for all my trips here before, only Kyle wasn't in the same room as last year. Still. Three flights. Two doors. Doable. I grasped the handle on Basic's harness more tightly, and my dog led me up the stairs.

I probably would've stood in front of his door forever if Basic hadn't whimpered. The door popped open, and I immediately was tackle hugged and kissed on both cheeks by Pavel. I recognized his scent more than ever. That thing about the other senses getting better when you go blind is totally true, but my brain was still trying to process the massive amounts of new information.

"And she has come to us at last," Pavel said, stepping back. "With a dog."

I heard him kneel down and I cleared my throat. "This is Basic."

"You named your dog Basic?"

A choked sound escaped my throat. *Kyle.* His voice was so much better than on the radio. So much better than I had ever heard it. I wanted him to tackle hug me too. But he stayed put, just inside the door by the sound of it.

"Yeah. Because he is . . . basic, that is. The trainer said he was a very functional dog." But in a week he'd turned into a lot more than just a dog.

Pavel laughed from the ground. "He's a good-looking dog. You should see him."

"I can't," I blurted out at the same time Kyle said, "She can't."

I felt Pavel pop up. "Oh, good. It's all good here. You are back to talking on top of each other. This is very good. Hailey, Kyle has been very patient."

Half my mouth tipped up. "Yeah. Me too."

Pavel clapped. "Excellent. This is outstanding. I will take the dog for a walk."

Everything in me froze for a second. It was Pavel. Basic would be fine. I kneeled and Basic's nose touched my cheek. Then I quickly stood, clipping Basic's leash onto his collar, so he'd know Pavel wouldn't need his help.

"Okay," I said, my voice scratching a bit. "No treats. And be careful with him."

I rubbed Basic's head again and handed the lead to Pavel. He squeezed my arm as he passed, and it gave me enough of a boost to stumble into Kyle's room.

Kyle touched my shoulder and drew his hand down until it reached mine. "You can take my arm."

"Have you been researching, Kyle?" I couldn't keep the bitter out of my voice.

"A little."

I didn't expect his honesty, and it silenced me for a second. "Oh."

"Being blind will be less scary with me," he said, and it was like a twist in my gut. The words from my letter used like this.

"Actually, it was *going* blind that would be less scary with you. Immediate blindness, as it turns out, is a real bitch. With or without someone along for the ride."

"I'm along for the ride, though. You know?"

I turned to him and slid my hands up his chest to touch the planes of his face. He froze and let me linger on each part of him. I waited to touch his lips till the very end. My fingers rubbing over soft dryness.

"I'm scared, Kyle."

He reached up and took my hand. "I know. Me too." He kissed my fingers, and the breath rushed out of me.

"I never thought you'd end up on my list," I said.

"You've always been on mine."

"But."

"But I've crossed most things off, Hailey. It's not a magic fix. The same things still scare me, but I found a way to move forward."

"I can cross off being blind, but that doesn't mean shit, really. I'm terrified I'll never see again. I hear miracle stories, and doctors are always working on new . . . You know what? Never mind. That's not this conversation."

"My point is," Kyle said, determination lacing every word, "we don't need the lists to move forward. They were always just this thing, another *thing* that kept us from each other. We don't need them."

"What *do* we need?"

Kyle stepped closer, took my hands in his. Slid his thumbs over the backs of my hands. "We need to want something more than we're afraid of it."

I didn't pull back when he leaned in to kiss me. I'd been expecting it, wanting it. His warmth hit first, and when his soft lips brushed up against mine, my hands tightened with his.

The kiss went on forever. No plundering or sloppiness like Chaz. Just this soft exploration that made me want to fall into Kyle. Nibbles on my bottom lip until I opened up and let him in to taste me completely.

It was everything I imagined. Better, really, because my senses were on fire. Hyperalert to his citrus smell and his touch and every moan and whimper coming from both of us. Finally, he pulled back.

"I'm a mess," I whispered.

"Me too."

"It was a deer, did you know that? A deer walked across the road, and she swerved, and . . ." And the car rolled and rolled and rolled.

"I know. I'm sorry. How's Tess?"

I shrugged. "Away. She's living with her aunt for a while in Florida. Might go to college there."

"Good for her." He stepped away and I almost wanted to lunge for him, pulling him back into the moment of our kiss.

"Are you okay?" I asked.

"You've got stuff to work out. I've got stuff to work out. Doesn't change how I feel."

"Really?"

"Of course. It's part of the journey, and I happen to want to take it with you." His voice was farther now. Lower. Like he'd sat on his bed.

I needed him closer. But it was like I couldn't find the words to ask. Like I needed to go to him, especially after a summer of him making unreturned phone calls. I stepped forward, and my foot caught on something. I fell hard and my leg banged against the edge of his bed.

"Jesus, I'm sorry, Hailey. I wasn't . . . I should've . . . I'm sorry. Here. Let me."

I waved my hands, blinking past the tears from the stabbing shin pain. "I got it. It's fine. I got it. I've got to learn your room. Basic won't always be with me. What was that?"

"Books," he said. "I didn't even see them." He grabbed my wrist and pulled me onto the bed next to him.

I lifted my leg up and felt the damage to my shin. "I didn't see them either."

He laughed, but the whole thing was awkward and I could tell everything we'd experienced with our first big kiss had turned to crap in less than a minute.

Scooting back, I tugged my knees to my chest. "We might not make it."

"We will," he answered, and the certainty in his voice made my breath stop in my lungs.

I placed my hand next to where I thought his was at the same time he lifted his to rub his fingers over my shin. His fingers pushed slightly too hard, and I winced.

"Sorry," he said, and I was about to reach out to take his hand again when he dropped it from my leg.

"It's okay." I rolled my pant leg down and tugged my legs closer.

I'd made my way here. For this? This awkwardness? All these misses? Had I waited too long? Should I have asked him to come to me?

"Of course it is."

"What are you talking about? I was talking about you pushing too hard on my leg."

He shifted. "Sorry. God, I'm screwing this up. I didn't mean to hurt your leg."

"What did you say 'of course it is' to?"

I felt a slight movement, but I could only guess it was a shoulder shrug. He'd already forgotten I couldn't see those things.

"I meant we're okay. We're going to be okay. I mean after everything else, this is almost nothing."

"Yeah, almost," I said, then shifted to the left and turned away, nearly missing his lean to kiss me again. His warmth gave it away. But before I could turn back, he snatched my hand and kissed that instead.

"We're going to be okay."

"And if we're not?"

He squeezed my hand, and I squeezed back. The comfort soothed me long enough to wait for his words.

"One day at a time, Hailey. It doesn't all work exactly as you expect. We don't get that. It's not in the cards for either of us."

"Then what do we get?" The hitch in my voice had to be as obvious to him as it was to me.

"We get now."

This time I leaned into him, until my cheek found his shoulder. It was less bony than I remembered. There would be subtle changes in Kyle that I'd feel, and some I wouldn't notice at all.

"Now," I echoed. And that would have to be enough.

~~List of Things to Do for Hailey~~

Kyle's List

X Learn to drive a stick

X Ask for a letter of rec from a teacher at school

X Get the number of a girl in history (Hailey got
   the number, but I did use it)

X Talk to Pavel about freshman year

~~DJ~~

X Talk to Mom about Dad

Do something with my writing aside from leaving
   it in boxes

X Be a good friend to Hailey

~~Spiders~~

X Get a job

Drive across the country

X Go to college

X Live in dorms. Get a roommate.

Get my PhD

Tell Hailey I love her

Be happy

Acknowledgments

Deepest gratitude to our agents who worked on *Love Blind*, to Liesa Abrams and the entire Simon Pulse team, and to all the people who graciously read this novel in its early stages and offered feedback.

Always a monstrous hug to our families who didn't get upset by our endless phone calls and online chats regarding Kyle and Hailey. We love you all so much.

This story truly belongs to the people we lost along the way, and to the people who began as acquaintances, who became friends, and then family, and to all the people we haven't met yet, who will impact our futures in profound ways.

Turn the page for a look
at another gripping
read from C. Desir.

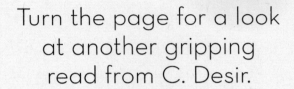

BLEED LIKE ME

Their worst addiction is each other.

C. DESIR, author of *Fault Line*

referee arguments between Mom and my brothers when one of the neighbors called about the noise. Or to help when Mom gave me the ragged, desperate face she had on now as I stood at the open front door. Her gray roots were an inch thick at the crown of her head, and she was wearing the same outfit she slipped on every day after work: stained, discolored T-shirt, saggy sweatpants with too-loose elastic at the waist.

"Luis has locked himself in the bathroom again and Alex won't eat any of his snack until Luis comes out." Her exhausted voice passed through me. I'd heard it for almost five years, too long to even remember what the Mom of my childhood sounded like.

I dropped my messenger bag at my feet and opened the drawer of the small side table next to the overloaded coat-rack in the hall. I plucked one of the emergency hotel key cards from its box and took the stairs two at a time. My heavy boots squeaked on the scuffed hardwood. The loud explosions from Miguel's Call of Duty game echoed from the living room.

I pounded on the bathroom door at the top of the stairs. "Luis. Get out of there."

"Fuck off."

Jesus. What did the other fifth graders think of this kid? He spent more time in the guidance counselor's office than in his own classroom. But no amount of "be respectful and

I wasn't supposed to be born. My mom's doctors had told her over and over that severe endometrial scarring would make it practically impossible for her to carry a baby. But my infant self didn't care about scarring. Or the partial hysterectomy Mom had to get after my delivery. And for most of my childhood, we were happy in our little pod of three—Mom, Dad, me. Until my parents got a different notion about the magic number three: adopting three boys from Guatemala.

And I learned to disappear.

It was easier for everyone. I became the quiet one. The one who didn't drain my parents of everything they had. Pathetic as it might sound, going to school and working at the Standard Hardware were the good things in my life. When I wasn't there, I was tucked away in my bedroom, coming out only to appropriate" lecturing from my parents or school officials made a dent in his colorful vocabulary.

I shimmied the card along the edge of the doorjamb, wiggling it into just the right spot. *Click.* I swung the door open. The bathroom was trashed. Toilet paper and shaving cream were everywhere. A bottle of cough syrup sat sideways on the sink, its contents spilled all over the toothpaste and toothbrushes. Not quite a childproof cap after all.

Luis stood with his arms crossed. Brown, unapologetic face, black eyes boring into me as if I were personally responsible for the crap state of his life. "That cunt won't let me play video games."

I squeezed my eyes shut. He'd trashed the bathroom over a video game? I shook my head. Mom didn't deserve this even if she did sign up for it. "Clean it up."

"Fuck off."

"Clean it up or I'll hide Alex's blankie."

His eyes flared in alarm and then burned in hatred. The kid didn't care one bit about himself, but threaten one of his brothers and he came out swinging. He snatched a washcloth from the drawer and dropped it onto the cough syrup mess. "I'm gonna get my brothers out of this shithole. Soon."

"I'm first," I mumbled.

"What?" he asked, pausing in his half-assed cleanup job. "What did you say?"

"Nothing."

I pointed to the washcloth and he started sopping up the mess again. His thin shoulders shook as he muttered curses. I called down the stairs to Mom, "He's out. Tell Alex he'll be there in five minutes."

"I need to go to the library to study," I said at dinner, pushing leftover spaghetti across my plastic plate.

Dinner was the worst time of the day. The "pretend we're a happy family" time where cell phones weren't allowed and we all had to announce two things we'd learned in school. Two. Things. Did my parents ever even go to high school?

Mom had become an expert in making every meal in under eighteen minutes. Eighteen minutes was the maximum allowable time she could leave the boys without chaos erupting. I had no idea how she'd figured this out statistically, but I trusted her on it and got used to dinners that came frozen in bags or popped out of the microwave. Family "together" time was loud boys barking orders at Mom.

My parents had adopted my brothers off the streets of Guatemala City when they were six, four, and three. They were only going to take one of them, but they could tell the brothers were bonded and they wanted to keep them as a unit. We'd had so many family discussions about the benefits of siblings. I was twelve then and just starting to get pissy about being the sole focus of my parents' relentless hovering. Mom stared at babies everywhere we went, then came home and gushed about how her sister had been her best friend growing up. The sister who'd moved to Germany and rarely called anymore. My dad said he'd always wanted brothers. They both promised it would change all our lives. It did, but not like any of us expected.

"I need to go to the library to study," I said again, between Luis's demands for more milk and Alex's complaints about how he got too many tomato chunks in his sauce.

"I need to go to the library to study." Repeating sentences three times gave me the best chance of them actually sinking in.

I hadn't been to the library since seventh grade. But I was testing out the ratio of success in getting away from my brothers. Good lies need to be tucked away for emergency use. Most people don't realize this and use them too frequently, so they're no longer effective. Big mistake.

"You can study here," Mom answered, the desperate "don't leave me with these monsters" look flashing across her face.

"It's too loud and—" Before I could finish, Luis snatched Miguel's dinner roll from his plate, and then Miguel punched him hard enough to make Luis squeal.

Cue sibling fistfight number three. A new record for family dinner.

I scraped my half-eaten spaghetti into the trash and ran upstairs while Mom pulled the boys apart. I glanced in the mirror: jeans, black T-shirt, hoodie, boots, stripy hair, chain necklaces, too-pale face, too-thin body. Still the same me. Sometimes I would squint when I looked in the mirror and imagine I was someone else living a different life, but the blur never lasted. The dinginess of my room and the hollowness of my eyes always broke the illusion.

My boots thunked on the stairs as I headed back down, grabbing my bag before returning to the kitchen. When I walked in, Mom was standing at the counter, dropping more dinner rolls onto a baking sheet and lecturing the boys about how they should just ask her to make more if they're still hungry.

"Okay, I'm going."

"Be back before ten." Mom waved at me and continued her lecture. Alex flashed his missing-tooth grin and then flipped me off as Mom turned away. Nice. Miguel and Luis were kicking each other under the kitchen table when I walked out. A crash followed by a shriek from Mom punctuated the door click behind me.

The skate park stayed open until eight on weeknights in September, closing for the season on October first. I walked to it on autopilot, having spent so many summer afternoons watching my brothers fly up and down the ramps. They bitched endlessly about the helmet requirement, but after two trips to the ER for stitches, they'd gotten the point about head injuries.

The night was cool and quiet. I parked myself on top of the high hill I normally sat on to watch the hard-core skaters practice. A chain-link fence surrounded the ramps, and on a clear night I could see the blinking lights of the Chicago skyline in the distance. I lit a menthol cigarette and blew rings of smoke toward the dusky sky. I shut my eyes and listened to the boards zipping down ramps and the low voices trash talking and laughing. Did my parents ever watch me at the skate park when I was younger? Before the boys and all the trouble? I couldn't remember.

"Skate girl, huh?" a voice broke into my cocoon, and I blinked the menthol buzz away. A tall, too-thin boy stood in front of me, smirking. A bright blue patch of hair dropped in front of his left eye, and a retro Sex Pistols shirt clung to his lanky frame.

"What?" I blinked again and shook my head.

He gave me a small smile and shrugged. His eyes traced over me, and it took everything I had not to cross my arms over my chest and move away.

"Why aren't you with the rest of the chain-smokers at the Punkin' Donuts?" he said. He took a step toward me, and I slid back so I could see him better. My eyes dropped to the aerosol can and paper bag he held.

"What are you doing with that?"

He sprayed the can into the bag and stuck his face into the fumes. His chest puffed out as he inhaled. I pressed my hand into the grass beneath me, plucking at the cool wetness. Wetness I could feel along the back of my jeans.

He coughed and dropped the bag to his side. "Livening up the evening."

I looked him over again. The rest of his hair was dark brown like his eyes. His jeans hung low on his hips, but not in the annoying way where they practically fall off. The bones of his shoulders jutted out from his shirt. He grinned at me, slightly dazed.

"Are you retarded?"

"Nope," he said, and the grin cocked up even higher on the side of his mouth not hidden by hair.

"You sure? No one huffs here. It's country."

"Country?" He shook the can again.

"Yeah, as in it's for idiots who can't find better drugs."

He chuckled, and I stared at the way his hair fell across his dark eyes and clear skin. No acne. How does this even happen to guys? He brushed his long fingers over his mouth, and I followed them as they fell back to his side. Hands have always been interesting to me, and his moved too gracefully in comparison to the rest of him. Like they didn't know they were on the end of a sloppy boy.

"Well," he said, dropping the can into the paper bag,

"huffing wouldn't be my first choice, but we're in the suburbs. Sometimes you gotta work with what you've got."

"We're like three El stops from Chicago. My grandmother could score drugs in this town."

He shrugged. "Maybe I like the fumes." I looked him over again. The thumb of his left hand hooked in his jean pocket while his other fingers drummed against the denim.

"Huh. My brothers huffed on the streets of Guatemala to keep from getting too hungry." Why'd I tell him that? Why was I even talking to him? Shit. Shit. Shit.

He took another half step toward me. "Yeah? Your brothers are from Guatemala?"

"Adopted."

"Obviously." He motioned to my pale face and blue eyes. Something was written on his palm. I squinted to see, but it was too blurred.

Enough. I stood up and grabbed my messenger bag. "Okay. Well, it was nice meeting you. I'm gonna go talk to some of the boarders."

"What's your name?" He reached out and fingered the hoops running up the side of my ear. I flinched and knocked his hand away. Goose bumps prickled along the back of my neck. It'd been too long since someone touched me.

I took a step around him. "Amelia Gannon. But no one calls me Amelia. It's just Gannon."

He pushed his hair off his face, and I saw a metal bar peeking from his eyebrow. "Gannon. Yeah, I like that."

"Glad you approve. I live to please. Really." I slid my pack of cigarettes into my pocket. I took a step to the side and he countered. People normally weren't this interested in having a conversation with me. I crossed my leg behind me and stared at him for an uncomfortable amount of time. "So?"

His eyes looked glazed, and it occurred to me his interest might be more from the fume high than anything else. It made sense. I wasn't exactly the kind of girl guys got in big conversations with, even random blue-haired boys with eyebrow piercings and nice hands.

"So what?" he said, reaching out to trace my hoops again.

"Dude, back off." I grabbed his wrist and dug my nails in. "Why are you touching me?"

He dropped his hand. "I like your hoops. They're sexy."

My cheeks heated, but I squinted my eyes at him. "Listen, whatever your name is, you can't just go around touching people. You'll get your ass handed to you."

He tilted his head back and laughed. His Adam's apple bobbed along his slender neck. I gulped as something warm pooled in my stomach. Shit.

"What are you doing here?" I asked. "Are you a boarder?"

He snorted. "Fuck, no. I was never sober enough to learn

when everyone else was figuring it out. Seems kind of stupid to try it now."

"You mean when everyone learned in, like, fifth grade? One of those child addicts, eh?"

His face froze for a half second, but then he grinned. "Something like that." He drummed his fingers on his jeans again. "So do you skate?"

"No. Not in a long time. Too busy working. I just come here for the amusement of watching guys fall on their asses."

He grinned. "One of those types, then?"

"What types?"

He looked me up and down, and my stomach knotted. "The angry girls."

My fingers tightened around the strap of my bag. "Not quite."

He leaned closer. "Then what type are you?"

"I'm not any type." I inched back. My strong instinct to bolt warred with the depressing realization that I had no place to go and the even sadder fact that this guy was the first guy in a long time to talk to me without asking for money or cigarettes.

"So where do you work?" he said, dropping to the grass and patting the spot next to him.

I didn't move. "Standard Hardware."

He patted the spot again. I stared at his fingers and tilted my head, trying to decide if he was being friendly or stalky. Chitchat wasn't my strong suit, so it was hard to say. He released a sigh before yanking me next to him. I scrambled to get up, but then his hand touched my side and I froze.

"Relax, Gannon. It's a nice night. I want to talk to you. You don't have to be so cagey."

I shifted away and narrowed my eyes. He offered me a goofy boy grin. I hugged my knees to my chest and focused on the boarders.

He grunted. "So a job at the hardware store must mean you know your way around tools?"

I couldn't help smiling. "Yeah. Pretty much."

His hands moved to the sleeve of my hoodie and he brushed away a piece of dried grass. His fingers lingered over the outside of my wrist before I snatched my hand away.

"I like girls who know their way around tools."

"Are you being gross?"

He laughed and nudged me with his elbow. "That's *your* head in the gutter, not mine."

"What did you say your name was?"

"Michael Brooks. But Brooks to you. Okay?"

I shrugged.

"So . . ."—he picked at a piece of loose string on the edge of my jeans—"do you want to hang out for a while?"

"Not really." I had nowhere to go, but I still wasn't sure

about Mr. Grabby Hands Brooks. Or my weird response to him.

He chuckled. "You don't like me?"

"You're a little handsy for my taste."

He laughed harder and pulled his hand back from the loose string. "Not normally. It must be something about you."

It was a line. It had to be. But why was I being singled out to be on the receiving end of cheesy lines? "What are you talking about? You just met me."

"I go to your school."

I stretched my legs out in front of me. "Since when?"

"Three weeks ago. Haven't you seen me?"

I turned to him and laughed in his face. "It's a big school. And why would I have noticed you?"

"I've seen you," he said, and shifted his knee so it touched mine. The warmth of his leg made me feel strange and, if I was being completely honest, a little bit good. "Come on. Let me walk you home."

"You're not walking me home. I'm not telling you where I live."

"Okay, I'll walk you somewhere else, then."

"Who even said I was leaving?"

He nodded to the flickering street lamp behind us. "Skate park's closing soon. What're your plans for the rest of the evening? Is there any place else you'd like to watch guys fall on their asses?"

I pulled my phone out of my messenger bag to check the time. It was too early to consider going home. My brothers would still be up.

"I think I'll stay here a little while longer."

He inched close enough that his whole thigh pressed fully against mine. "Me too, then."

I shrugged and tamped down the heat on my cheeks, grateful for the growing darkness. "Suit yourself." I held out my pack of cigarettes. "Want one?"

He scoffed. "Filtered menthols? I don't think so. I smoke real cigarettes."

I lit another cigarette and dropped my lighter into my pocket. Smoke curled around me, and wetness from the ground seeped further into the back of my pants. But the warmth of Brooks's too-close leg kept me from paying much attention to the cold discomfort. Neither of us said a word. I opened my mouth to ask what he was doing there in the first place, but somehow the question felt like an intrusion into the strange peace blanketing the night.

CHRISTA DESIR writes contemporary fiction for young adults. She lives with her family and overly enthusiastic dog outside of Chicago and works as a part-time independent bookseller and freelance editor. Two of her novels were chosen by the Illinois Reading Council as Illinois Reads' books for high school students. She has also twice been selected for the In the Margins list of top fiction books for youth living in poverty, on the streets, or in custody. She has been a rape victim activist for over twenty years, including providing advocacy services in hospital ERs, working with incarcerated teen survivors, and speaking to high school and college students about sexual violence. Visit her at www.christadesir.com.

JOLENE PERRY is a middle and high school teacher turned author. She married the guy she kissed on her high school graduation night, lives in the mountains of Alaska, and has spent months sailing in the Caribbean. Her previous novels for young adults include *The Summer I Found You* and *Has to Be Love*.

DISCOVER NEW YA READS

READ BOOKS FOR FREE

WIN NEW & UPCOMING RELEASES

RIVETED

YA FICTION IS OUR ADDICTION

JOIN THE COMMUNITY

DISCUSS WITH THE COMMUNITY

WRITE FOR THE COMMUNITY

CONNECT WITH US ON RIVETEDLIT.COM

AND @RIVETEDLIT